W9-BUD-467

DIRT BIKES, DRONES, AND OTHER WAYS TO FLY

DIRT BIKES, DRONES, AND OTHER WAYS TO FLY

CONRAD WESSELHOEFT

HOUGHTON MIFFLIN HARCOURT
BOSTON NEW YORK

www.hmhco.com

The text of this book is set in Minion Pro.

Library of Congress Cataloging-in-Publication Data
Wesselhoeft, Conrad, 1953–
Dirt Bikes, Drones, and Other Ways to Fly / by Conrad Wesselhoeft.
p. cm.
Summary: "Seventeen year-old dirt-bike-riding daredevil Arlo Santiago catches the eye of the U.S. military with his first-place ranking on a video game featuring drone warfare, and must reconcile the work they want him to do with the emotional scars he has suffered following a violent death in his family."
—Provided by publisher.
ISBN 978-0-544-23269-3
[1. Video games—Fiction. 2. Trail bikes—Fiction. 3. Drone aircraft—Fiction. 4. Special forces (Military science)—Fiction. 5.Death—Fiction. 6. Single-parent families—Fiction. 7. Family life—New Mexico—Fiction. 8. New Mexico—Fiction.] I. Title.
PZ7.W5166Dro 2014
[Fic]—dc23
2013034542

Manufactured in the United States of America
DOC 10 9 8 7 6 5 4 3 2 1
4500461720

Remembering LWW

"The future was calling."

CHAPTER 1

KENYA MAN EXPLODES out of my phone:

> *L.A. . . . L.A. . . . L.A.*
> *Gonna get my junk in play*
> *At the corner of Sunset and La Brea.*

I jerk out of REM sleep, level nine. Scramble and find my phone wedged under El Guapo's ass, punch in.

"Dude," I rasp, "be right out."

But instead of Cam or Lobo on the other end, it's some space cowboy.

"Hello, is this Arlo Santiago?"

Everything about the voice sounds like a jail door clanging shut.

"Am I speaking with Arlo Spencer Santiago?"

"Uhhhhhhhmm . . ."

El Guapo—"The Handsome One"—arches his back and starts to hump me, his way of saying good morning. I shove him, and he tumbles ass-over-floppy-ears onto the floor. Then he pops up and grins at me.

He's always grinning. Humping and grinning. He's the grinningest, humpingest dog in the world. Probably the only standard poodle in all northeast New Mexico.

"Guess so," I say.

"Good morning, Arlo. I'm Major Keith Anderson, United States Air Force. How are you today?"

I glance at the clock—6:55 a.m. Damn, just what I need, a recruiter calling me at this hour. Messing with my routine.

I've polished my mornings to perfection. On the one hand, I give myself Maximum Sleep (MS)—sleep to the very last millisecond. On the other hand, once Kenya Man starts rapping, I'm up, moving fast. In five seconds, I've accelerated to Maximum Efficiency (ME). Not to say I'm totally awake; I'm not. But my body knows all the moves, how to cut the corners.

On a blackboard, you can write it this way:

MS + ME = success

. . . with success being getting to school before the 7:29 a.m. bell.

I have exactly two minutes and twenty-seven seconds to piss, slap water on my face, get dressed, and eat breakfast.

But first I've got to deal with this tool.

"It's an honor to speak with a world champion," the man says.

I rub sleep off my face. "Hey, who is this again?"

"Nice job yesterday on Drone Pilot," he says. "You finally beat him."

"Beat who?"

"SergeiTashkent, of course.'"

Now he has my attention.

"What are you," I ask, "the CIA or something?"

The jail door laughs. "No, Arlo. Merely the United States Air Force."

"Listen, dude . . . Major . . . whoever you are . . ." I roll out of bed and whip a T-shirt off the floor. "I'm running late for school."

"Sure, I'll get to the point. We want you to fly with us."

"No thanks. I'm only seventeen. Call me in a year."

El Guapo leaps onto the bed and thrusts his shaggy hips at me. Hump and grin, hump and grin—only God knows the mind of a high desert poodle.

"Arlo, we've been following you on the leaderboards for some time," the man says. "Last night, we watched you knock Sergei out of the number one position on Drone Pilot. Sergei's a superb UAV pilot, technically the best we've ever seen. And you beat him. That was *extremely* smart flying."

I clamp my hand on El Guapo's snout. He freezes mid-hump.

"Look," I say, glancing around for my jeans. "I don't want to join the air force."

"Arlo, I'm not a recruiter."

"Well, who are you, man?"

"I'd like to invite you to join us for war games this Saturday at White Sands."

"War games?"

I glance at the clock—6:57 a.m. *Damn!*

"You'll get to test your skills against real pilots—some of our very best."

"Hold up! If you mean fly real planes, uh-uh, no way. I have no idea how to fly a plane."

"Not a plane, Arlo, a drone. You definitely know how to fly one of those. We know that very well. It's just like your game Drone Pilot. The difference is, we make it real."

"Dude," I say, "this is way too much information. And I'm late for school."

"Sure, Arlo, I'll check in later. Start thinking about Saturday."

Click!

"Yeah," I say, tossing my phone. "Peace to you too."

Then it hits me — it's Lobo's Uncle Sal again — our local joker and genius entrepreneur. Owner of the best coffee shop in town, and my sky-diving instructor for the past three years.

Uncle Sal has a gift for faking voices. For some reason, I'm one of his favorite targets. Last time, he wanted me to enter a Rocky Mountain oyster eating contest sponsored by the Daughters of the American Revolution.

Lobo would've told him about my win yesterday. About seriously kicking SergeiTashkent's butt, knocking him to number two on the Drone Pilot leaderboard, which I've been trying to do all year.

I am now the number one drone combat pilot in the world — the virtual world, that is — until somebody kicks my butt.

In video games, when you reach number one, your butt is out there, cheeks flapping in the wind, for anybody to kick — SergeiTashkent, ToshiOshi, IpanemaGirl, anybody.

There are seven billion anybodies in the world.

Just the thought of Uncle Sal . . . I start to laugh. In fact, I laugh so hard I trip putting on my jeans. Damn, I'm late.

Dad walks in, all frayed, scratching, and barely employed. He taps his watch.

"Ass in gear, Arlo."

"Can I have five bucks for lunch?"

He winces, opens his wallet — puffy with poverty — and holds out three faded ones. Says his daily mantra: "Spend it wisely."

"Always do," I say, and snatch the money.

"Don't forget," he says. "Snack Shack tomorrow night."

Dad runs the concession stand at Rio Loco Field. It's a huge comedown after running a newspaper, but, hey, it pays a few bills.

"Who we playing?" I ask.

"*Jeopardy,*" he says.

"Yeah!" I say, and smack a fist into my palm.

Jeopardy is one of the highlights of the football season. The halftime show is ten times better than the game itself.

I dig two unmatched socks from under my bed and sniff them. It's been five months since I've found clean, folded, matching socks in my top drawer. That's one little difference in not having a mom anymore.

There are many — *many!* — little differences.

"And I want to get up to Burro Mesa again," Dad says.

"Not me," I say. "You know where I stand on that, philosophically and spiritually and all."

"Overruled," Dad says.

I jam on my Old Gringos. Stomp 'em in place. Great boots, like great art, get better with time.

"She wouldn't've wanted a damn tombstone anyway."

"Not a tombstone, Arlo. A monument. Get your nomenclature right."

Five months ago — on May fifteenth, at two-fifty in the afternoon — Mom walked into the EZ Stop on South Main to buy a bottle of grape Gatorade and never walked out.

Siouxsie, waiting in the car, heard the shots and saw the holdup guy run.

Siouxsie's thirst for grape Gatorade — and Mom's swinging through that door to buy a bottle — changed day to night.

No sunset, twilight, or dusk in between.

Just — *whomp!* — night.

Dad and I have a standing disagreement over whether to build a "monument" to Mom on Burro Mesa. He's already sketched it out, bought the sand. Ordered a chunk of Bandelier stone "yay high by yay wide." Written the epitaph, or inscription, or whatever you call it, a hundred times.

It gets longer and longer.

Then shorter and shorter.

He's never satisfied.

Dad was a journalist for eighteen years, but he can't seem to write that damn epitaph. It's beyond all his powers of creation. How can he ever expect to finish a novel if he can't write a frickin' epitaph?

Me? I believe the sky is Mom's monument, and the grass and wind her epitaph. Burro Mesa is perfect the way it is, untouched by manmade shit. To the north, you can see deep into Colorado, all the way to Pike's Peak. Look south, and you can see halfway to Mexico. Up there, it's all space, space, space. Green, blue, and forever. The air just shines.

Last summer, we spread Mom's ashes along the rim rocks, mixed them in with the lilies, Indian paintbrush, and shooting stars. I ride up there sometimes with El Guapo. Watch him run amok and hump the herd while I sit and ponder. A monument would desecrate everything—like building a McDonald's at the bottom of the Grand Canyon.

Kenya Man raps out of my phone.

L.A . . . L.A. . . . L.A.

Me, I live in *C.A . . . C.A. . . . C.A.*—Clay Allison, New Mexico, located just south of Butt Crack, Nowhere, at the intersection of mesa dust and tractor rust.

This time it's Cam. "Dude! What the—?"

"Be out in a minute," I say. "Kick it for me."

I grab a sausage off the stove, bite it, toss the rest to El Guapo, and shoulder my backpack.

"Mornin', Texas Slim."

Siouxsie—my twelve-year-old sister—sits at the kitchen table. Her hearing aids look like tiny fortune cookies beside her cereal bowl.

"Put those in your ears," I say.

She doesn't move. Maybe she doesn't hear me. Maybe she does. I'm never exactly sure.

I raise my voice. "And don't forget to feed the mares. Remember, one and a half quarts of oats, not two. Always feed Big Z first. She's the alpha."

Siouxsie rolls her eyes. "Have faith, Texas Slim. I won't forget."

"Yeah, right," I say. "You can't hear a damn word I'm saying."

"You said feed 'em five and a half gallons."

"ONE AND A HALF QUARTS!"

She stirs me away with her spoon.

"And do NOT bring any of those barn kittens into the house again," I say. "Guapo'll catch fleas."

She clamps her hands over her ears. "Can't hear a damn word you're sayin', Texas Slim."

Siouxsie's got Mom's go-your-own-way gene and nickel-hard stubbornness. Plus, she's got another gene — some trait that's popped up in Chromosome 4.

At first, the doctors didn't know what to call it. They hemmed and hawed, scratched and twitched, then gave it a name: Huntington's disease. Basically, HD creeps like a glacier, neuro-degeneratively crushing a few cells at a time. Siouxsie's main symptoms, so far, are stiffness, some loss of coordination, and some hearing loss.

Dad doesn't open the medical bills anymore. Just stuffs them in the drawer beneath the microwave.

I grab my helmet and bang outside.

Cam and Lobo are out by the barn. Cam's revving my bike — my green Yamaha 250 four-stroke. Super-strong frame, which I've tricked out with heavy-duty shocks.

I bought my Yam 250 in Santa Fe using my chunk of the life insurance money. It's a little banged up and scarred, but a great bike. Mega-fast acceleration. Profound off-road and scramble capability. Able to handle all my abuse. Never wiped out or spilled any tools.

Not yet, anyway.

I mount up, pull on my helmet. Adjust my shades. Grind the throttle. Listen like a doctor to the *thump-thump-thump* of the engine. Dirt bikes congest the way people do — they wake up coughing and hacking. Grinding acts like a decongestant, but the best decongestant is the open road.

Two of the mares — Queen Zenobia and Blue Dancer — stare at me from the corral. When I rev again, they flatten back their ears. They disapprove of my grinding Yamaha, and they disapprove of Lobo and Cam.

Cam throws a leg over his Kawasaki KLX.

Lobo, decked out in his "Ride Naked" T-shirt, is saddled on his Bandit 350.

"Top of the mornin'," he says over the throbbing engines.

"Hey, I just talked to your Uncle Sal," I say. "He wants me to join the air force. The dude is crazy."

Lobo nods. "All us Focazios are batshit."

The screen door slaps. "Good morning, Homo sapiens!" Siouxsie shouts from the porch.

She wraps an arm around the post. Without her hearing aids, she probably can't hear us talking, but she can definitely hear us revving — even the dead can hear us revving.

Lobo lifts his voice. "Hey, how's the prettiest girl in all Orphan County today?"

"Hey, Lobo," Siouxsie says. "Ride careful — and take care of Texas Slim."

"Oh, yeah, we always do," Lobo says. "Don't we, Texas Slim?"

El Guapo barks, and we're gone.

CHAPTER 2

WE ARE THREE BIKES SPINNING dust.

My favorite time of day.

A time of grinding engines and drone silence.

Dew, dust, and desert grit.

Grease smoke and sage.

Pure testosterone perfume.

Now I'm really waking up, New Mexico–style. The northern plain stretches purple to Eagle Tail Mesa, then all the way to Raton Pass and the Sangre de Cristo Mountains — the Blood of Christ, always dying for our sins.

New Mexico paints this for you — the Land of Enchantment is more enchanting in the morning. The colors washed, torn, and bled, the slow-burning fuse of a sky. The thousand dusty shadows. I was born here, in Clay Allison, New Mexico, a scabby dog of a town that sleeps on the high plateau, snug up against Colorado's mountainous ass.

Cam, Lobo, and I cut across the back acres. Slip down into an arroyo and shoot up — sailing over the toppled fence — onto Lew Lopez's property. We pass Lew's squatting doublewide, his rusted pickup, weed-shrouded tractor, and unpruned pomegranate orchard.

I glance to make sure the light's on in his kitchen — it is. Lew's somewhere in his nineties. A World War II vet — Iwo Jima wounded and decorated. He's half Mexican, half Navajo, half Irish, half everything, which means he's all New Mexican. And he's all alone since Inez died a few years ago. A gnarled, shriveled man in red suspenders, turquoise bolo, thick glasses, and a veteran's cap.

"Arlo," he tells me whenever I see him, "you boys sound like a swarm of bees a-comin'. Slow down or you'll break your necks."

We swerve onto Lew's access road and slow at the intersection of gravel and highway. Wait, as always, for Lobo to catch up. Then we open the throttles. The engines scream as we buck and rocket up the blacktop.

This morning, the highway is perfect and dry. At Gobblers Knob, the grade eases downhill. There's a semi ahead. Cam pulls alongside me and gives me the finger — his way of challenging me. I give him a thumbs up.

We close in on the semi at about eighty miles per hour. Then we crank it. I glance at the speedometer. The needle jumps to ninety, which is as far as the speedometer goes on my bike. But speedometers are paper walls. You can break through them easily. You just have to know the road, the texture of the air that touches it, and how to ride the grade. A thousand little factors come into play, but you can't analyze them. Analyzing weakens you. Too much thinking weakens you. The secret is to feel, sense, and react. Simultaneously. To trust your instincts.

The highway bends like a hunter's bow and starts to dip. For a stretch, we're blind to oncoming traffic. I make my move — my leap around the semi. It's an extremely stupid and dangerous move — for anybody else. Today it feels exactly right.

Wouldn't you know, here comes another semi rushing at me. An alarm explodes in my head. Cam fades back.

I jam off the alarm. Shove everything out of my mind — fear, worries, Dad, Siouxsie — and enter the Drone Zone.

Now I'm Leif Ericson standing at the prow of my Viking ship.

I'm Neil Armstrong bouncing on the moon.

In the Drone Zone, speed and adrenaline morph into . . .

Peace.

And eternity.

The space between the trucks at the passing point is tight. I duck my head, hunch my shoulders. The oncoming semi blasts its horn.

Blasts!

Blasts!

BLASTS!

The driver looms large in the window, drops his jaw, rises in his seat until he's almost standing. I can practically see the beads of sweat on his forehead.

Now I'm at the center of the Zone. Everything's a blur. Everything is clear.

Yea, though I fly through the valley of the shadow . . .

I shoot like an arrow down the line, between flashing silver sidings. Taste the warm, diesel-ly air rushing up from the swirling underbellies. Feel the calm that lives in pure speed.

It's over in an instant. I whip out ahead, the semis screaming at me from both directions, and bomb up the highway. Go more than two miles on sheer adrenaline. I'm truly blazed on speed. At the shortcut, I veer off the highway.

As I grind down and brake to a stop, all the alarms I turned off jump back on and ring like crazy. My heart is pounding.

Cam pulls up. Lifts off his helmet. Glares at me. He looks like an Old West Apache with his bandanna rolled across his forehead, and his long hair flowing. He spits. Wipes an arm across his mouth.

"*Very* uncool, dude!" he says. "Even for you. A new low. Don't *ever* do that again. Not if you want to ride with me."

Lobo pulls up. "*Hombre*! You scared the shiz out of me. Seriously, what was that! You just about died."

Fact is, I'm feeling more alive than ever. The hair on my arms springs for joy. But I hide it. Make humble. "Sorry, dudes," I say. "I went temporarily insane."

Cam aims a finger between my eyes. "Insanity will kill you," he says, pulling the trigger.

I don't say what they can't understand. I don't tell them that I had to do it.

I wasn't at risk; everybody else was. Maybe I regret putting those drivers in a tight place, for a second or two, but that's all. As for me, I was in the Drone Zone.

Flying fat.

Invincible.

Cam might've made it, with luck, but not Lobo. He would've freaked out. If you ride too cautiously, or your nerves get in the way, or you think too much, you're dead.

Cam, on the other hand, is willing to ride the edge, but he lacks the reflexes. Split-second timing is not good enough. A second before split-second is what you need. It's the speed of a fly versus the speed of a bee.

"Aighhht!" Lobo says. "Let's ride."

We grind throttle. Shred sand.

The shortcut takes us up and over Little Piñon Mesa. It's scarred with a thousand bike grooves — the whoriest-looking mesa in all northeast New Mexico. That's why every dirt rider comes here. Because it's all humps, jumps, gullies, falloffs, and loose sand.

Plus two little wooden crosses.

On Little Piñon, we earn our air miles. I take flight on my favorite jump, Davy, named in memory of Lobo's older brother, Army Specialist David Focazio, who shot himself after getting back from Afghanistan.

Even Lobo catches some decent air.

We land in the school parking lot at 7:27 a.m., a whole two minutes before the bell. We're sitting at our homeroom desks, studiously, at 7:29 a.m.

Just as the bell rings, a new girl walks in.

Everything twitches and stops, including the clock.

CHAPTER 3

"HOLD UP, LEE," MR. MARTINEZ SAYS. "I want to introduce you."

The new girl is torqued lanky like a runway model, but she hides under a loose T-shirt, untucked flannel, and slightly baggy "guy" jeans — a sure sign that she's not from Orphan County. But it works. It definitely works.

She steps beside Mr. Martinez and thrusts back her shoulders. Her eyes spark.

"Class," Mr. Martinez says, "this is Lee Fields. She comes to us from Seattle, Washington. All the way from the Great Northwest to the Great Southwest. Class, what do we know about Seattle?"

"Rain," Michelle Pappas says.

"Bill Gates," Vonz Trujillo says.

"Sasquatch country," Lobo says.

"Right," Mr. Martinez says. "Though the jury is still out on the Sasquatches." He turns to the new girl. "Lee, we here in Clay Allison don't get much rain, and sometimes we get too much sun —"

"We got adobe brains," Vonz blurts out.

Mr. Martinez frowns. He's been teaching eleventh-grade history and language arts for thirty-nine years. He taught Dad. Five years later he taught Mom. He's taught one NASA astronaut, two governors of New Mexico, three psychopathic killers, and ten thousand truckers, wranglers, keno girls, fry cooks, and motel desk assistants. We can mess with him only so much.

"Lee," he says, steepling his fingers, "forgive us our occasional lapses and minor trespasses. We more than compensate with our pieties and niceties."

Lee smiles. "I forgive you."

Some of us laugh. Some of us snicker. Pure oxygen fizzes into my brain.

What stops the clock is her hair. It plunges like Niagara Falls, a cascade of red-gold. Clay Allison is a poor town. There's a played-out, hope-burned shabbiness here. A long-past-its-prime-ness. But we're used to it. And when you're used to it, you don't notice the shabbiness anymore — until somebody new shows up. A new person is like a mirror of reality, somebody who opens your eyes and shames you at the same time.

Just looking at Lee Fields makes me wish I were from anyplace else. In my mind, I'm already telling her where I'm from.

"L.A.," I say. "I'm just here for the semester. Then it's back to L.A."

I can't take my eyes off her hair.

Homeroom consists of twelve girls and eleven boys. The closest to honest-to-god gold hair is Latoya Solaño's drugstore lemon with candy-pink highlights and original black roots. We're about one-third Hispanic, one-third Caucasian, and one-third hyphenated. Lots of Catholic, too.

Me, I'm authentic, pure-grade New Mexican salsa: Hispanic

(through Dad); Caucasian (through Mom); lapsed Catholic (through Dad); daredevil (through Mom).

Add onions, tomatoes, and a teaspoon of salt.

Plus a few drops of Navajo (through Dad) for extra zest.

Blend and puree.

When I look in the mirror, I see it all — curly black hair, blue outcast eyes, guilty-white eyeballs.

Lee's hair is brushed and proper — except for one glaring fact, of which she seems completely oblivious: the ends curl like wicked fingers and tickle her ass. I glance over at Cam and Lobo. They're staring too. Already, like me, they're wishing they were those wicked fingers.

Lobo catches my eye. Bangs his head against an imaginary light pole. *Swack!*

"Alfalfa, dude," he whispers.

Peach, plum, alfalfa — the three degrees of kiss-worthiness. Peach — peck softly; plum — taste the polished insides of her mouth; alfalfa — probe deep as an alfalfa stalk is long.

"Lee is staying with her aunt, Lupita Fields, up in Chicorica Canyon," Mr. Martinez tells us.

Lupita Fields! She was Mom's oldest friend. Back in their high school days, they rode the canyon together. On horses, not dirt bikes. Chicorica Canyon is prime dirt-bike country, full of arroyo washes, mazes, and old mining towns. It was prime ranch country too, until the Town of Clay Allison dammed Chicorica Creek and built a pipeline.

I ponder the name Lee. New Mexico is a land of Tanyas, Donnas, and Jamie Lynns. Lee is often part of a name — like Brenda

Lee or Sammi Lee — but usually not a name by itself. To my ear, Lee sounds unfinished and masculine. She needs more dip for her chip. Hmm. Rocky Lee, Wynona Lee — those would work.

I lean back to see if she's wearing Northwest hiking boots. Uh-uh, she's wearing pink athletic shoes. Pumas. City-girl spotless. New Mexico will dust her up, that's for sure.

Mr. Martinez points to the class motto framed above the door: CHARACTER IS FOREVER.

It's one of dozens of quotes posted on the walls — the sacred words of Aristotle, Harriet Tubman, Helen Keller, Nelson Mandela, Dr. Seuss, Pink Floyd, Anonymous. On and on.

He calls them his "wall sages."

"Character Is Forever" — his own contribution — hangs above the door so we can ponder it every time we leave the room.

"Lee, I ask all my students to embrace this principle," Mr. Martinez says. "Not merely for the academic year but for a lifetime. I'd like you to embrace it as well, because —"

"Oh, I totally embrace it," Lee shoots back.

"Well, then . . . *ahem!*" Mr. Martinez scowls at the rest of us. "Most of your classmates think James Bond got it right — *diamonds* are forever."

"James Bond can go jump off a mesa," Lee Fields says.

Mr. Martinez beams. "Class, we have a visionary in our midst. Do you have any questions for Lee?"

Michelle Pappas flaps a hand. "Why are you here?" she asks in a pissy tone.

"Michelle!" Mr. Martinez snaps. "Rewind. Respect."

Michelle pastes on a smile. "Why are you here?" she asks again.

"My dad's stationed overseas," Lee says.

Nothing shy in those eyes. Nothing shaky in those hands. Not like some first-day students.

"Like, deployed stationed?" Michelle asks.

"Yup," Lee says. "He's a Sergeant First Class in Arapaho Company, Second Platoon, Pakistan. This is his fifth combat tour."

We are silent. Five tours is a lot. We all know this. In Clay Allison, people are always shipping out. Lobo's brother, Davy, shipped out on three tours.

Vonz jacks up a hand. "What's he do out there? You know, his MO and all that."

"Explosive ordnance disposal," Lee says.

"What's that mean, exactly?" Sharon Blossburg asks.

Lee hooks a corn-silk strand behind an ear. "It means he sweeps for roadside bombs and IEDs — you know, improvised explosive devices — and deactivates them. But what it really means is, he's helping all the guys over there, even the locals, stay safe."

"The locals! What's the point of that?" Sharon asks.

Lee bristles. "The point is to stay alive. In one piece. And for our guys to come back home. And get on with their lives. Obviously."

Mr. Martinez clears his throat. "Yes, well . . . Just to add to that, the main mission of our military intervention in that part of the world is to stifle the threat of terror," he says. "Also to expand the footprint of democracy. But to those with their boots on the ground, like Lee's father, the mission can be as basic as survive today so you can return home safely tomorrow. And, Lee, that is our sincerest hope for your father."

"Thank you," Lee says.

"How 'bout your mom?" Leah Castenado asks.

"She's out in California with her new husband and baby."

My hand shoots up. "Where in Pakistan? I mean, where's your dad stationed?"

"The North-West Frontier."

"Oh, yeah, I know that country."

It just slips out. Everybody stares at me like I'm an idiot. Lee looks at me funny too. I sink into my chair.

The fact is, I've flown over the North-West Frontier a thousand times. When you cross the last river and hurtle out of the valley, the mountains leap up. You'd swear they were the Front Range of the Rockies. Same dog-jaw silhouette. It looks and feels like home.

"What're your interests?" Latoya Solaño asks.

"I'm sort of obsessed with the war these days," Lee says. "The BBC does the best job at covering things, like the day-to-day fighting and the search for terrorists."

"The search for Caracal, you mean," Vonz mumbles. "He's the father of all terrorists."

"Yeah, him," Lee says.

Latoya raises her hand. "When my uncle was stationed over there, we did that too," she says. "We kept the news on all the time. I used to have a thing for that British reporter guy. I forget his name."

Lee smiles. "Ethan Shackleton."

"Yeah, Ethan, that's him," Latoya says. "I could watch him all day. That boy needs motherin' and lovin' like nobody else."

"Back in Seattle I had a motorcycle," Lee says.

Lobo snickers. "Like a Vespa?"

"Harley," Lee says.

Cam, Lobo, and I twitch respectfully. Harleys are like grandfathers — you honor their legacy despite their limitations.

"What model?" Cam asks.

"SS 350," Lee says.

I picture her on an SS 350 bombing up the road, hair flying. She should be wearing a helmet, but I leave that out.

"Hey," Lobo says. "It's a good thing you left that guzzie behind. 'Cuz hogs break down out here. This ain't street-scramble country. It's dirt-ridin' country. We're iron butts. And proud of it."

"What shampoo do you use?" Dolores de la Cruz asks.

"That's enough," Mr. Martinez says. "Let's give Lee a warm Clay Allison High School welcome."

We all clap, smile, and say "Yeah, welcome — welcome." But it's a honeymoon moment. It won't last. If she were fat and ugly, it might.

But she ain't.

CHAPTER 4

FOR LUNCH, WE MOUNT UP and peel for the Sonic drive-in. Cam invites Michelle Pappas to ride double. Lobo invites Latoya Solaño. There's something about bikes and breasts. They just go together, like strawberries and shortcake.

I ponder inviting Lee Fields. Looking at her makes me ache. But I have to wonder the eternal question — the one that always stops me:

If you wore your heart on your face, what would you really look like?

Then there's the pecking order.

In Clay Allison, you have your first string, second string, and third string, all suited up and dripping gonad juice. Then you have your fourth string — those who do not play football.

I am fourth string.

If the United States were drawn in the form of a naked man, then Clay Allison would be located in the moist crotch. The sign coming into town reads WELCOME TO CLAY ALLISON, HOME OF THE OUTLAWS, STATE HIGH SCHOOL FOOTBALL CHAMPIONS, and seven of the past ten years are listed.

Not that I couldn't play football — I'm fast and nimble enough. Probably a natural wide receiver.

It's just that I'm not into collisions, or anything that slams into you, slows you, or is too gravity based. Football basically boils down to gravity and contact, and I'm into antigravity — flight and freedom.

Yeah, I am definitely fourth string.

Being so much in the minority can be hard in a town like Clay. People look at you funny, like your nose is upside down on your face.

Who am I to even think of asking Lee Fields to get on my bike?

Vonz swaggers up to her. He's the spittin' image of a llama in wraparound shades. Lee gives him a cautionary smile, part stop, part go.

I slide on my helmet, slam down on the starter, grind the throttle till all 250 ccs are screaming. Lee Fields glances my way and flips her red-gold hair. This time when she smiles at Vonz, it's green light — go!

Didn't they write about this in the book of Genesis? "In the beginning was the football player and the beautiful girl."

Hey, Lee Fields, is that all you got?

'Cuz it ain't enough for me.

"Go forth and multiply, dudes," I say.

And I'm gone.

« « « » » »

THE SONIC HAS A COUPLE advantages over the other pit stops vying for our lunch money. First, three dollars goes a long way here — it buys me a burger and small fries. Second, it's just a few steps away from TunzaFunza.

TunzaFunza — or the TunzaFunza (Plus Caffeine) Cyber Café — started life as a gas station about the time Bonnie and Clyde were robbing banks. When I was a little kid, it was a Christian thrift store, which nobody I know ever, *ever* went to. Then it became the TunzaFunza Arcade, which included a mini bowling alley, a basketball shoot, and some video games.

I was a TunzaFunza kid. It's where I discovered the Drone Zone.

A few years ago, Lobo's Uncle Sal bought the arcade and turned it into a cyber café. In those days, not many cowboys cared what a latte was. Today — thanks to Uncle Sal — every bony-assed wrangler who can barely speak a full sentence gets finicky about his caffeine: "Er . . . make it a semi-wet cappuccino, partner."

Uncle Sal installed Wi-Fi and a game box, making TunzaFunza the heart of "cyber" in Orphan County. It's only a frog-size heart, but it beats.

I bum some quarters from the others, scoop up my burger, fries, and helmet, and mosey on over.

I'm walking away, but I'm also walking toward.

Few people understand this concept. They walk away from something, but they don't walk toward something else. They don't feel their destination. They don't shed a world as they walk away and gain a world as they walk toward.

I do.

Because I am walking toward the best place of all.

The Drone Zone.

Not even sex feels as good. But, hey, I shouldn't be talking because I'm still a virgin. Unless you count Orphan County Tonsil Hockey, which is how some girls thank you for a little high flying on a dirt bike.

TunzaFunza is crowded today. Uncle Sal stands behind the counter driving the espresso machine, all five hands flying. Behind him hangs a poster-size photo of his plane, the *Hi-O Silver,* complete with missing door and other skydiving features. I know that plane well.

"Hey there, Arlo!" he booms as I walk up. "How's my favorite diamond in the rough today?"

"Dude," I say. "That was a sweet one this morning."

He blasts the steam wand into a pitcher of milk. "Sweet one? What are you talking about?"

"You know, White Sands, war games—all that."

Uncle Sal rattles his head. "Arlo, you mystify me."

A freebie Americano skates across the counter into my hand.

"Now get outta here," he says. "I'm a busy man."

I doubt that I mystify him, but he is a busy man.

I take my Americano and lunch over to the game corner. A senior named Rafe Rudolpi is in my seat. He's playing something called Mob War 2080, a futuristic look at the dark alleys of crime. You pick the city, the warrior, and the weapon.

Rafe's a football player, defensive end. Steroid mustache. Ugly, even by Clay standards. But he poses like next week's *Sports Illustrated* cover. Unless you play football, you do not exist to Rafe. He does, however, make an exception for gamers, but only if you play at least at his level.

He senses me watching and immediately his ego fires up. Now he's playing for an audience. Always a mistake. When you're conscious of others, even semi, you lose focus. Focus is everything. And true focus is the doorway to intuitive transcendence. It finds impossible targets, saves your life, and lifts you thousands of notches higher on the leaderboard.

It explodes my mind to think what the world would be like if all seven billion of us found true focus.

I hover there, sipping my Americano, munching my fries, and trying not to let my pity show. But Rafe's weaknesses are so glaring: he's slow to fire at the hovercraft; he forgets to look behind him in the alleys; he doesn't know how to see in the dark, instinctively, as any warrior must.

In the end, he survives. He kills a midlevel mob leader, pulverizing him, raining brain matter over half of Hong Kong, including the roof of a Chinese pagoda, where seagulls flock down and eat it. But he also kills 232 civilians.

Rafe seems pleased with himself. Maybe it's an above-average score for Clay Allison, but on a world scale, it sucks. He doesn't even rank in the top thousand.

He glances up, hoping to bask in some admiration. Then he sees it's me. He grabs his root beer from the cup holder and makes way.

"Show me how it's done, junior," he says.

"Happy to," I say, sliding into the seat.

I punch in my coins and log on. Download my game, Drone Pilot.

Select my UAV — unmanned aerial vehicle. Lots of designs to choose from: flying wing, rotorcraft, missile, hawk. On and on. Some drones are the size of a commercial jet; some are as small as a hummingbird.

Yesterday, my big day against Sergei, I shot into the sky as an MQ-9 Reaper, a pure hunter-killer, with a sixty-six-foot wingspan and a maximum speed of three hundred miles per hour, which I pushed to well over four hundred.

Today, I choose a MQ-3 Rapier, a twelve-foot-long missile-shaped drone designed for maximum expendable destruction. I want to challenge myself—to push to greater speeds. I'll be harder to hit and harder to detect. But flying with rudimentary wings—"wingstubs," as they're called—will make it much harder to maneuver. So it's a tradeoff. There's always a tradeoff.

The default design sucks, so I start to tinker. Most gamers are in such a hurry to play that they don't bother with this step—the customizing—and that's a major reason why they don't win.

Gaming has taught me this: that the more you individualize and tailor the game to you, and not somebody else's default idea of you, the higher-farther-faster you can go.

When you individualize and personalize, you play the real game. Just a few people out there truly get this.

I start to redraw my drone. I modify the carbon-fiber skin from one-half inch thick to one-quarter inch. This shaves exactly 162 pounds from my total weight—it will give me more time in the air, more precious seconds. On the downside, a thinner skin means I'm more vulnerable to attack—to the inevitable tracers and popping flak.

"Dude, what're you doing?"

It's Rafe, the human mosquito.

"Shut it, man," I say.

What I'm doing is this: I'm mounting a machine gun—borrowing ideas from an F-15E fighter—and welding it onto my nose. To pare my weight even more, I delete one whole barrel. The default is for one thousand shells. I cut this to two hundred. On second thought, I make it one hundred.

"Dude! You're crazy!"

Rafe's voice is getting punier.

Now I'm light — and fast. I can defend, but mostly I can offend.

I dump fuel, siphoning off a third of my load. I'm as light as can be. This will be a fast game — "surgically swift," as they say in the promotional docs.

In drone flying, the law of opposites applies: less is more. Never attack with more firepower than you need. Heavy guns and big shells are for amateurs. Your aircraft needs to be at least as fast as your instincts. Plus — and this is so obvious you'd think every gamer would know it, but few do — all it takes to kill an enemy is one well-aimed shell, even a little one, a tiny bullet. A fight can be won with one move. You just gotta know how, and when, to make it.

Now I'm Sir Lancelot riding to battle without armor — and carrying just a dagger. I'm *very* vulnerable, but I'm also way faster than any other knight out there. I can truly rack up a genius score.

It's a tradeoff, and today I have traded everything for speed.

Of course, speed is a sensation. To say it tingles up and down my spine and glows in my fingertips is an understatement.

While I'm gearing up, Rafe sees my user name — ClayMadSwooper — on the leaderboard.

He leans close and studies the numbers. More than two million people have played this version of Drone Pilot, and exactly three thousand are ranked. The top ten are listed on the screen by user name, and the top three are listed in bold lights: Ipanema-Girl is number three. SergeiTashkent is now number two. Clay-MadSwooper — that's me — is number one.

Rafe looks shocked. "Dude, when did this happen?"

"Last night."

"Is that ranking local?"

"Hey, don't insult me."

He gapes. "I'm profoundly speechless."

"Keep it that way," I say.

It's a crass thing to say to a senior and a defensive end on the football team, but Rafe really does need to shut up.

I choose a war zone. The game is extremely biased — every zone is a Muslim country:

Afghanistan
Iran
Iraq
Libya
Pakistan

I choose Pakistan, the North-West Frontier — the region around the Swat Valley. It's my favorite place to fly because it feels like home. When you fly drone or ride dirt, you get to know country. The orchards and groves, and farther up the spiny canyons, following the narrow washes and dry riverbeds that always lead to something.

Pakistan's Swat Valley looks and feels like Orphan County's canyon country. Loamy green bottomland rolling up to craggy granite palisades. Far-off snowy mountains. You can practically smell the river trout. And the sudden shadows. Oh my God, those shadows.

Yea, though I fly through the valley of the shadow of death . . .

Some guy with a kick-ass bass voice — in a tone half warning, half prayer — opens the game with these words. I could skip them, but I never do.

. . . I will fear no evil.

I fire up my engines. Count down. Blast off. Pull into the blue.

The soundtrack soars along with me. Subdued yet symphonic. Layered with a slow Hawaiian steel guitar to introduce all that death. It's both frightening and beautiful.

I'm up, up — gone.

I'm cruising at three thousand feet, homing on the Swat, when three enemy aircraft pop up at eleven o'clock — a sweet pod of death.

These craft are some duck-brained designer's idea of terrifying. They've got the wings of an F-22 Raptor and the aft fuselage of the *Millennial Falcon* — in other words, wide-assed but extremely fast.

One banks, dives, and blasts away. Red tracers carve up the sky.

Here's the problem: I can fly high and evasively or swoop and lose him in the canyons, but that'll cost fuel.

Since I don't have the fuel to mess with, I turn on the enemy plane and become the attacker.

In air combat, this is the moment of "shift."

When you shift, and defense becomes offense, you confuse the enemy, if only for a moment — and that's all it takes. Confusion is opportunity.

I fire a burst of shells. At least three hit the belly of the plane. One penetrates the fuel tank. Smoke pours out. At first, it's just a thin stream. Then he catches fire. The plane explodes, disintegrating into raining fireballs.

Rafe is freaking out in my ear: "Dude-dude-dude! Way to go!"

I block him out.

The two other planes come at me like rottweilers. I can't aim at one without showing my ass to the other, so I swoop low, flush against the ground.

Even little changes in land surface — a knoll, a boulder, a mesquite shrub — will end it all. So I slide into the trough of a dry riverbed pissed smooth by time.

When you're flying at the speed of blur, everything is surreal. You're never more than a millisecond from obliteration. It's pure, adrenalized, instinct flying — and it's the gateway to the Drone Zone.

One of these dogs can't handle my low-flying moves. He tries to pull out, clips a wing, pinwheels, and slams into the canyon wall. I shoot into the blue, straight up, with the last enemy jet sniffing my ass. Pop a loop and now I'm on *his* ass.

I feel the chill of death rush up his spine. Before he can twitch, I've fixed him in my sights and plowed the last of my shells into his carbureted guts.

As I split off, he explodes, raining molten steel over the Swat Valley.

Now I'm free — but I'm also out of ammo. Plus, I'm extremely low on fuel — just a needle's width from empty. Some drones can stay aloft forever powered by a single hydrogen cell, but when you operate on jet fuel or batteries, you can burn out fast.

The rule is, always — *Always!* — know your fuel level. Get so you can sense it down to the last lickable drop.

How you use fuel is the greatest challenge in drone flying. That's why I lighten my load, befriend the wind, glide the thermal, and lick the tank dry. I would lie, cheat, and steal from my grandmother to gain a few more seconds in the air.

Fuel is gold. Ammo is silver. All else is crap.

I close on my target, a biological weapons plant located in the village of Quaziristan. Ground guns open up. Flak pops all over. I'm getting scarred and nicked, but nothing penetrates my quarter-inch-thick skin. Not yet, anyway.

I brush the rooftops of the village. The thing about Pakistani villages is, almost all the structures are just one or two stories. If they were multiple heights, it would be death. But they are basically the same height, thank God.

Before she can even hear me, I blast over the head of a black-veiled woman hanging clothes on a rooftop. I can't actually see it, but I know I've just shredded every last robe and T-shirt on the line. I just hope my sonic *smack* hasn't knocked her off her feet.

Thirty seconds to an empty tank . . . twenty-nine . . . twenty-eight . . .

Now I'm in the heart of the Zone. A place of peace and calm. Instinct and prayer. A whisper from death, yet more alive than ever. Part of something bigger.

At fifteen seconds, I shoot into the sky, get my first naked-eye look at the weapons plant. The ground guns blast away. I can barely see through the flak. I'm nicked . . . nicked . . . nicked. But my skin holds.

Twelve . . . eleven . . . ten . . .

I fix a laser on my target. I'm going to rack up an extremely high score, cement my number one position on the leaderboard. Put more distance between me and the great Sergei.

My thumb slides to "Activate."

Just one little push of a button.

"Five . . . four . . . three . . ."

A bell rings, and children swarm out of the building next to the weapons plant.

My thumb twitches, leaps left. I hit Self-Destruct.

My drone pulverizes, showering down as molten particulate. Many little children are cut and burned. All are covered with soot and dust. The last image on the screen is of a cluster of saucer-eyed kids.

Trembling.

MISSION OVER. GAME OVER. POWER DOWN.

My score rolls up:

PILOTING: AWESOME.

MARKSMANSHIP: AWESOME.

STRATEGY: UNKNOWN.

CHECKLIST: INSUFFICIENT FUEL, INSUFFICIENT ARMOR, INSUFFICIENT AMMUNITION.

MISSION OUTCOME: ABORTED TO SAVE LIVES.

I get a good score—some would say great—but it's a long ways from my best. Six months ago, I would've been happy with it. Now I'm disappointed, because I've raised my performance level to the upper reaches of the game's exosphere.

Still, I'm pretty sure I've held the lead. When the leaderboard reconfigures, sure enough, there I am on top: ClayMadSwooper.

"*Hoo-woosh!*" somebody says.

"*Daaaamn!*" somebody else says.

I become aware of everybody around me—Cam, Lobo, Michelle, Latoya, Rafe. Even a few stray wranglers, holding their little cappuccino cups. Everybody's been watching.

"Dude, that was a helluva game," Rafe says. "But why'd you self-destruct? You coulda taken out that plant. You coulda scored off the charts."

It's pointless to point out the obvious to some people.

Cam claps my shoulder. "You made the right call, man. You saved that school. You saved those little kids."

"Quite a show, *hombre*," one of the wranglers says. "I'd say you've played this one before."

"It's just a game," I say. "No big deal."

CHAPTER 5

A SHINY BLACK FORD CROWN Victoria LX is parked in front of our house. Two men are talking to Dad. I brake outside the front gate and ponder the scene.

One of the dudes has on a crisp uniform — the dark blue of the United States Air Force. He looks like a recruiting poster: tall, cropped, and ripped. The other dude is older, bulkier, not quite so tall. He's dressed in chinos and a brown leather jacket. No military decals or insignias. He's bald, but "good bald" — bone shaved.

Dad's quite the contrast to these two. He's thin, unbuff, and a bit slouched. His jeans ride low. Not butt-crack low. Just don't-give-a-damn-anymore low. His hair, which he's taken to cutting himself, has the look of burnt range grass, with a little ash mixed in.

Dad's let go in stages. Stage one was May, when Mom died. He started holding himself differently, slouchier. He started dressing . . . not like a bum, but like a bum a week before he becomes a bum. Stage two was July, when the newspaper folded. He stopped doing the everyday stuff — doing it right, at least.

For the first sixteen and a half years of my life, Dad was a somebody in northeast New Mexico. Editor in chief of the *Orphan County Gunslinger* — "The Straightest-Shooting Newspaper in the Southwest, founded in 1887."

The *Gunslinger* died the way every business in Clay Allison dies — it dried up. As Dad's always telling me, you can't squeeze lime juice out of limestone.

Dad got offered media jobs in Albuquerque and Denver, but he didn't want to leave Clay. Didn't want to go far from Burro Mesa.

Now he owns and operates the Snack Shack down at Rio Loco Field. On football Fridays, I'm right there beside him, tonging hot dogs, pouring coffee, juggling Skittles.

Some weeks, this adds up to less than a hundred bucks. Even for Orphan County, New Mexico, that's slim, especially because of Siouxsie and all her needs.

What's saved us are the mares — Queen Zenobia, Blue Dancer, and I Love Cornflakes. These pregnant, snorting ladies wander between the barn and corral, getting fatter by the day. You'd never know they were once sleek, Kentucky-bred racers, or that Queen Zenobia came in fourth at the Preakness.

I take care of them. In exchange, Mr. Wasserman, of Gunnison, Colorado, takes care of our mortgage. But the deal lasts only until they drop their foals, which is going to happen in twelve to fourteen weeks — or sometime in January or early February. That's the point; they will be winter babies, and it's warmer here than in the Gunnison Valley. We'll hold on to those babies until spring.

After that, God only knows.

I sputter toward the military dudes. Dad walks out to meet me, slices a finger across his throat. I kill the motor.

"You know anything about this, Arlo?" he says, glancing back at the dudes.

"'Bout what?"

He plants his hands on his hips. "Don't mess with me. These guys seem to know all about you."

I pull off my helmet. Peer over my shades. "Nah, never seen 'em before."

"What's all this about some shootout down at White Sands?"

I check out the dudes again. "You serious?"

"Mmm-hm," Dad says. "I thought so."

A gust of wind blasts into us. It darts across the field and hops the fence. A black curtain hangs over Eagle Tail Mesa.

"Looks like it's gonna drop and slop," Dad says. "C'mon, we better hear them out."

I lean my Yam 250 against the side of the house, under the eaves. We go over to the dudes.

"Hello, Arlo," the man in uniform says. "I'm Major Keith Anderson. We spoke this morning."

"Yeah, I actually remember."

"Hope you made it to school on time."

"Yeah, got there early."

"This is Colonel Carl Kincaid," Major Anderson says. "We're on the same team."

I'm trying to wrap my brain around the fact these guys are real and not one of Uncle Sal's jokes. I shake the colonel's hand. He's a knuckle cracker.

"What team would that be?" Dad asks.

"ARI," Colonel Kincaid says.

Dad looks puzzled. "You government boys and your acronyms."

"ARI — Applied Robotic Interdiction," Colonel Kincaid says.

"Yes, of course," Dad says. "Let's go inside before it hauls down. We can interdict ourselves over some coffee."

We go up into the kitchen. I'm thinking about what Major Anderson said this morning on the phone — about war games and White Sands. Just the thought . . . Something soars inside me. If it's true, this could be profound.

Dad gets the Mr. Coffee going, and I clear the table of Siouxsie's homeschool stuff. It's a mess, with spilled juice and scattered worksheets. The old Siouxsie was all about neat stacks and parallel pencils. The new Siouxsie's a slob.

"Just wondering," I say. "If you're a colonel, how come you're not wearing a uniform?"

Colonel Kincaid smiles. Actually, it's more like a facial tic.

"I'm old army, Arlo. I wore a uniform for twenty-two years — Persian Gulf to the Pentagon. These days, I work independently."

"Ah," Dad says, setting out the mugs. "An independent contractor."

"That's right," the colonel says.

The Mr. Coffee drips down. Dad fills the mugs and hands them out, sniff-checking the half-and-half before he plants it on the table. He drops a pack of Chips Ahoy! cookies beside it — the original hard variety, not the phony chewy ones. Dad doesn't bother to put anything in a pitcher or on a plate. Mom would've had a fit.

"So what's the big deal?" Dad says. "I mean, why are you interested in Arlo? Has he broken any law?"

"Hey, please!" I say. "I don't break laws. I ride and abide."

It's a load of crap. I break laws every day, if you count the speed limit.

Everybody's staring at me. It feels like something's going to drop: a hammer, a shoe, a guillotine blade.

"Arlo's captured our attention," Colonel Kincaid says. "You see, ARI has evolved into an important part of our strategy, especially in one war zone."

"ARI?" Dad says. "Tell me again."

"Applied . . . Robotic . . . Interdiction," the colonel says.

"He means drones," I tell Dad.

"Ah, yes, well, we know about those, don't we," Dad says. "And which war zone are we talking about?"

Colonel Kincaid starts to answer, then stops. "Why don't you tell him, Arlo."

The reason for this visit is starting to explode my mind. At the same time, it's so off my beaten path, I have to wonder.

"Pakistan," I say.

"Can you be more specific?" Colonel Kincaid asks.

Thanks to Drone Pilot, I can.

"The North-West Frontier," I say.

Colonel Kincaid smiles — it's more than a tic this time. It's almost warm.

"Pakistan!" Dad says. "We're not at war with Pakistan."

"Not officially," Colonel Kincaid says. "Our war is not against the Pakistani people or government but rather against an extreme mindset that breeds in that region."

"Sir," Major Anderson says, "the North-West Frontier is one of the world's most dangerous landscapes, both topographically and politically."

"It's a godforsaken snake pit," Colonel Kincaid says. "In three thousand years, nobody — not Alexander the Great, not the mogul warlords, not the British Empire, not even the Soviet Union — has been able to control the Frontier. Today, it's occupied by insurgent groups and outlaw tribes. Depending on the day of the week, they're either in bed with each other or cutting each other's throats."

"Sounds like a great place to raise kids," Dad says. "But I still don't get it. Why are you here?"

Yeah, I say to myself. *Why* are *you here?*

I grab the sugar jar. The near-infinity of white crystals seems to capture the surrealness of this conversation — the relationship between micro and macro, nothing and everything.

"Mr. Santiago — may I call you Hector?" Colonel Kincaid asks.

"You may."

"Hector . . . Arlo . . . we know that key elements of the insurgency — those responsible for attacks against our personnel and facilities — are based in the mountains of the North-West Frontier."

"Yeah, mostly in the Swat Valley," I say.

"Correct," Colonel Kincaid says. "That's common knowledge. The media reports it every day. The Swat is our main area of interest."

I'm watching Colonel Kincaid as he talks. He looks both worn down and alert. Like he's spent most of his life missing sleep, eating meat, drinking coffee, and smoking cigarettes. Or more accurately, like he's tried to cut back on all those but failed. He also looks like he's pumped some iron, though maybe not this year.

"These insurgents," he goes on, "hide in remote compounds, slipping back and forth across the border. They plan missions, train operatives, and carry out their mayhem with virtual impunity."

Major Anderson clears his throat. "One of our jobs is to monitor all communications pertaining to UAVs—"

"There you go again with your acronyms," Dad says.

"UAVs," the major says. "Unmanned aerial vehicles."

"Drones," I tell Dad. "All these acronyms are about drones."

Dad scratches his head.

Major Anderson says, "The DOD—Department of Defense—"

"I know what the DOD is," Dad grumbles.

"Yes, sir. Well, the DOD tracks the entire universe of air combat and defense scenarios. One area we monitor is video games—the type that involves covert observation and strike."

"Video games!"

Dad fixes me with his "squinch"—his pinched, squinty look that combines doubt and disgust with a twinkle of amusement. Over the years, as editor of the *Gunslinger*, he spent a lot of time squinching at mayors, governors, rodeo stars, and other people who might not be telling the truth.

Colonel Kincaid picks up. "New games come on the market every day. As far as we're concerned, ninety-nine-point-nine-nine percent are pure shit. Forgive my French."

"Forgiven," Dad says.

He swings around and opens a cupboard. Plants a bottle of

Cutty Sark Scotch whiskey on the table. "More authority for your coffee, gentlemen?"

"Not for me, thanks," Major Anderson says.

"How about you, Colonel? It's the real McCoy. Double rectified."

Colonel Kincaid places a hand over his mug.

Dad shrugs and spikes his own coffee. "Keep going," he says. "I want to know more about these video games that involve 'covert observation and strike.'"

Colonel Kincaid sips his coffee. "Most are conceived and designed by twenty-two-year-old kids dressed in black T-shirts," he says. "In my opinion, they've cracked their skulls in one too many skateboard falls. They know nothing about us."

"'Us'?" Dad asks.

"That's right." The colonel coughs—a boggy, old-smoker cough. "Those of us on the front lines—from Colorado Springs to Cambridge to Kabul—who study military operations, history, technology, strategy, logistics . . . These kids know squat about flying. Flying is the supreme skill, Hector. It's the sublime marriage of science and art. 'The touch'—that's what you need. These damn video games rarely rise above the level of cartoons."

"There's one exception," Major Anderson says.

"Yeah," I say. "A big one."

"Go on, Arlo," the colonel says. "Tell us about it."

I set the sugar jar on the table. "It's called Drone Pilot," I say. "Actually, that's the short name. The full name is Drone Pilot World War III: In the Valley of the Shadow."

"Isn't that the game you're always playing?" Dad asks.

"Not always," I say.

"Like hell," Dad says. "That game eats you for breakfast and spits you out for lunch."

It's actually a fair statement. When I'm not sleeping or at school, I'm either hitting the mesas on my 250 or playing Drone Pilot. I can pinpoint the start of my meteoric rise on the leaderboard to May, about when Mom died. It's just a coincidence, as far as I know.

Dad turns to the military dudes. "Is it me, or is our country spawning a generation of couch-potato slackers? Thomas Jefferson must be weeping in his grave."

"He's not weeping over Arlo," Colonel Kincaid says. "You see, Hector, we think your son may be a highly capable drone pilot."

These words buzz up and down my spine.

"Sir, we'd like to invite Arlo down to White Sands to test him," Major Anderson says. "If he performs well, he may be of value to us."

"Of value?" Dad looks puzzled. "Are you sure this isn't one of Uncle Sal Focazio's practical jokes? Who are you, a couple of his old paratrooping buddies?"

The colonel glares at Dad.

"Sir," Major Anderson says, "as of today — correction, yesterday — Arlo is the top drone pilot."

"Top drone pilot where?" Dad asks.

"In the world."

"You mean, the video game world," Dad says.

"Yes," Major Anderson says.

"Hell, that's not the world."

"Let me break it down for you," Colonel Kincaid says. "The game Drone Pilot is based on our technology. God knows how they got it — the algorithms and such — but it's ours. This game is not like any other video game out there. It replicates one of the most effective and lethal weapons systems ever devised, a system that delivers profound capability with zero vulnerability. If you can fly a UAV — excuse me, a *drone* — in the game Drone Pilot, you can fly a real one. If you can pinpoint and destroy a level-fourteen target, you can pinpoint and destroy a real target. Something the size of, say, a pickup truck from half a world away."

"Or the size of a single person," I say.

Dad doesn't look impressed. "Capability without vulnerability? Where are the heroics in that?"

"We're not interested in heroics," Colonel Kincaid says. "Only in results."

Dad gulps his coffee. "Surely you can find someone at least eighteen years old."

The colonel shrugs. "Let me tell you, Hector, what does *not* interest me: talent. I see talent every day and it bores the hell out of me. What I'm looking for is far more rare."

"And what would that be?" Dad asks.

The colonel's eyes spark. "Rapture."

"Rapture?" Dad says.

"Someone with 'the touch,' Hector."

"And you think Arlo has 'the touch'?"

"I do," Colonel Kincaid says. "Assuming the leaderboard is accurate."

"Hey, it's accurate," I say. "It's sacred."

Right now, my mind is on fire. Because Colonel Kincaid gets it. He actually understands what I've done. And respects it. Major Anderson, too.

Dad scratches his neck. "White Sands, that's a long ways down the pike. A night or two in Alamogordo. Five or six meals. I don't exactly relish all that. And I sure as hell don't have the budget for it."

"Sir," Major Anderson says, snapping open his briefcase. "We've taken that into consideration." He hands Dad an envelope.

Dad props it up — unopened — against the pepper mill.

"I'm going to level with you," he tells the officers. "We've had a lousy year — book of Job lousy."

It's strange to hear him say this, because he almost never talks about it.

"In what way?" the colonel asks.

"Every way," Dad says. "Lost my wife. Lost my job. And my daughter has been diagnosed . . ."

"Diagnosed with what?" the colonel asks.

Dad shakes his head. Sunken.

"She's got Huntington's disease," I say.

"HD," Colonel Kincaid says. "A tough one."

Dad's trembling now. He doesn't usually let it show. He's proud — a proud man. But since the newspaper folded, people see him as half gone to hell. That's the way it works in Clay Allison, New Mexico — you're as shiny as your last victory or as dog-assed as your last defeat.

He looks at the officers. "So I must ask you, what's in it for us? Because, you see, I'm sitting on a mountain of debt the size of

Pike's Peak. And due to geological instabilities, Pike's is getting higher every day. Boy, what a view!"

Dad looks half ready to laugh, half ready to cry, and half ready to lunge across the table and kick the crap out of Colonel Kincaid. He would definitely lose.

Dad and the colonel go eye to eye, 'nad to 'nad — first to blink, first to twitch and all that. The colonel blinks first.

"What's in it for you, Hector? Well, it all depends. If Arlo can help us . . . if his skills can translate . . . if he can perform at the highest level . . . then —"

"Then what?" I blurt.

The colonel faces me. His look goes deep, like he's trying to see some magic spark inside me.

"Then, Arlo, your father will no longer be sitting atop Pike's Peak."

Dad looks stunned. I'm feeling it too.

Dad says, "Do you *want* to do this, Arlo?"

The truth is, going to White Sands to play the military version of Drone Pilot sounds amazing in itself. But the idea that we might lower Pike's Peak feels like an answered prayer.

I don't explode out of my chair. Got to keep the seesaw balanced between Dad and the dudes.

"Yeah," I say, like it's nothing.

"I'm curious about something, Arlo," Colonel Kincaid says. "What makes you so good?"

So good? It's not that I don't have an answer. It's that I don't fully grasp what's behind my answer. Plus, it's kind of personal.

I open my mouth to speak, but nothing comes out.

"Take a minute," the colonel says.

I grab the sugar jar again and roll it in my hands. Stare at the tumbling crystals as they bury the soda cracker, then fall away, revealing the cracker again.

Fact is, I could sum up my answer in two words—*Drone Zone.* The Drone Zone is that special place on the right side of my brain where the clutch is always wet and the engine always purrs.

Like when I crank my Yam 250 and take to the air on Little Piñon.

Or when I play Drone Pilot.

It wasn't easy getting here. For a long time, I measured progress in inches—one inch higher. One foot farther. One kill more.

Do that a hundred times. Do it a thousand. Do it five thousand. Don't try to be better than others. Just push yourself to be better than the last time.

On a blackboard, you can write it this way:

> The more you push yourself + the more you push yourself = the better you get.

One day, you go past the point where your senses work in greased harmony. You slip out of your skin. You free yourself from gravitational pull.

You enter the Drone Zone.

When I'm in the Drone Zone, I function better than I'm capable of. Brain chatter dies. Life shit fades. Something inside me lines up with something in the universe.

I break through.

Maybe it's God letting me peek at the light.

Maybe it's the spirit of Mom pulling me from the dark.

Maybe I'm delusional.

But whenever I enter the Drone Zone, when I reach my limit, I realize it's not a limit. It's a door. All I have to do is open it.

Nobody — including me — knows what I can do when I enter the Drone Zone, and *truly* push myself.

Because I never have.

But I don't tell this to the officers — it's way too much information.

I set the sugar jar back on the table.

"Why am I so good? Um, maybe because I'm not afraid to go fast or high. Lobo and Cam — my friends — *are* afraid, which is normal. But I'm not, which is probably abnormal. Like there's a broken fear wire in me. I'm more aware of things when I leave the ground. The higher I go, the more aware I am."

Colonel Kincaid looks at me like I'm freakin' Mona Lisa. "A broken fear wire," he says. "I like that."

Dad frowns. "Well, I don't."

CHAPTER 6

A RAINDROP—ONE SINGLE DROP—splats at my feet. We definitely need this rain. Most of Mom's plants have died of thirst. They stand in the dust and rustle in the wind. But after that one drop, nothing.

The sky scowls down. But it can't darken me.

I'm feeling too good.

I watch the Crown Vic roll up our driveway, go left on the access road, and head toward Interstate 25.

"Damn!" I say, smacking my fist. *"Daaaamn!"*

I wheel my Yam 250 over to the shed. Dad's turned this weathered-plank shack into a garage for all our nags. We keep five here—the oldest dating back to Dad's dusty-rusty motorcycle days, before he and Mom got married.

The only actual living bikes are my own two, my Yamaha 250 and my YZ 125.

Dad's bikes—his Harley Fat Boy, his Indian Chief, and his Triumph Bonneville—died slow deaths, cannibalized to keep each other alive. Still, even in death, these old bikes are beautiful machines, majestic and muscular. You can tell they once ruled the open roads. They make my two bikes look like wimps. But then, my bikes can do things these old nags could never do.

I park my 250, close the shed door, and slip the bolt. It's getting darker and darker. It's truly going to piss and float cow pies.

I stroll over to the barn — our giant green-sided, silver-roofed aluminum lunch box, all prefab and permanently new, with none of the grainy-plank-truth feel and smell of the shed. Nothing like the old barns of Orphan County that sag like mule backs and make you wonder, did Billy the Kid or even Clay Allison himself sleep in that hayloft?

Radio music is blaring inside. I open the door and squeeze in, barring the way for El Guapo, who will only harass the kittens.

Siouxsie's sitting on the alfalfa. Four bales high, an easy climb because the bales are stacked like bleacher seats. She used to do standing flips off the bales. Now, just getting up on the stack is a major achievement. The black kitten in her lap stares at me with yellow eyes.

"Sioux-Sioux-how-do-you-do?" I say.

She snaps off the radio, reaches into her pocket for the fortune-cookie-shaped hearing aids, tilts her head like she's hooking earrings, and pops them in.

"All done," she says, nodding toward the ladies. The mares snort and stare at me, luminously, from their stalls. "Fed 'em one and a half quarts, just like you said."

I go over and check the stalls. The oat and alfalfa levels are about right. The water buckets are wet. Manure's even shoveled. That couldn't have been easy.

The mares seem content. Blue Dancer flares her nostrils. Queen Zenobia — "Big Z," sixteen hands tall — leans over the rail and nudges me. Cornflakes snuffles my hand, searching for a treat. They're good ladies, doing the quiet, important work of the belly, growing new life. I'll miss them, when their time comes.

"Who were those men, Texas Slim?"

I climb onto the alfalfa stack and roost my ass beside her.

"Nobody," I say. "Just a couple of military dudes."

She twists a few strands of her hair, licks the ends, and flicks the point at the kitten, like a sword. The kitten parries.

"They want you to join up?" she asks.

"Nah. Just play some video games down at White Sands."

"Video games! How come?"

I pull a stalk of alfalfa out of the bale under me and join the sword fight. The kitten pivots and swipes a paw at me. He and I go at it like musketeers.

"'Cuz I'm good," I say. "That's how come."

I baffle the kitten with a flurry of thrusts.

"Wanna know how good?"

"Uh-uh," Siouxsie says. "Not if you're gonna brag about it."

"Best in the world," I say, and jab the kitten in the belly.

Now I've done it—committed the sin of arrogance. Mr. Martinez likes to quote Herodotus: "All arrogance will reap a harvest rich in tears."

He may be right. Arrogance has been stalking me for months. It's probably why the sky is scowling right now.

Siouxsie hacks up and spits. "Biggest head in the world, you mean."

"Hey, I'm the best frickin' drone pilot you'll ever see. And it's your lucky day to be talking to me. Want my autograph?"

"Yuck-o," Siouxsie says. "You think ugly."

She's right, I do think ugly. As soon as you let arrogance in the door, you're dead. Arrogance lowers your guard, pierces your shield. Humility, on the other hand, is your friend. Don't brag, don't think about your skills, don't even talk about them, and they will grow. Like a beanstalk. Brag, and that beanstalk will topple. Any movie I've ever seen, when a guy starts bragging, he gets it — a bullet, a knife, a shove down the elevator shaft.

This time when I poke the kitten, he hooks a claw into my finger. A drop of blood appears. *"Damn!"*

I grab his scruff and fling him in the general direction of the chopped hay.

"Don't do that!" Siouxsie says. "You got a problem, kick a stump."

"What're you talkin' about?" I say. "That was the high point of that little Jedi's day."

A terrified mew comes from inside the hay.

"Go get him," Siouxsie says.

I jump off the bales, go over and dig the kitten out, dust him off, carry him back, and perch myself beside Siouxsie again, kitten in lap. He's just a scrawny thing, a fur-covered skeleton, totally barn born and bred. I stroke him, and he starts to purr.

"See what I mean? One happy kitten."

Siouxsie scoops him back.

I notice that she's wearing the headband Mom made for her — the one decorated with tie-dyed ripples of blue.

"Hey, mind if I see this?"

Before she can answer, I've slipped it off.

"Stop being a jerk, Arlo."

I am being a jerk. Why, I don't know.

Of the three of us, Siouxsie's been hit hardest by Mom's death. Dad and I can function okay, like with one kidney or half your liver, but for Siouxsie, Mom was both kidneys and the whole liver.

The first time we noticed a change in her — started thinking that she wasn't just accident prone — was about eighteen months ago, when she fell on the basketball court during a game against Springer. She was rushing down court and — *bang!* — she was flat on her ass.

Mom was everywhere for her. Took her to doctors in Denver and Albuquerque. Got her into an occupational therapy program in Raton. Started homeschooling her.

She also sat me down and explained about Huntington's disease. How it's caused by nerve cells dying in the brain. They waste away slower than autumn leaves. Huntington's can get you in many ways — hearing that fades, muscles that jumble, moods that darken. On and on. It's a long list. There can be progress, but no cure.

The other thing is, Huntington's is hereditary. After Siouxsie was diagnosed, Mom had me tested up in Denver. Not only is my chromosome 4 normal — every corkscrew of my DNA is in shiny, mint condition.

Mom made the house "Siouxsie friendly." Got her on an extra-nutritious diet. Walked with her every day — laps around the barn and house. Most days, you barely noticed anything was wrong. But some days, Siouxsie tripped over her own shadow.

Mom was just starting to convert the downstairs den into a bedroom when she died. The hooks for hanging Siouxsie's posters are still where she left them on the windowsill. The new lamp is still in its box.

"How come you never talk about her?" Siouxsie asks.

"Hey, I talk about her."

"No, you don't."

"What do you mean? Just yesterday I needed her socket wrench for my 250. I asked Dad where it was."

"That's stupid," Siouxsie says.

She runs a finger along the arc of the headband, and we hold it, like a wishbone. The dyed ripples range from sky to turquoise to midnight.

"She's on my mind all the time," Siouxsie says. "Mostly, I think about that day."

"Big mistake," I say. "Delete 'that day' from your memory. All it does is cut things open. Why bleed if you don't have to?"

"I can't delete it," Siouxsie says. "I'm the one who made her go to the EZ Stop. If it wasn't for me . . . I saw her lying there, Arlo."

"Yeah, well, maybe I saw her lying there too."

I didn't, of course. But in my mind, I've seen her lying in that pool many times. And every time, I hit Delete.

How long did it take — one hundredth of a second? Five seconds? And look what happened — not just to her, but to all of us. To Siouxsie, Dad, and me.

Day to night.

No sunset or twilight in between.

Just — *whomp!* — night.

"I hate violence," Siouxsie says.

"Me, too," I say.

"Liar," Siouxsie says. "If you hated violence, you wouldn't play Drone Pilot all the time."

“Nah, don’t confuse it,” I say. “That’s just a game. Just make-believe.”

In fact, Drone Pilot is pretty violent. But that has nothing to do with why I play it. For me, it isn’t about violence and darkness. It’s about getting *through* violence and darkness.

I stare out the window. The sky swirls gray, black, and yellow. I wait for it to break open. But nothing.

“Here’s what I do,” I say, snapping back. “Just get on my 250 and bomb the mesas, blast the bumps. That’s how I deal with it. It’s a lot better than that grief counselor. A lot better than talking.”

“For you, maybe,” Siouxsie says.

“Definitely for me,” I say.

I pop the headband back on her head. “It’s cool that you wear this,” I say. “Kind of a memory thing.”

“Not just that,” Siouxsie says. “I can’t do braids anymore.”

Tears brim in her eyes.

I give her a nudge. “Hey, I’ll do your braids for you.”

“You don’t get it, Arlo.”

“Get what?”

She shakes her head.

“Get what?” I ask again.

Siouxsie pulls the buds out of her ears and clenches them in her fist.

I raise my voice. “Hey, we’re headed down to White Sands on Saturday. Bet we can get Dad to stop at the Tularosa Café for some chocolate churros. Best in the West, and you know it.”

The old Siouxsie did know it. The new Siouxsie can’t even hear me — or refuses to. I’m never sure.

She stares at some invisible point above the barn door, about twelve feet up, some mystical portal through which, maybe, spirits come and go between worlds.

Tin-poom-pah!

Now it begins. Little fingers tap the roof, roll into drums. Out the window, the sky flashes. Hail bounces under the barn door. The mares twitch, stomp, and bang their asses against the stalls.

Siouxsie stares at the invisible point.

I jump off the bales, hoist her up—*"Hup!"*—and swing her onto my back. But her legs barely hold on. I haul her over to the chopped hay and dump her.

She should be laughing. All the thunder-clatter and stomp-shifting, all the sky energy—even the deaf can hear that. We should both be in hysterics. Because you should never waste a storm. But Siouxsie sinks into the hay. Eyes lit and lost.

You don't get it.

She's right, I don't.

Mom, let this storm wake you up. Glue you back together from all the scattered dust up on Burro Mesa. You need to be here NOW! If only to deal with this one thing—this shining, staring lostness.

CHAPTER 7

"CLASS, WHO CAN DEFINE *MATRIARCHY?*"

Mr. Martinez tweaks the knot on his necktie. Everybody ducks, shifts, or squirms. It's not that we can't define *matriarchy*, it's that Mr. Martinez likes to lure you with an easy question, hook you under the gill, reel you in, and make you wriggle in front of everybody.

He waits for hands. Nobody raises one.

"You blocks, you stones, you worse than senseless things," he says, quoting from *Julius Caesar*. "Latoya! Speak to me."

Latoya straightens up. "Matriarchy . . . *umm* . . . well . . . that's, like, when women rule and stuff."

"Correct," Mr. Martinez says. "A matriarchy is a society in which women play the leading role. Not merely the central role, the *leading* role. Can you give us an example of a such a society from chapter seventeen?"

"Not really," Latoya says. "Only . . . only, it's the way it should be. I mean, women actually *should* rule."

The light glints off Mr. Martinez's glasses. "Because . . . ?"

Latoya shrugs. "Because we're smarter. Just look around this room."

"Bull!" Vonz says. "No society in history's ever been a real matriarchy."

"Are you sure of that?" Mr. Martinez asks.

"I can prove it," Vonz says.

He slides up his T-shirt sleeve and flexes his bicep. It bulges into a mound. "Women don't have this. And you can't rule without it."

Michelle shakes her shoulders. "Yeah, but we have our own stuff."

"Go ahead, Michelle," Mr. Martinez says. "Speak to us."

"What about those tall women who carried bows and cut off their breasts, like Xena? Weren't they stronger than men?"

"Oh, you're thinking of the Amazons," Mr. Martinez says. "The mythological tribe of female warriors. But let's not confuse history with myth."

Lobo leans over and whispers, "Dude, did Xena cut off her jugs?"

I jerk an elbow at him.

Cam levitates a hand. "Aren't beehives a matriarchy? I mean, all those male worker drones doing the grunt lifting for the queen?"

"Good example, Camerado," Mr. Martinez says. "Now who can give us a human example?"

Mr. Martinez scans the room again, and this time his glasses glint at me.

"Arlo, please give us an example of a matriarchy?"

Unfortunately, I didn't get around to reading chapter seventeen. Still, I try to think of an example. What enters my head is this: matriarchy was when Mom was alive and everything ran smooth in our house, like on my Yam 250 when I wirebrush the sparks. Patriarchy's like now — Dad's running things. Everything still works, but it doesn't fire exactly right, because the sparks are a bit gunked up. So when I need that extra kick, like going over Raton Pass or just before a jump — maybe I get it, maybe I don't. That's patriarchy.

I'm so lost in this thought that I don't notice everybody staring at me. Lobo smacks my arm. "Dude, wake up!"

I shake out of it.

"Class," Mr. Martinez says, "please open your books and read from chapter seventeen — *silently*!"

He gestures, and I follow him out of the room. He closes the door. We stand there. Mr. Martinez smells of pipe smoke and tuna fish, his basic lunch for the past forty years.

"How you doin', son?"

"Me? Fine."

Sadness pools in his eyes.

"Siouxsie — how's she doin'?"

"Great."

"Homeschool workin' out for her?"

"Seems to be."

"That Siouxsie — her smile can brighten a room quicker than the General Electric grid. How's your dad?"

"We're all doing really well," I say, hoping this will end it.

But nothing ends until Mr. Martinez wants it to.

"I sure miss the ol' *Gunslinger*," he says. "Straightest shootin' newspaper in the Wild West. Times change, but not always for the better."

"For sure," I say.

"How's that family therapy coming along — the grief counselor and all? Did you finish up the sessions?"

"Nah," I say. "Waste of time."

Which is true. You don't get anywhere hugging pillows and screaming at walls. I sure didn't.

Mr. Martinez takes off his glasses and polishes the lenses with his handerchief.

"Arlo, some things we can never understand. What happened is unfair. It's unfairest of all to you and Siouxsie. If I were walking around in your boots, I'd probably see the world as a senseless, tormented, even murderous place."

Something rises in me — something halfway between a fist and a sob. I hold it back.

"Look in there," he says, peering through the little window into our classroom. "Up on our walls. All those stars. Long-dead, but still shining. I'd like to reach up and pull one down just for you. Who should it be? Who best to speak the words *you* need to hear? Because I cannot. I don't know the right words. Sometimes all the wisdom of the ages is not enough. Time is what we need. Time is your friend, Arlo. Time will sort it out. Just go about your days. Follow your norms. And don't do anything rash. Promise me?"

"Yeah, sure," I say.

"And for God's sake stay safe on that motorcycle. Don't end up like Evel Knievel — all 'scar tissue and surgical steel.'"

"Hey, I'm actually pretty cautious."

"I can think of many words to describe you, Arlo, but 'cautious' is not one."

A light sparks in his eye. "Let's pull down Martin Luther King, Jr. The night before he was killed he told an audience, 'Longevity has its place. I may not get there with you.' Wasn't that prophetic! I'd like you to have longevity, Arlo. I'd like that very much. But here's the rub: longevity alone isn't enough."

"It isn't?"

"Not half enough," he says.

He peers again into our classroom. "Let's pull down William Faulkner. Do you know who he was?"

"Yeah, some writer. Long time ago."

"That's right, Arlo. One of our greatest. He said that 'man will not merely endure, he will prevail.' I prefer the Spanish: *Aguente primero, luego prevalezca*. First, endure. Then, prevail."

"Nice," I say. "But what's it really mean?"

"It means this," Mr. Martinez says. He draws back the string of an imaginary hunter's bow. "You, Arlo, are one of my most magnificent arrows. I notch you, aim at the horizon, and—*ffffffffftt*—off you go, to soar long after I'm gone. That's what it means."

He sticks out his hand.

"Another reason I miss the old days," he says, "they let you hug your students."

We shake.

"Tell your dad I'm still working my way through that manuscript of his. I'll get back to him with my comments—in a year or two." He winks. "And tell Siouxsie 'hi.'"

"Yeah, I will."

Mr. Martinez could've retired long ago. Dad says he's the only person in all Orphan County whose character and reputation are the same. Everybody else, there's a difference, like a fat tree throwing off a thin shadow. But Mr. Martinez's shadow fits exactly who he is.

He opens the door, and as he strides to the front of the room, I slip back into my seat. I can feel the eyes on me, each pair an added weight on the barbell.

"Well, now, where were we?" he says, in his classroom voice.

Lee Fields shoots up a hand.

"Go ahead, Lee."

"The Berbers of North Africa."

"Ah-ha!"

"And the Hopi of Arizona," she says. "Both societies are characterized by rites and rituals that exalt women over men, especially mothers and grandmothers."

We stare at the torqued golden girl who does not advertise her torsion, and who talks like an anchorwoman.

"At last!" Mr. Martinez says. "A flower blooms in the desert. Thank you, Lee. Class, let us discuss the Berbers of North Africa and our Hopi friends to the west. Hold on to your hats."

CHAPTER 8

WHEN THE BELL RINGS, I blast out of the room. Somebody calls after me, but I ain't stopping. I pound down the hall and bust through the doors. As far as I'm concerned, school is over for the day, even if it's just second period. I go straight to my bike, unlock the chain, fling it in my backpack, jam on my helmet, pop my shades.

Saddle up. Kick it.

Grind!

Hear the strong *thump-thump-thump* of the four-stroke.

GRIND!

Feel the mustangs running up my spine.

I'm about to gallop off when there's a knock on my helmet.

"Hello in there."

I ease off the throttle. Angle my head because all I can see is a silhouette. Slide down my shades. It's Lee Fields. The girl from Seattle and the book of Genesis. She who talks of Berbers and Hopi.

"Can I ask you about your motorcycle?"

Two kinds of energy flow out of Lee: beautiful-girl energy and snaky, Garden-of-Eden energy. At least, that's how I see her now, standing with Tinaja Mesa on her shoulder. I don't kill the engine.

"Yeah, what about it?"

"Know where I can find one?"

Motorcycles are another thing. I can talk about them with anybody, from fools to smiling rattlers. So I kill the motor. Tug off my helmet.

"Clay's a boneyard," I say. "If you want a decent bike, check out Raton or Trinidad. Better yet, check out Santa Fe or Albuquerque, wherever there's online ads or newspapers. There sure's no newspaper here in Clay."

"Your dad was the editor, wasn't he?"

"Was," I sniff.

Lee hunkers down for a better view of my bike. Up close, Lee Fields isn't all that scary. Or perfect. There's a strawberry welt on her neck. *Damn,* does she have a boyfriend already? But those pink Pumas. Not a smudge or speck of dirt. How can anybody keep their shoes *that* clean?

"Word of mouth," I say, "is best. But I can tell you, from my own mouth, Clay's dead—not just dying, dead. I know every bike in the county, from the fattest hog to the skinniest Honda. How much you wanna spend?"

Lee thinks a moment. "Hmm, I don't know."

I'm pondering whether to say the next thing, because I haven't thought it through. But before I can make up my mind, I hear myself say:

"I got another bike, a Yamaha YZ 125. Been saving it for my little sister, but—"

Lee waves off my thought. "Oh, definitely. You *should* save it for her."

"She's not too interested these days," I say. "So it might be for sale."

Lee perks up. "What's the condition?"

"Scratched and nicked," I say. "All the paint's basically worn off. She's definitely broken in. Got a wet clutch."

"Wet clutch?"

"An oil drip that keeps everything running smooth," I say. "You can't find a better bike in all northeast New Mexico. Plus, she's lucky. Never wiped out or bit the dust. And she's a high flier. Kind of a minor genius on the bumps. This one's a major genius." I pat my 250 four-stroke.

Lee moves around, studying my machine. "Think I should get a dirt bike or a road bike?" she asks.

"No offense," I say, "but that's a tragic question. Do you wanna stay stuck on asphalt all your life? Or . . ." I sweep my hand from the Spanish Peaks to Tinaja Mesa — 180 degrees, north to south. "Or do you wanna ride all this? 'Cuz that's northeast New Mexico. On a dirt bike, it's all yours. Every square mile."

Lee nods. "I see your point."

"Always — *always* — go with the dirt," I say. "Give your bike all the rein it wants, and it'll love you right back. You got miles of good dirt up in Chicorica Canyon — all those arroyos and washes."

Lee looks off in the direction of the canyon. "We've got horses for the arroyos and washes," she says.

"Nah," I say. "A horse has a mind of its own. A dirt bike is an extension of *your* mind. All the speed and freedom of a wild mustang, with none of the orneriness."

"You seem to have a strong opinion about this," Lee says.

"Hey, if you really want to know what I think—"

Lee plants a hand on her hip. "Yes, what *do* you think, Arlo Santiago?"

It's a nice shift—a sweet torque, halfway between righteous mom and jutting runway model. I smile. Despite myself.

"Okay, I'm gonna give you my little speech on life here in Orphan County," I say. "This is what the Chamber of Commerce *won't* tell you, so listen up."

Lee makes a serious face. "I'm listening."

"Here it is," I say. "In this neck of the desert, everybody—everybody!—needs three things: more money, more water, and better shocks. There you go, that's my little speech. That's everything you need to know about Orphan County, New Mexico, boiled down to the grit."

"Well, we sure need more water," Lee says.

"Hey, I know all about that," I say. "My sister and I used to swim up at your aunt's ranch, in the part of the creek called the Punch Bowl."

"It's barely a trickle now," Lee says.

"Yeah, well, your Aunt Lupita got seriously robbed."

Which is true. Chicorica Creek used to tumble across Lupita Fields's property and then down to the ranches below, watering their land and herds. That was the natural flow of Chicorica Creek. Then the Town of Clay Allison started tinkering around with the law.

"What they did was unconscionable," Lee says.

"Wait," I say. "You're in New Mexico now. Just say what they did was *wrong*."

Lee shrugs. "It *was* wrong."

And she's right. The town—in its infinite greed—hired a Denver lawyer, and they built a concrete dam across the creek on Lupita's property. Now her water supply funnels into a copper pipe, elbows ninety degrees, and rushes down the canyon into the town reservoir.

Everybody below in Clay Allison gets more water and better water pressure. We're all singing in the shower and whistling when we flush our toilets. The only problem is, we stole the water from Lupita Fields and her rancher neighbors.

"Where I come from, you can't take something and call it your own," Lee says.

"Maybe not up in Seattle," I say. "But you're in the Land of Enchantment now. The Crotch of the West."

"The Crotch of the—" Lee laughs. "I don't remember seeing that on the license plates."

"Yeah, well, people here do what they like," I say. "It's a tradition. When you pack a gun in your pickup, you can pretty much do anything. That's the beauty and truth of it."

Lee shakes her head. "That's the ugliness and lies of it. They definitely don't know my aunt."

"Well, we sure know her," I say. "My mom and her were best friends. Going back to, like, kindergarten. But that dam is here to stay. Concrete is concrete."

Lee checks her watch. "Will you be at the game tomorrow night?" she asks.

"I'm always at the game," I say.

"What position do you play?"

"Hot dog salesman."

She blinks. "Any veggie dogs?"

"Veggie!" I sneer. "You'd better get that foreign word out of your vocabulary. You're in prime beef and hog-gut country now."

"I wouldn't touch one of your hot dogs," Lee says.

"Oh, yeah? Why's that?"

"The fat and sodium," she says. "Then there's the nitrates. And the ni*trites*. And the—"

The second-period bell rings. Lee glances back, then quirks a smile at me. "Hey, can you bring your YZ 125 to the game?" she asks. "I'd like to check it out."

"Yeah, maybe."

The fact that I'm even talking about selling my 125 staggers me. Because I love that bike.

"See you tomorrow night," Lee says.

She pivots on her Pumas and walks away, the ends of her red-gold hair whisking back and forth.

Shimmering.

CHAPTER 9

I'M FLOPPED ON MY BED sucking an orange and watching the four o'clock news — the *BBC World Update.* I don't usually watch the news — and never the British Broadcasting Corporation news — but Lee's such a big fan, why not have a look?

"We go now to Pakistan's North-West Frontier, where correspondent Ethan Shackleton has filed this report."

The North-West Frontier — a good start.

A dark-haired dude appears on screen. He's probably late twenties, but if you count the mileage on his face, he's more like mid-thirties. He's decked out in a safari jacket with a BBC logo. He's got that three-day-beard thing going.

"The question persists — where is Caracal? We have an abundance of speculation and theory, but no definite answer."

Caracal — that's twice in one day.

"He remains the quintessential shadow warrior. Let us review . . ."

I tug off my boots, stack some pillows, and settle back with my orange.

"Caracal takes his name from the elusive Asian mountain lion. Like his feline counterpart, he is intensely secretive and fiercely territorial.

"He is best known as the architect of terrorist attacks that have killed thousands on three continents. Today, he is believed to be the insurgency's top commander on the North-West Frontier."

The camera pulls back, and Ethan starts to mosey along a riverbank, all the while talking to his TV audience. Below him, the river flows frothy and fast. On the far horizon stand snowy mountains. I recognize them as the Hindu Kush. The tallest peak — the one that looks like a shark's fin — is more than twenty-five thousand feet high. I know all this from Drone Pilot.

"For several years, Caracal has remained invisible to our eyes. We received reports last year that he was killed in a drone strike outside Peshawar. However, follow-up reports suggested that he was alive and well — or at least sufficiently recovered from his wounds to commit further acts against Western personnel and interests."

They cut to an old photo of Caracal. He looks like a college professor, lean and serious.

"What do we know about this man? He was born in a tribal village on the North-West Frontier and moved at age twelve to England, where he was educated at top private schools. At Cambridge University, he excelled in chemistry and philosophy. Here he became affiliated with the 'Sixth Pillar,' an organization fueled by the idea of 'holy war,' which it defined as 'the internal and external struggle to defend the faith.'

"During two years of graduate study in Washington, DC, he wrote a dissertation on the relationship between religion and terrorism, which he later expanded and published under the title A Declaration of War Against All Oppressors. *Today, this volume is regarded by sympathizers as the insurgency's strongest statement advocating the use of violence and terror as a means to an end.*

"Although he inherited family wealth, he lives simply and modestly, adhering to the strictures of his faith.

"Former teachers, classmates, and neighbors paint a divergent portrait. Some remember him as 'polite and soft-spoken,' others as 'brilliant,' and still others as 'ideologically inflexible' and 'clearly a bad man.' While he is known to have ordered the execution of enemy prisoners, he is also a

provider of food, medicine, and other forms of aid to war-torn villages on the North-West Frontier."

A photo pops up showing Caracal with his wife and three kids. His expression is a mix of pride, love, and deer-in-headlights bewilderment. I've seen family pictures of Dad looking pretty much the same.

"He was widowed one year ago as the result of the same targeted drone strike that was thought to have killed him. He has three children — a seven-year-old son and twin daughters, age three.

"But where is he? Assuming he is alive — and most intelligence experts I've spoken with do assume that — he is in deep hiding. He likely limits his movements to keep out of sight of even the most discerning surveillance craft. When he moves, it is thought to be with the help of a support network, including loyal tribal leaders.

"Recent reports suggest that he is based at an outpost in the Hindu Kush mountains that rise out of the Swat Valley. It's possible that he moves between outposts under cover of night. From here, he likely executes his tactical program of assault on Western personnel while plotting the next strategic strike on foreign soil.

"Caracal has always been fixated on the United States and

its global interests. It is widely believed within the intelligence community that he is planning to launch a large-scale attack on Western interests in the near future.

"This is Ethan Shackleton, BBC World Update, *reporting from Pakistan's North-West Frontier."*

« « « » » »

IT'S MIDNIGHT. I'M STRIPPED TO my boxers, brushing my teeth, shaking my ass to Kenya Man's "Kaleidoscope Mirror" . . .

"Chrome is the color
of my mouth and mind.
I'm black like a storm,
Blue like a chime . . ."

. . . when my laptop pings. It's an e-mail from Colonel Kincaid.

Arlo, The attached memo contains a reference to you. Have a look.

I pop open the memo. Most of it is blotted out — or redacted, as they say in various anally retentive circles. I turn down Kenya Man and read:

Date sent: (redacted)
From: (redacted)
To: (redacted).

The first three pages are completely redacted. However, at the bottom of the last page is a single buck-naked sentence:

> *The pilot is a seventeen-year-old American citizen remarkable for his ability to handle a diverse range of drone aircraft in extreme terrain and erratic atmospheric conditions, and for his extensive knowledge of the North-West Frontier.*

I read this again.

Then I crank Kenya Man and shake my ass.

But after a while, I start wondering. How does he know I'm "remarkable"? Because I've never actually flown a drone — unless you count the game — in which case, I've flown a million.

If Colonel Kincaid is right, and Drone Pilot truly "replicates" the act of flying a real drone, then White Sands could be profound.

I flop on my bed, redact the light, and grin at the night.

CHAPTER 10

DAD AND I ARE PACKING the pickup, getting ready for tonight's game — Clay Allison (the Outlaws, 9–0) vs. Jeopardy (the Saints, 8–1). The rivalry between Clay and Jeopardy is famous and bitter. Dating back to the stone ages.

Dad adjusts his Snack Shack ball cap. Studies his checklist.

"Tamales — four dozen — check. Hot dogs — ten dozen — check. Candy . . . hmm . . . Arlo, where the hell're my Gummi Bears?"

"Under the Styrofoam cups."

"Check."

On and on until we get everything packed in the pickup and bungeed under a plastic sheet.

Each time I open the door of the truck, El Guapo jumps in. No matter how carefully I guard the door, he makes it into the driver's seat. I grab his collar, drag him out. But he jumps back in.

This goes on and on, one of his little games. Drives me crazy. Which is why he loves it.

Finally, I give up and leave that humping shag carpet right

where he wants to be, sitting behind the wheel, ready to drive off.

Dad turns toward the porch, snaps, "C'mon, Siouxsie!"

He closes his eyes, regretting his tone. Wills the hurry out of his bones. Sets down his clipboard and goes up the porch steps into the kitchen. He comes out carrying Siouxsie in his arms.

"Hey, I can walk," she says.

"Not fast enough," Dad grumbles.

She slams a fist into his shoulder.

Dad sucks it in.

El Guapo sees all this and jumps out of the pickup to make way for them. Dad sets Siouxsie in the passenger seat.

Under her breath, she says, "Just for the record, I don't want to be here."

"Duly noted," Dad says. "But just for the record, I'm not leaving you alone."

I look at my sister, getting worse one molecule at a time. God knows what Huntington's has crushed today. Will crush tomorrow.

"You boys ride in back," Dad says.

"Guapo too?" I ask.

"Why the hell not."

I grab Guapo, hoist him, and place him in back. Then I glance over at the shed.

"Hey, Dad! Hold up a sec."

I duck into the shed and wheel out my YZ 125, into which I've poured miles and hills beyond counting. You can barely make out "Yamaha" on the front shock guard. Mom bought me the bike for my tenth birthday. Grinding the throttle that first time—*whoa!* And when I hit my first bump—*damn!*

I didn't know it then, but I was knocking on the door of the Drone Zone.

Why I'm even thinking of selling my old YZ is beyond me, because I love her. Right now more than ever.

I love her like a sister, and I shouldn't be selling any member of my family when there are so few of us left.

Even so, I fetch a plank and run her up into the bed of the pickup.

Dad gives me a *what-the-hell?* look.

"Might be sellin'," I say.

"Selling! I don't believe it. But if it's true, it's the best idea you've had all year."

We peel out. The cold and wind stab through my jeans jacket. El Guapo presses against me for warmth. Drops his head in my lap. I forgive him for everything, for all his sins of mud rolling, skunk chasing, and humping disobedience, because he's basically a great dog. The best standard poodle in all northeast New Mexico.

Somewhere in the back of Mom's mind, when she picked him out of the litter, the fattest puppy, she knew this.

I think.

We ramp onto Interstate 25 and bomb north. I can see the first snow on the Spanish Peaks—the Breasts of the World, as Grandpa Spencer likes to call them. Fresh whiteness sparkles through the layers of gray afternoon. The peaks look both near and far. Real and fake.

El Guapo doesn't like the cold air blasting his back, so he

burrows under the plastic sheet. I don't blame him. If I'd thought of it first, I'd have done the same. But there's only room for one of us.

I turn up my collar and settle back for the ride to Rio Loco Field.

CHAPTER 11

"HEY, WHAT THE . . . !"

Dad rips off the plastic sheet and glares at me.

Turns out El Guapo wasn't snoozing after all. Nearly half of our hot dogs are gone. We're down from ten dozen to six dozen, if you count the partially eaten ones. Also gone are the plastic wrappers, except for a few shreds. Guapo was just beginning to sample the tamales when we pulled up to the Snack Shack.

Dad lunges at Guapo, who darts away.

"Thief!" he shouts. "Bastard!"

He opens his wallet, pulls out some cash.

"Arlo, fire up your bike and buy me all the hot dogs you can. Quick."

I crank my 125 and blast off. My old dirt rider feels good. How could I even think of selling it? I can't—I won't.

At the Super 24, I ask Tony the clerk if he's got any hot dogs without nitrates.

"Say what?"

"How 'bout veggie dogs?"

"Not in this lifetime."

I buy the whole stock of hot dogs, six packs, and button the bag into my shirt. The traffic heading back to Rio Loco Field is heavy. I weave in and out and ride the shoulder.

As I cut through the parking lot, I notice that Dad has moved the pickup to a better spot to beat the crowd. I can see El Guapo sitting on the driver's side and Siouxsie sitting next to him. It's funny in a way, because Guapo's such a clown that even his sad face makes me laugh. But Siouxsie — there's nothing funny about her.

I brake to a stop and ponder whether I should sit with her for a minute. But just then *Winged Victory* — the bus carrying the Jeopardy Saints — pulls into the lot. The players clatter off amid cheers from Jeopardy fans and hoots from Clay fans. Tonight, these players are big stars. They clop across the parking lot, their 'nads clacking in time with their cleats.

This stardom would make sense if they were saving lives or curing cancer, but all they're going to do is crack their helmets and catch a few passes.

No, I'm no football fan. I glance again at my sister, grind my throttle, and am gone.

"Quite a crowd," Dad says when I hand him the shopping bag. He's got the coffee brewing, the cider steeping. He's got both grills fired up, and he's filled them with two dozen dogs each. They're beginning to glisten. The Snack Shack is really cooking.

"I'm worried about your sister, Arlo."

"Me too," I say.

A minute later we're too busy to worry. People are lining up outside the Snack Shack, blowing on their fingers, eager to wrap them around something warm.

I do my hot dog dance:

Tong it,
bun it,
drop it in a trough.
Ring it!
Ching it!
"Mustard on your left."

About every third dog, I glance into the bleachers, searching for Lee.

At kickoff, everybody goes drunk on football. Two great teams, sworn enemies. Jeopardy hasn't beaten Clay in five years. This is the high noon of county football.

We are the Outlaws, dressed in black.

Jeopardy is the Saints, dressed in white.

At the half, Clay leads 24 to 14. Now it's time for "the show." I have witnessed "the show" nearly every year of my life. It might even be my earliest memory. It's definitely the high point of the football season. Better than any Christmas pageant or Fourth of July parade.

The mascots take the field. The "Outlaw Clay Allison" wears fringed buckskin chaps, a black leather vest, and a black cowboy hat. The "Saint" wears a white robe with coat-hanger wings and a Styrofoam halo. She carries a giant papier-mâché Bible.

This year, Clay Allison is played by senior Ben Gigliano. He saunters about twirling six-shooters, pausing to swig from a bottle he keeps in his chaps.

The Saint is portrayed by Ramona Solaño, Latoya's cousin. She's a senior at Jeopardy High School.

Clay shoots up a storm, each bullet exploding out of the

loudspeakers, but nothing hits the Saint. So Clay reaches back and fingers the last bullet from the loop in his belt, kisses it, chambers it, cocks, aims, and fires. The Saint snatches the bullet in midflight, holds it up for all to see — an oversized Styrofoam bullet she has slipped from her sleeve. Clay drops his head in defeat.

The Saint pulls the smoking guns from his fingers, flings them away, and raises the Bible over Clay's head. She says into her mike:

"Will you mend your ways and grace your days?"

Clay bows his head. "Sure will."

"Will you take the path of the pure and follow in the footsteps of the Lord?"

"Sure will."

The Saint touches Clay's shoulders. He falls to his knees and says into his collar mike:

"Praise the Lord in the highest! Amen."

Everybody at Rio Loco Field loves it, because Clay gets to ham it up and shoot all sorts of blanks, and the Bible-toting Saint gets to cast a spell over him.

But as the Saint leads the Outlaw off the field in victory, a posse of cowboys races out from the sidelines twirling lassos. They rope her. The Bible falls to the ground.

Will Clay stay redeemed? Hell, no!

He picks up his guns and shoots up a storm all over again. Somehow, he has found more bullets.

And that is how the halftime show ends: Clay yipping and *kay-yai-yai*-ing, and the Saint hogtied and helpless. Next year, Jeopardy will host, and Clay won't be so lucky.

Ben Gigliano and Ramona Solaño have done a bang-up job, one of the best. They have caught a truth, and that's probably why we're all so mesmerized, even me.

Their little performance is all about Orphan County's two most powerful urges — the urge to be purified and the urge to follow a wild hair up your ass.

We all feel those urges, that conflict.

I sure do.

« « « » » »

DURING THE THIRD QUARTER, the Saints fight back. The score is now tied 31 to 31. A hush falls over the bleachers. Everybody stops breathing. Business at the Snack Shack goes slack.

Dad bumps me. "Better go check on your sister."

"Good idea," I say.

I flip open the counter hatch and hike through the pedestrian tunnel to the parking lot. Closing in on the pickup, I can see El Guapo sitting behind the wheel but no sign of Siouxsie. I open the door thinking she's lying down, or maybe curled on the floor, trying to return to the womb. But she's gone.

Guapo ducks between my left arm and the hand brake.

Slips out of the truck.

Trots a few yards, turns, and grins at me.

There's a moment when I might be able to entice him back — if I had a chew stick or cheese snack. Or better yet, a hot dog. But I don't.

"Get back in, you bum!"

Guapo tilts his head. I soften my tone.

"Hey, when we get home, I'll give you five chew sticks — original bacon flavor. Just get in the damn truck."

But he sniffs freedom and bolts, his white flanks and fluffy ears strobing between the parked cars. He's headed for the pedestrian tunnel to Rio Loco Field.

"GUAPO!"

I take off after him. See his tail bob into the tunnel. There's still a chance he'll come back, if I don't chase him. So I slow down. And pray this thought:

Please, God — please! Don't do this to me.

I rush into the tunnel, and about midway the walls begin to buzz. By the time I step into the stadium the buzz has morphed into a gigantic, cackling groan.

At first, I can't bring myself to lift my eyes and look out at the field. I would give anything to be dogless. *Guapo*-less.

Then I look up.

There, under the bright glare of the football night on the too-green field, El Guapo is darting about. Uncoiling all his wound-up energy.

He is doing this in front of twenty-two players and three refs. Plus the students, faculty, staff, and parents of two high schools sardined into the Rio Loco bleachers. Plus all the grandparents and other fans — all the anybodies and nobodies who could make the game tonight. About two thousand people.

El Guapo is out on the field expressing himself.

Several players go after him. In Guapo's mind, this is like an invitation to celebrate. He switches to goof mode. Dodges, leaps, and even appears to buck. No player can catch him. El Guapo is by far the best athlete on the field.

Dad is screaming at me. It's way too loud to actually hear him, but I feel his screams in my bones. When I look in the direction of the Snack Shack, he's flailing his arms at me.

Get out there — and get that dog!

Every fiber of me says "No!" But El Guapo is my dog. He was Mom's, but he's mine now. Not that I asked for him, but he latched on to me. Made me his primary human. You can't go against that grain.

I step across the sideline into the harsh lights.

"Hey, Santiago! Get your stupid-ass dog off the field!"

I whistle. "Guapo! Hey!"

He stops. The players stop, sensing a plan.

I fist my hand and crank it to my shoulder. "Sit, Guapie!"

He sits obediently on the Jeopardy thirty-five-yard line. As I amble closer, he tilts his head and grins, his tongue looking surrealistically pink under the Friday-night lights.

"Who's a good boy, good boy, good boyyyyy."

I ease across the Clay thirty to the forty. Then I cross the border into Jeopardy country. Here the grass looks different. An ominous shade of green.

I keep my arm bent and fist raised — the sit command — and stroll toward El Guapo as casually as if I'm strolling along the banks of the Rio Loco itself, hearing the water gurgle and smelling the prickly pear. Because if Guapie senses a trick, he'll be off again. That's how his brain works. Life is a game. Gnaw the bone. Chase the squirrel. Hump the knee.

“Hey, Guapo,” I say, striding closer. “You’re the greatest thing on four legs.”

But he’s past the point of flattery. His eyes glaze. His grin fades. He looks at the laughing bleachers.

He rises up and shakes himself. Yawns. Sniffs the grass. Circles.

Arching.

Sniffing.

Rocking on bowed legs.

Dilating.

Crowning.

Spreading.

Hunkering.

He plants himself just south of the Jeopardy thirty.

Closes his eyes.

Squeezes out a load.

It’s a big one.

CHAPTER 12

EVEN THE BLADES OF GRASS groan.

It's time to die.

I dive and catch Guapo by the collar. Referee Ray Sandoval rushes up with a bucket of cleaning products. Somebody else is beside me with a scrub brush, Windex, and plastic bags.

Everything is thrust into my arms. Every voice howls in my ears.

It's the worst day — the worst!

No, not the worst.

Ray grabs Guapo's collar, leads him away, shouting: "Clean it up!"

I melt to my knees and go to work. Just south of the Jeopardy thirty-yard line. In the deepest level of hell, where the devil himself craps.

Two thousand sets of eyes watch my every scoop, swab, scrape, and hand rotation.

One giant mind with one puny thought: how big a fool I am.

Never has so much brightness felt so dark.

I try to shut them out — to find some kind of wisdom inside me to get through this. What would Socrates do? Mahatma Gandhi?

Cackling loudest of all, halfway up the bleachers, on Clay's side, are Lobo and Uncle Sal. Somehow, the familiar sound of their idiocy comforts me.

A chant is born: "*Scoop the poop!*"

It swells until both sides are united.

"*SCOOP THE POOP!*"

Only not everybody's saying "poop."

The spirit of Charles Darwin must be hovering over Rio Loco Field. Because you can feel evolution at work. Or more accurately, reverse evolution.

"*Scoop the poop . . . Scoop the poop . . . Scoop the . . . !*

"*Scoo-PER! . . .*

"*Scoo-PER! . . .*

"*Scoo-PERRR!*"

The announcer crackles through the loudspeakers.

"Uh, ladies and gentlemen, uh . . . Clay Allison's very own Arlo Santiago is . . . uh . . . proudly taking care of business on behalf of the family dog. Let's hear it for Arlo."

I hear it.

Man, do I hear it.

I'm pretty sure they hear it in Texas, too.

And western Louisiana.

« « « » » »

NOBODY SCORES AFTER THIS. Both teams tiptoe around the spot where El Guapo unloaded. Even though I super-buffed the grass with Windex.

The game ends in a 31 to 31 tie.

Clay's die-hard fans shove by me. But the non-die-hard fans

seem upbeat. Nobody wants to shake my hand, but I get clapped on the back a lot. The mood is that it's Clay's victory, symbolically speaking.

Over and over, I get called "Scooper."

"Hey, Scooper." "Yo, Scooper." "Scooper-duper-dude."

Already it feels permanent, like an epitaph. I smile and roll with it. But if my gut were on my face, my jaw would be dragging on the ground.

At the Snack Shack, everything that was so organized and careful before is sloppy now. Dad hurls stuff into the pickup, including the hot dog grills. El Guapo sits at the wheel, looking sheepish and scolded.

"Once upon a time," Dad says, jerking open the door and shoving Guapo to the passenger side, "my name in this town was not associated with dog shit."

He points to the bleachers. "Take your sister home. Do you both good."

He gets in, slams the door, and peels out.

Maybe it *is* the worst day.

No, it will never be that.

I scan the bleachers for Siouxsie and spot her a few rows up, wedged between Lupita Fields and Lupita's niece, Lee, of the cascading red-gold hair and pink Pumas. A blue and red Navajo blanket covers all three laps.

I cruise over on my Yam. Stop just below them. Pull off my helmet.

"Arlo!" Lupita calls down. "Get up here."

I cut the ignition, hop the rail, and climb the bleachers. Lupita stands and throws her arms around me. She's a great hugger — smells of lavender and bucked hay. If only I could stay here, wrapped and warm, for a year or two.

"Way to go," Siouxsie says, breaking the spell. "Now we're all famous."

"Yeah, well . . ." I aim a finger at her. "You're coming home with me."

"Wait!" Lee says. "Aren't you gonna show me your bike?"

She looks at me like nothing just happened. But everything happened. Her shimmering blondness falls flat.

"Nah," I say. "Gotta get home."

"Oh, go on, show her the bike," Lupita says. "Siouxsie and I'll wait here. We still have some catching up to do."

It's nice that Lupita uses the word "wait," because Siouxsie's not about to jump off the bench.

Fact is, I haven't seen Lupita Fields for five months, not since Mom's service. She wrote me a letter — so short, I haven't forgotten:

Dear Arlo, If ever you need to talk, laugh, cry, or just sort it out, you let me know. I am here. Love, Lupita

As far back as I can remember, Lupita's been a loner up in Chicorica Canyon, preferring life with her thirsty cows and dusty horses to hanging out in town.

She's actually a nice-looking woman, tanned with peppery-dark hair and glowing dark eyes, slim but strong, no-nonsense in business, somewhat cold if you don't know her, but easy and warm around friends. She's part denim and leather, part turquoise and silver. Basically, she's Orphan County royalty.

Overall, though, she's a bit too sun-dried from living with herds at nine thousand feet. She was married a couple of times — and kicked both her husbands out. Then she decided, to hell with it, animals are better than people.

When the town dammed her creek and stole her water, she kind of disappeared. But having her niece here means Lupita's starting to come to town again.

Before I can say no, Lee slips out of the Navajo blanket and grabs my hand. We go down the bleachers and hop the rail.

"Say hello to six gears of greatness," I say, introducing Lee to my Yam 125.

"Hello, six gears of greatness," Lee says.

I mount up, fire up, and pop a wheelie, rolling down the track, U-turning, spinning into a three-sixty, tricking it all the way to a five-forty, never once touching my foot to the ground. Very few riders can do this — Cam and Lobo sure as hell can't. Then I roll back, all on one wheel.

Up in the stands, Lupita claps. "Ride 'em, cowboy."

Siouxsie lifts her voice: "Somebody's showin' off again."

Behind us, we hear: "Hell, that ain't showin' off."

CHAPTER 13

"SCOOPER!"

It's Uncle Sal. He and Lobo stride over. "That was one helluva show," Uncle Sal says. "I'll never forget it. Not as long as I live."

He shakes my hand, then, remembering, wipes it on my shoulder.

"*Scoo-PER! . . . Scoo-PER! . . . Scoo-PER!*" Lobo chants. "Nobody'll forget it, dude. Watching you scoop, man, that was the high point of my life."

"Shut up, man," I grumble.

Lobo catches my eye and does.

"Sponsors!" Uncle Sal says. "How many times I got to say it, Arlo, you were born for sponsors. Way I figure, tonight you got free publicity, but not the kind of publicity you want. Now listen—listen! Everything you do in the spotlight forms your reputation. Tonight—and I'm just speaking plain, uncle to nephew—you soiled your reputation. I'm sorry to say, you will be remembered for this. More than for all the good deeds you have ever done. People here tonight will remember your moment in the spotlight. You are left with two choices: you can fight back or move to Antarctica."

"Antarctica," I say.

"Ho-whoa! Whoa-whoa-WHOA!" Uncle Sal says, noticing Lee. "Who is this?"

"She's the new girl, Uncle," Lobo says.

"Hands off, Salvatore!" Lupita shouts from her bleacher seat. "That's my niece."

Uncle Sal lifts his visor.

"Why, hello up there, Lupita! Hello, Siouxsie! Lupita, may I say that sublime loveliness blooms upon every twig of your family tree?"

"You may," Lupita says. "But just this once."

Uncle Sal digs a business card out of his wallet and plants it in Lee's hand. "I am your Uncle Sal."

Lee looks at the card. "I don't have an uncle," she says.

"Ah, don't worry," Lobo says. "He's everybody's uncle — I mean, he's my real uncle, but he's everybody else's too."

"My nephew is correct," Uncle Sal says. "I am *zio al mondo* — uncle to the world."

He raises his voice into the bleachers. "Lupita, how long's it been since we went upstairs for a little crop-dustin'?"

Lupita's talking with Siouxsie. Without looking at him, she pops a finger, slits her throat.

"Twenty years, I bet," Uncle Sal booms. "Got a new plane now — a Cessna 182, the *Hi-O Silver.* More legroom to maneuver. Hey, how 'bout we fly over the Santa Fe Trail some Saturday and check out the wagon ruts, for old time's sake?"

"Salvatore," Lupita says, "you are a filthy man!"

She folds herself toward Siouxsie and blocks him out.

Uncle Sal tips his cap and grins.

"Dude," Lobo says, "what're ya doin' on your 125?"

"Just showing it to her, man," I say. "Might sell it."

"Sell it!" Lobo gapes. "Nah, you can't sell it. She's your baby."

His words ring true. I decide right then that my old Yam YZ 125 is not for sale. Not to Lee or anybody else. And never will be. When the time comes, I'll give it away.

"Young lady," Uncle Sal says to Lee, "let me tell you about Arlo here. He rides dirt like nobody else. Many times I've sat in a folding chair at the base of Little Piñon Mesa, with a glass of Chianti and a good Cupido cigar, and watched these boys ride. I've watched them grow up this way. You ask me, who are my favorite composers? Well, Mozart and Rossini come to mind. But my truly favorite composers are Yamaha and Kawasaki. I've never seen Arlo choke. Never seen him bite the dust or scatter his tools. Everybody else ends up in a ditch or in the emergency room sooner or later, with a sprained ankle or broken neck, but not Arlo. He just goes faster and higher. One day he will simply fly away."

"Or break his neck," Lee says.

Uncle Sal shrugs. "Destiny is destiny, and Arlo has more destiny than anybody I've ever known."

"Hey, show her some lip," Lobo says.

Rio Loco Stadium is shaped like a horseshoe. At the opening, just beyond the end zone, is a steep bluff that shoots up to the height of a five- or six-story building. The double mound of dirt at the top looks like a woman's puckered mouth. These are "The Lips." At night, the field lights glaze them.

Over the years, the Lips have been our Angelina Jolie, Jennifer Lopez, and even a few local girls. It's actually two different jumps — the Lower Lip, bigger and sexier but a killer, which I've been meaning to try — and the Upper Lip, girl-next-door friendly, which I've flown off maybe thirty times, always against school orders and cop warnings. But it's been more than a year since the last time, and that was in full daylight.

"Oh, yes!" Uncle Sal says. "We would all like to see some lip."

A natural, hard-clay ramp runs up the bluff. The ground where I would land is inky black. It's junky on top, as I recall, with broken bottles, tin cans, and brambles strewn all around.

Lobo reads my mind. "No worries, dude, I'll clear it for you. Wait for my signal."

Before I can say no, he rushes off and scrambles up the bank into the darkness. Pretty soon, we see him waving his arms. *"Aighhht!"* he shouts. "Good to go! Over and out."

My mind doubts — but my spirit leaps. Before I can decide, I have decided. I shake a finger at Lee. "Don't you *ever* try this."

"I just might," she says.

Uncle Sal winks at me. "Over the moon, Arlo."

I loop onto the field. I'm not supposed to drive on the gridiron, but what the hell. Hardly anybody's around to stop me — all the cops and refs have gone home. Plus, I need the long approach, if only to center myself.

I cruise to the fifty-yard line. Circle and plant myself dead center of Rio Loco Field. It's the epicenter of the whole county. Many have gotten drunk on this spot. Lost their virginity. Found God.

I rev the throttle and stare at the Lips. I'm strongly tempted to try the killer Lower Lip — but it's too dark on top. That would be crazy, even for me.

I feel the energy of my old Yam run up my arms, ding like a

pinball in my brain, then race down my spine. Some bikes are born to go and some are born to sit in sheds. My old Yam is born to go.

Yea, though I fly through the valley of the shadow . . .

I ease off on the clutch. Shift. Grind. Shift. Grind. Fly past the goalpost and bounce onto hard pack. The ground shudders. I open the throttle. Blast across hard clay and swoop up the bank. Shoot like a yo-yo up a string. The ground is brittle, but I'm riding loose. My tires bite the clay.

When I hit the Upper Lip, I spring into the air. Take wing and sail across the last drops of milky light from Rio Loco Field.

I rise on my pedals and wing my arms, spread them all the way, wide and free. Smell sage and a hint of mesquite. Feel the breeze on my face. Feel the absurdity and stupidity of not knowing where I am in logical, left-brained relationship to the ground. Because I am flying blind.

Only I'm not blind.

I'm conscious of the danger, of the possibility of broken femurs and neck, but I'm not afraid. Just the opposite. I shed all my fears and worries. What happened on the field tonight is ancient history. Mom's death is ancient history. Dad's and Siouxsie's problems — all gone. Every ache in every cell of my body stops hurting.

I am in the Zone.

Full Drone.

Happy.

Free.

I grab the handles. Slam to the ground, skid, catching my balance with my left foot, bump blindly over rocks and ruts and weeds. The shocks soak it all in. Every penny I've ever pumped into these shocks is paying me back a thousand bucks.

God bless good shocks.

I brake to a stop.

Pull off my helmet. Just sit there, in the darkness, my old Yam purring under me.

It's so peaceful up here. The stars and constellations so much closer. Orion the Hunter. His faithful dog, Sirius. If only El Guapo were as faithful.

I want to stay here. Above the madness. Closer to heaven. Closer to Mom. Right now, I could as easily cry as laugh. Both are inside me, equidistant from my center of balance.

Here, it feels like everything in the universe is hitched together.

"Duuuuuuuude!" Lobo says, rushing up, a black shadow in the darkness.

We go down into the lights.

CHAPTER 14

LEE SWATS MY SHOULDER. "Well done, Arlo Knievel!"

"Didn't I tell ya!" Uncle Sal says, brimming with tears. "That was beautiful, bucko! The way you spread your arms—you looked like Christ on the cross. Listen! All of you, listen! Listen *boldly!* These are the times that rock our souls. Seeing you up there, Arlo, catching the big air, it came to me. We're gonna bust it up, partner. You won't have to go to Antarctica after all. What am I always telling you—what's my motto?"

"Defecare due volte," I say.

Uncle Sal grabs my shoulders. *"Defecare due volte!"* he says.

Lobo turns to Lee. "That's Italian for 'shit twice.' It means don't hold back. Get it all out of you. Go for broke."

"Nice to know," Lee says.

Uncle Sal's eyes look ready to pop. "Already I can think of two sponsors," he says. "Hurtado Toyota and Wingo Lumber. And that's just local. Now everybody *listen!* Lobo, you and Lee pay special close attention, because I see you as indispensably connected with this initiative. We are going to do this again, next Friday, at halftime. With one major difference." Uncle Sal points to the pouty Lower Lip. "Arlo, this time, you're going to jump that one."

"The killer?" I say.

He pats my shoulder. "You've jumped plenty of killers. It's about time you got some recognition. Lobo, who we playin' next Friday?"

"Clayton, away."

"Away—dammit! How about the week after?"

Lobo scratches his neck, thinking. "Raton, at home."

"The Tigers! Hold on, isn't that the homecoming game?"

"Sure is," Lobo says.

Uncle Sal smashes a fist into his palm. "Another packed house. Only this time, everybody—everybody!—will see you, Arlo. They will see the names of our sponsors—Hurtado! Wingo!" Uncle Sal sweeps his hand. "And they will see you flying in defiance of all things gravitational. Because, yes, everything will be floodlit. We'll put one light at the bottom of the bluff, right there. We'll put one at the top, and a third—yes, a third!—over there on the shoulder. This will make it possible to triangulate."

"Wait!" I say. "This is ridiculous. Why would I even do it?"

"Why!" Uncle Sal squints at me. "Arlo, how long have I known you?"

I shrug. "All my life."

"That's right. I smoked a Montecristo Number Two in your honor the day you were born. Fifty bucks a stick. Burned like a dream. Now, listen, all of you! We are remembered for our highest and lowest deeds. Neil Armstrong for walking on the moon, Brutus for killing Caesar. Unfortunately, Arlo, shit rolls downhill.

If you don't do something to stop it you'll be remembered forever as 'Scooper' Santiago, this town's most famous spring-activated shit pan. Is that what you want? Is that your destiny?"

I shrug. "Hey, I don't know my destiny."

"Well, I do," Uncle Sal says. "And it ain't 'Scooper.'"

"What are Lee and me supposed to do, Uncle?" Lobo asks.

"You two will be my principal distributors at the grassroots level," Uncle Sal says. "I'll work with the business community. Arlo, please tell me you still have your Yamaha 250—that you haven't sold it or done something stupid with it."

"Yeah, I still have it."

"Good. Because this has to be bolder. What do you call that bigger jump?"

"The Lower Lip," I say.

"Ah, yes, the Lower Lip. Smooch it, baby!" Uncle Sal looks around. "Where the hell is Cam? We'll need him to amp and trick your 250. It's gotta fly. Now, listen-listen! Destiny has just let us peek at her hand. We have to do this, Arlo, before the memory of your scooping hardens like a petrified turd in the public mind."

"Will he get paid?" Lee asks.

Uncle Sal frowns. "No need to push Arlo's civil rights, Lee. We already march to that drum."

"I just want to be clear about this," Lee says. "Because it sounds like Arlo's going to risk his neck out there. If somebody's going to profit, it should be him."

"Lee, this isn't about money," Uncle Sal says.

"So what's it about?" Lee asks.

Uncle Sal lowers his voice to a rasp. "It's about reputation. And reputation, as the preacher sayeth, is a precious ointment." He throttles up. "Now, listen, all of you. Meet me at Two Hole on Monday after school. We'll discuss this on a granular level. One more thing, Arlo: you will need to change your name."

"What!" I shake my head. "No way."

"It's all about marquee impact," Uncle Sal says. "If we are going to succeed — *breakout* succeed, which is the only kind of success that interests me — then we will need all the help we can get."

Uncle Sal turns to Lee. "Arlo's mom and dad were a little behind the times. They named their kids after a folk singer and a gothic rocker girl. 'Arlo Santiago' is okay if you want to sell tractors. But it's not marquee worthy."

"I like the name Arlo Santiago," Lee says. "It's honest."

"So is an old potato," Uncle Sal says. "We need a name you can write sideways on a scorecard. A good marquee name is just that much more velvet."

Uncle Sal pivots and rushes off. Mumbling ecstatically.

"Fully batshit crazy," Lobo says. "But some of his ideas . . . Dude, tell her about Jeopardy."

We watch Lobo shamble after Uncle Sal.

Lee arches an eyebrow. "Please tell me about Jeopardy, Arlo Santiago."

"I can tell you this," I say. "Jeopardy — the town — is named after *Jeopardy!* — the TV game show. You know, Alex Trebek and all. It used to be Sulphur Springs, New Mexico. Then a few years ago Uncle Sal hammered out this deal and got the game show people to pay the town to change its name to Jeopardy."

Lee looks puzzled. "Why would a town want to name itself after a game show?"

"Three million bucks, that's why. The town's used that money to fix a lot of potholes and build a public swimming pool."

"What does the show get out of it?"

"Publicity," I say. "Now the name Jeopardy is splattered over every freeway sign for a hundred miles. Everybody says Jeopardy all day long. They're cruising down the interstate — 'Hey, let's make a pit stop in Jeopardy.'"

Lee says, "It's gonna take me a while to get used to the Land of Enchantment."

"Yeah," I say. "The laws of common sense don't apply here. Depending on who you talk to, Uncle Sal got somewhere between two and twenty percent. There's also a Truth or Consequences, New Mexico. And he's working on a Wheel of Fortune down in Doña Ana County."

Lee turns and studies my YZ 125. I can tell she's hungry to ride it.

"You sure you've done this before?" I ask.

"I'm sure."

"So you know rule number one?"

Lee pulls off her ski hat and shakes loose her hair, all that bouncy-slow-motion hair you see from a mile away. It's the real reason men throughout history have searched for gold.

But what I see, in a fractional shadow, is the burden of that gold. A wishing she didn't glitter so much. Maybe I'm just imagining things. I hope not.

"Rule number one, wear a helmet," she says, sliding my helmet onto her head. "Any more rules?"

"Yeah, don't do what I do," I say.

She snaps the chin strap. "I just might."

She throws a leg over the bike. Kicks it. Grinds some pepper. Frowns.

"I'm used to more horsepower," she says.

"Horsepower's overrated," I say. "Ever see a horse fly?"

Lee shoves off. Traces a figure eight. Cuts away and rides easy. Born for the saddle, or so it looks. I attribute this more to my YZ 125 than to her, because it's such a great machine. Perfectly broken in. Just not strong enough for the highest flying. That's where my 250 comes in.

Lee rolls off the field onto the weed-studded hard pack at the base of the Lips. I go over and lean on the goalpost. It's rare for me to stand on two feet and watch somebody else ride. I feel a twinge because Lee looks so good on the bike. Yet by natural ascension and legacy, my YZ 125 belongs to Siouxsie. I always meant to give it to her. I never told her so, and she never asked, but she knows. At least, she knew. I wonder what she thinks now.

Lee cruises back and forth along a stretch of about sixty yards of scrabble. She leans over, checking the texture of the ground for anything that might throw her. When she reaches the end of the stretch a second time, she finds her mark, grinds all the way, and blasts off, lofting into a long, sweet wheelie.

I figure she's cleaning out all the small-town crap she's had to put up with since moving to Clay Allison.

Of course, you can do this lots of ways: meditate, sit in a sauna, go to church, hug a tree, take a laxative. But a dirt rider is the best way. Speed, open ground, and a sweet run-up with nothing but horizon on the far side, that's God for me.

I watch Lee blast wheelie after wheelie.

Just when I'm thinking she's worthy of some respect, though

not much, she hits a rut and bounces off the bike. My old Yam, which has never ditched, pranged, or wiped out, now runs riderless. It goes and goes. Then for the first time, my sweet YZ trembles, wobbles, and slams to the ground, skidding to a stop on its side.

I rush over, but Lee's already up, dusting off her ass. "I didn't see that ditch. I'm *soooo* sorry. I hope I didn't mess up your bike."

"You did," I say.

I go over and toe-stop the spinning wheel. Hoist my YZ from its dusty bed. Squat and eyeball the alignment. Doesn't look damaged. But the engine's caked. God knows, the carburetor's probably totally gunked. I clean what I can with spit, sleeve, and cuss. Then I mount up and kick it. She coughs a little, but when I rev, she hums like always. God, I love this bike.

Lee's limping over to pick up the pink Puma she lost in the fall. I blast ahead, cowboy down, and snatch it before she gets there. Then I ride back, bending to drag the shoe along the ground—blotting out that Seattle pink.

I brake and fling the Puma at Lee.

"Welcome to Orphan County."

CHAPTER 15

"GET UP, ARLO! LONG ROAD today."

Dad's shaking my foot. I open my eyes in darkness. Hear him go down the hall to Siouxsie's room and rap twice. "White Sands, little girl."

I wait for Siouxsie to answer. When she doesn't, Dad raps louder. "Shake a leg, Siouxsie."

The house holds its breath.

From behind her door comes a puny "Okay."

That one word makes all the difference.

I toss off my covers and sit up. Something sparks inside me. Today's the day.

I accelerate to Maximum Efficiency (ME). Slide into my jeans, white T-shirt, black T-shirt, green flannel—the one I've washed and left hanging on my doorknob. Pull on socks, stomp into my Old Gringos. Stumble into the bathroom, piss, splash water on my face, rake fingers through my hair. Brush the gutter out of my mouth.

Dad likes his coffee "black as hell," so I get that going. Then I slip on his duster and head to the barn.

“Mornin’, ladies!” I say, sliding open the door. “Big day ahead. Gonna fly some drones with the air force boys.”

The ladies stare at me as I fork alfalfa into their stalls, careful to obey the pecking order: Queen Zenobia first, then Blue Dancer, then Cornflakes. I’ve learned not to mess this up or they’ll get nippy.

I scoop one and a half quarts of oats per pregnant lady. I’m very conscious that I’m nurturing their babies, too. They watch me approvingly as I measure the oats.

“Lobo’ll come by today,” I tell them. “Cam’s gonna come tomorrow. I know they’re not your favorite people. But they’re gonna feed you, so don’t get too ornery.”

Cornflakes snorts. Blue Dancer shakes her head. But they listen. They’re very nice ladies. Well mannered. Of a higher social standing in their world than I am in mine.

I can’t wait to see their babies. Just three more months. But in the spring they will go — the ladies and their stick-legged foals — up to the Gunnison Valley of Colorado, and new pastures.

Damn, I miss them already. It busts me up to think about it. Why does everybody have to go?

I smooth my palm down Queen Zenobia’s blaze. Scratch the muscles on Blue Dancer’s chest, the way she likes. Cornflakes and I press our foreheads together. I respect the pecking order, but I don’t play favorites. Because they’re all my favorite.

“Wish me luck,” I say.

And they do, those mares.

I warm up the pickup and get a bead on 95.9 KLAY. Dad’s tossed his briefcase behind the seat. It bulges with his novel — God knows what that’s all about. He’s jammed Siouxsie’s homeschool books under the seat. And he's stuffed in some extra sweaters, jackets, and raincoats. "Contingency clothes," he calls them.

When I go back into the kitchen, he's humming over the stove: frying eggs and bacon, grinding pepper, splashing Tabasco. It's a sight I haven't seen for a while. An English muffin pops out of the toaster. Siouxsie's at the table mopping up her eggs. I sit down, and Dad sets a plate in front of me.

"Well, since they're paying for this trip, we're goin' in style," he says. "We'll stay at the Travelodge in Alamogordo, so bring your swimsuits. Oh, yes, on the way back, what do you say we stop at the Tularosa Café for some chocolate churros?"

It feels like old times. That's the thing about a journey—it pops you into focus and sweeps the mess of your life under the rug, if only for a brief time. Yesterday's worry is just that.

Plus, the fact that I'll be flying drones with the air force boys buzzes all through me.

Dad slips me a mug of coffee, splashed with milk and hazelnut. "That dog of yours is looking mighty morose," he says.

Guapo is curled in the corner, face to the wall. He knows that we are leaving—and knows that he is staying.

He ignores Siouxsie as she struggles into her jacket, opens the kitchen door, and eases down the steps, holding the rail with both hands.

He ignores Dad's parting words: "Guapie, I'm placing you in command of the fort."

I fill his water dish to the brim, pour a mountain of kibble, lift the dog gate, check to see that the bathroom door is open and toilet seat up. When I dangle a piece of bacon in his face, he ignores it. When I bend down and stick my face in his, he aims his sad eyes away.

I knuckle his bony head. "See you Sunday night, Fat Boy. Hump all the sagebrush you like."

« « « » » »

WE BOMB SOUTH ON I-25, Siouxsie wedged between Dad and me. It's starry dark out my window, but out Dad's, above Eagle Tail Mesa, you can see the dancing gypsy skirts of dawn.

"You guys remember that audio book the grief counselor gave us?" Dad asks.

I groan. *Soul Fire: Meditations on Grief and Healing* was rammed down our throats. It's basically a collection of confessional stories, inspirational poems, and Native American flute solos.

"Yeah, what about it?" Siouxsie asks.

Dad fishes the audio book out from under his seat.

"Thought we'd try this again," he says. "We're just a three-ring circus now. We've suffered, all of us, and we don't know what to say or how to say it."

I crank the volume on the radio. A song all twang and silicone spills out.

Dad snaps it off, cuts me a look. "Here we are, together for the first time in quite a while," he says. "Sort of trapped, in a way. But let's not kid ourselves: silence isn't golden."

"It's leaden," Siouxsie says.

Dad ponders the dancing gypsy skirts. "I can accept the fact that she's gone," he says. "But I still can't comprehend it, even after all these months. What gets me — where it really sticks — is the suddenness. We're just not built for that."

"The suddenness is because of me," Siouxsie mumbles.

I elbow her.

We drive a ways in leaden silence, Siouxsie narrowing herself so that she doesn't touch me.

"Well, what should we do about it?" Dad says at last. "Go back to the counselor?"

"No way," I say. "I'm done hugging pillows and screaming at walls."

"Then what?" Dad says. "Give me some help here, because my compass is broken."

"It's not all that hard," Siouxsie says. "Just talk about it — talk about how you feel."

Dad looks confused. "Isn't that what we're trying to do now?"

Siouxsie groans. "You don't get it. You either, Arlo. And until you do — you're just gonna live on different sides of the mountain from me."

"Mountain?" I say. "We don't live on a mountain."

Siouxsie glazes over and folds in. Dad doesn't speak either. If we were talking about New Mexico politics or Kit Carson and the Navajo Trail of Tears, he would have lots to say. But about Mom's death, only stuttered beginnings. Or nothing.

I'm the same way.

Fact is, we've never really talked about Mom and how her staggeringly sudden, incoherently violent death has shaped us into the stunted people that we are. It just hasn't happened. I doubt it ever will.

Maybe Siouxsie's right — we live on different sides of the mountain and follow different streams toward different oceans.

That's what it does, this world. It turns you into a mountain hermit.

I pop in *Soul Fire,* and we listen to some uplifting crap about Buddha, the Apostle Paul of Tarsus, the Roman emperor Marcus Aurelius, and Teddy Roosevelt — how they handled grief and adversity.

Bottom line: all life is suffering, but you can triumph over it if you follow some simple rules. For example: get up early in the morning — early risers tend to be happier people.

If that's true, then I'm ecstatic.

« « « » » »

WE PULL INTO THE ALAMOGORDO Travelodge at ten forty-five a.m. Dad checks us in and calls Major Anderson.

"Hmm," he says after hanging up. "Seems there's a ride ready to take you out to the post."

"Do I have time for a swim?"

"Doesn't sound like it," Dad says.

Five minutes later my ride pulls into the Travelodge parking lot. Except instead of a shiny limo, it's a flatbed truck. The driver's bagged out in military camouflage. "Hop in, Arlo," he says, opening the passenger door for me. "I'm Specialist Mullins." He taps his name tape. "I'm unforgettable."

CHAPTER 16

WHITE SANDS—OR OFFICIALLY, THE White Sands Missile Range—is a huge expanse of sugary sand, sharply different from the desert scab surrounding it.

"Those spiky peaks over there are the Organ Mountains," Mullins says as we approach the entrance to the post. "Man, you gotta see them at sunset—they look like bloody knives."

They look like bloody knives to me now, and it's still morning.

"I'm headed up that way as soon as I drop you off," Mullins goes on. "Gotta pick up a load of creosoted four-by-fours. I'd ask you to tag along, but, hey, you're a big shot. You'll be too busy flying drones."

At the gate, Mullins shows the guard some papers. We get waved through.

"We're riding on sacred gypsum now," Mullins says. "This is the largest military installation in the whole country, bigger than the state of Delaware. It's prime proving ground for rockets, missiles, and drones."

He points to a road sign: TRINITY SITE 42 MILES.

"Ever hear of Trinity?" he asks.

"You mean the atomic bomb tests?"

"Yeah, that's it," he says. "Happened just up the road in July of '45. Guess what happened a month later?"

"Hiroshima," I say.

"Yup, and Nagasaki. *Ka-blammo-whammo!* The whole world changed because of what happened right here, on this white sand, for better or worse."

He points to a turnoff. "Just up there a few miles is Northrup Strip, where the space shuttle used to land. Man, we're just full of sand and history."

"Any secret stuff?" I ask. "Like UFOs or aliens?"

"Plenty of secret stuff," Mullins says. "But all the UFOs and aliens are over in Roswell."

We roll down into a sand-washed valley scattered with windowless concrete buildings.

"Right there's the test center," Mullins says, pointing to the building on the right. "We call it the Skunkworks, 'cuz they're always skunkin' around inside."

We park in front of the Skunkworks, and Mullins guides me to a big room. The sign outside the door says UAV COMMAND AND CONTROL. I peer in and see about eighteen flight suits seated in front of monitors.

"One thing to remember about White Sands," Mullins says. "We're an army post, which means we're punctual. You're done today at eighteen-hundred hours. That's six o'clock post meridian, not six-oh-one. Which gives me just enough time to run out to the Organ Mountains, grab my creosoted load, and get back in time to pick you up. Hey, when you're up there — in the wild blue — do me a favor."

"Just name it," I say.

“T-FOG for me, Arlo.”

“T-what?”

“T-FOG — touch the face of God.”

“Touch the . . . Hey, no offense. But I’m not even sure —”

“You don’t have to be sure,” he says. “Just think about it, if only for a few seconds. Reach out and touch whatever’s up there.”

“Do my best,” I say.

“I know you will, Arlo.”

Mullins salutes me, slyly bumps my fist, and is gone.

« « « » » »

“WELCOME, ARLO! GLAD YOU MADE it.”

I look around for the voice.

“On your right. Through the glass.”

The right wall of the room is tinted glass. Major Anderson waves to me from the other side. Shadowy people stand beside him, in some kind of control room. I try to make out Colonel Kincaid, but it’s too dark to see much.

“Take any station you like,” Major Anderson says through the mike. “Just click enter and follow the prompts. The password is *swatvalley.* We’ll get started soon.”

I take a seat in back. Stretch, yawn, and check out these “real pilots.” They range in age from twenty-something to forty-something, give or take a few years. Half should be using Chinese hair-growth herbs.

At the same time, they’re glancing at me. A moose-faced pilot grins. A short-haired female pilot winks. A pilot with the bulging eyes of a Gila monster grumbles:

“DOD — Department of Desperation.”

Somebody else says, "Department of Diapers."

One minute, that's all I've been here. And I'm already taking flak.

I log on and mess with the joystick. It's a little different from the Drone Pilot stick, so I memorize the differences and practice them until they become reflex.

Deeper down, though, I'm wishing I hadn't come. Give me pregnant mares over arrogant pilots any day.

A technician comes over and pastes jellied wafers on me. As he wires me, I study the others — my competition. I notice their posture. Not a hint of lazy spine. Flight suits blazed with military patches saying "100 missions," "Enduring Freedom," "Desert Storm." On and on.

I don't have any patches on my flannel shirt, but if I did, they would read:

"Enduring Sloucher."

"Zero Missions."

"Orphan County Scooper."

Major Anderson steps through a door in the glass wall and goes to the front of the room. He faces us, crisp and straight. The room goes quiet.

"Welcome to the White Sands Test Facility," Major Anderson says. "This is Ground Zero for testing the most powerful defense systems the world has ever known."

He lets that sink in. The room gets even quieter. I straighten up a bit.

"First, I want to say why you are here. You're here because you are the best at what you do — which is fly. With two exceptions, you represent the four branches of the United States military.

Exception one . . ." He points to the short-haired woman who winked at me. ". . . Lieutenant Judy Clark, astronaut in training with NASA, based in Houston. Exception two . . ." He points to me. ". . . Arlo Santiago, from Clay Allison, New Mexico. A town up north famous for football."

Major Anderson doesn't say that I'm a high school junior. Or that I've never flown before, except in video games. The other pilots glance at me again. I feel myself go up in value. If only by a few cents.

"Today," Major Anderson says, "we are going to take you out of your comfort zones. You won't be sitting in the cockpit of a Tomcat or an F-15. You won't be blasting off the flight deck of the *Enterprise* or *Abraham Lincoln*. Instead, your butts will be glued to your chairs. You will fly remotely.

"I want you all to lock on that word:

"Remotely."

I lock on it. It's easy, because *remotely* is *my* comfort zone.

"Make no mistake," Major Anderson goes on. "Drone flying is not airborne flying. Many of your skills and instincts will translate, but some will not. In fact, some may get in the way. Score the points today, and you'll be back tomorrow. Score the points tomorrow, and you'll be eligible to fly drones for the United States of America. In the most conflicted hot spots in the world. Protecting and defending our liberties."

For a moment, the air crackles with patriotism. Even I feel it.

A PowerPoint image pops up. It shows a line of military flatbed trucks — just like Mullins's. The difference is, standing on each flatbed is a pneumatic launch tower. And locked into each tower is a drone aircraft.

"Today, you'll fly three missions," Major Anderson says. "Mission one will be an actual drone flight, using a lightweight remote-controlled aerial vehicle. Missions two and three will be video-simulated flights using far more powerful craft."

He catches my eye. "Although the experience of missions two and three is much the same as a video game, do not think of them as such. The stakes are far higher. We are talking air surveillance and attack as an art form."

Major Anderson points to the screen. "Let's get started with mission one. You'll launch here, at our drone air station, three miles to the north of our present location. You will follow posted coordinates in a westerly direction to your target here, in the Organ Mountains."

Organ Mountains.

An image of the spiky peaks that Mullins pointed out appears on the screen. A long, straight highway rolls toward them.

"We've cut your fuel supply to a bare minimum," Major Anderson says. "We want to see how you deal with scarcity — how your mind works, how your body works. If there's a spirit involved, we want to see how that works. In the event of an emergency, one of our command instructors will take over. At any time, you can communicate with us by clicking 'Message.' Meantime, we will monitor you — your stress level, reflexes, and to the extent possible, your thought processes."

He pauses to let us lock on all this information. I look at my hands — my fingers. They are very still. Very ready. I think of the phrase *calm before the storm.*

"Ladies and gentlemen, these aircraft are real — they are not toys. They have a combined price tag of $3.7 million, paid for by the American people. We cannot afford to lose a single vehicle. So fly smart."

A Red Dart 200 pops up on my monitor.

It's kind of a letdown. Red Darts are wimps. The 200 is barely bigger than a model airplane. Just a bit of foam covered with a fiberglass composite. Length: two feet. Wingspan: just over four feet. Dinky-as-hell motor. There's a camera turret mounted in the nose. A second camera in the belly.

I'm guessing everybody here—like me—is a muscle flier. High thrust, turbofan, mach speed, that sort of thing. Flying a five-horsepower Red Dart is like handing a nickel to Donald Trump and saying "Go invest." But maybe that's the point—to see what you can buy with a nickel.

I decide to give it my best.

"Ladies and gentlemen!" Major Anderson says, snapping me back. "Until I say 'launch,' you will give me your full attention."

I sit up straighter.

"The success of your first mission," he says, "depends upon your reaching the target, capturing key photographic intelligence, and returning to point of origin.

"Each craft has just enough power to get you there and back, with no more than a few minutes to spare. We will rate you in four areas: flying ability, efficient use of fuel, strategic value of photographs, and general resourcefulness.

"One cautionary note: Many top guns have performed well on this exercise only to run out of gas and belly-land in the desert a mile or two short of the airstrip. This is automatic disqualification from our program. If you want the high scores, you must return to point of origin. In other words, spend your power wisely. Questions?"

My hand slinks into the air.

"Arlo?"

"Are there any rules? I mean, anything you can't do?"

"Good question," Major Anderson says. "The answer is no. There are no rules. Just bring your Red Dart home in one piece."

He scans the room, sees no more hands.

"Game on!" he says. "Launch at will."

Bang! I launch my Red Dart 200. From a pneumatic catapult mounted on a flatbed truck located three miles to the north of the Skunkworks.

I'm flying.

I'm flying!

Even if I'm sitting in a chair in a cinderblock building. And even if it is just a dinky Red Dart.

My fingers tingle.

My mind aches with joy.

I am wide awake.

I rock my wing. Pull up. Nose down. Try a chandelle turn.

I'm tempted to try a loop, but that would cost time and energy. Besides, on my screen I can see the other Red Darts climbing. Already, they've jumped ahead. Already, I am last of the flock.

I bank west toward the Organ Mountains — those bloody knives on the horizon — and slam into a wall of headwind. I'm bumping all over the place. That's the problem with these little drones: no thrust, no turbo. Gaining altitude is like doing chin-ups when you're out of shape.

The others are fighting too. Trying to decide: go high, above the turbulence. Or go around. These are the obvious choices.

But obvious has never gotten me anywhere. It's always the unobvious — that hummingbird of a thought — that has taken me farthest, fastest, closest. That's true when I hit the mesas on my Yam 250, and it's true when I play Drone Pilot.

Now a hummingbird flits across my mind. Tickles my central nervous system. Tweets in my ear.

I peel away from the flock. And point my Red Dart due south. A warning light pulses on my screen: "Off course. Rectify."

The sender is "Capt. Charles H. (Chip) Pearson, Command Flight Testing." He must be one of those shadows behind the glass wall. He pings:

"Arlo, turn 38 degrees north."

I hold to my southern course.

He pings again. "Baffled. Explain."

No time to explain, Chip.

I click "Message," type "Trust me," and hold my breath.

The reply comes in an instant: "Godspeed, Arlo."

Thank you, Chip!

I slip to an altitude of sixty feet and step my way down to thirty. I can do this because here the wind is just a few knots, puffing to eight or ten. Plus, I love to fly low. To skim across the ground and feel it breathe.

Trouble is, I'm pointing my Red Dart in the wrong direction — south, toward Mexico, not west, toward the Organ Mountains. It's too late to turn back — to chase the others on their obvious course. There's a good chance I will fail, and post the lowest score in White Sands history.

Still, that hummingbird flutters in my ear.

The sand ripples, shifts, and rises. I wrestle my Red Dart to an altitude of ninety feet—back into the "turb"—and look down over a vast ocean of silky-white sand. I could gaze at this all day, but you've got to focus. Always focus. Fraction of second to fraction of second.

Ten minutes later, flying south, my fuel has dropped one quarter. I'm aware of Major Anderson watching me through the glass wall. But I'm also aware of what he said.

There are no rules.

Now I see it—the highway. A ribbon of black rolling west across the desert.

I see the truck too. At least, I think it's the truck. It's too far off to know for sure. Just a dot wavering in the desert light.

I bank and point my Red Dart due west.

Airspeed: eighty knots. I dip my nose.

A red light blinks on:

"Too steep. Pull up."

Sorry, Chip!

The dot crystallizes into a military flatbed truck. Lumbering up the highway. I need wing flaps for drag, but the Red Dart is a straight mono-wing design. It's not built for precision flying.

I lift my nose.

Lower my tail.

Square my wings.

This has to be perfect.

Because you can't scratch taxpayer property.

Usually, I enter the Drone Zone cranked at the speed of blur. Now I pull all the way back until I'm hovering over the flatbed.

Float down like a lazy kite. The earth pulls me. The airflow lifts me.

Seventy-eight knots.

Seventy-two.

Sixty-five.

Fifty-eight.

I tilt my nose steeply up.

Hunker my tail.

Fifty-seven.

Fifty-six.

Inch down . . .

Barely breathing.

I'm between earth and sky. Totally awake. Everything is clear.

I'm me. Nobody else.

Yea, though I fly through the valley of the shadow . . .

My wheels kiss flatbed metal.

The softest bounce.

Mom's peck on my forehead: "Good night, sweet prince."

Mullins doesn't even glance in the rearview mirror.

Now I'm hitching toward the Organ Mountains.

I may as well take a thirty-minute nap.

CHAPTER 17

MULLINS DROPS ME OFF at the Travelodge just after dark. I don't tell him about piggybacking on his flatbed — something stops me. I'll tell him in the morning.

In the lobby, I peer through a window into the pool area and see Dad and Siouxsie soaking in the Jacuzzi. The swimming pool is boiling with cannonballing kids trying to splash the ceiling and failing by at least five feet. The sign on the wall reads NO RUNNING. NO DIVING. But everybody's illiterate tonight.

I go to our room, change into my suit, grab a towel, and head back.

"Hey, it's the world's best drone pilot," Siouxsie says as I ease into the Jacuzzi.

Dad tries to read my face. "Well?"

I shrug. "All I know is, they want me back tomorrow."

Something passes between Siouxsie and Dad. Some flicker. The faintest sign of hope. Soaking in the hot water, just the three of us, amid the banshee screams and echoes, we don't say anything.

Because the last year's been nothing but bad news. That's what our bones, muscles, and cells remember. They don't remember good news. It's scrubbed from our DNA.

"So you scored high?" Siouxsie asks.

I lift my voice so she can hear: "Yeah."

Dad clamps a fist and squirts a jet of water into the air. "Let's celebrate," he says. "Where shall we have dinner?"

"Atomic Burger!" Siouxsie says.

"Totally," I say.

Dad nods. "Tonight all roads lead to the Atomic Burger."

He helps Siouxsie out of the Jacuzzi. She pauses before each step to find her balance. Dad's patient with her. Makes sure she has a rail to hold on to. Some of the splashing banshees notice Siouxsie. "What the hell is wrong with her?" one says.

I almost leap out of the Jacuzzi.

One more word.

Just say one more word.

But nobody says anything. They go back to cannonballing and their goal of a wet ceiling.

I sink into the hot water and close my eyes, wondering, what does it mean? Could I actually have beaten some of those pilots? Air force officers from Vandenburg? Navy officers who blast off the deck of the *Enterprise*?

It doesn't seem possible.

Mission one—piggybacking on Mullins's flatbed out to the target area—worked only because it didn't fail. My margin of error was tighter than the crack in a butterfly's ass.

Missions two and three were just video games—scenarios involving acrobatic flying, evading tracers, locking on targets, taking out targets. What I do all the time when I play Drone Pilot.

All it takes are the three "-itions" — ignition, intuition, and ammunition. Plus speed-of-a-fly reflexes.

I climb out of the Jacuzzi, go to the edge of the pool, curl my toes around the border tiles, and do a standing flip, which I pretzel into a can opener, leaning back just far enough to truly propel a geyser but not so far as to hit my head.

Going under, I hear maximal vacuum suckage. Everything shudders. An aquatic bomb explodes. I surface to see that I have drenched half the banshees.

They stare at me in saucer-eyed wonderment, because I have just done in one dive what they have failed to do in a hundred — shellacked the ceiling, which is now dripping wet, especially around the central light fixture.

I'm kind of disgusted with myself for showing off, but it's important to let them know that there are standards in the world.

« « « » » »

THE ATOMIC BURGER IS the most famous burger oasis in New Mexico. In fact, it's famous nationwide, due to the bumper sticker I DROPPED AN ATOMIC BURGER IN ALAMOGORDO, NM.

The walls are plastered with atomic bomb and space-age knickknacks: a picture of J. Robert Oppenheimer, the father of the atomic bomb; a model of the *Enola Gay*, which dropped Little Boy on Hiroshima; and a huge poster of a mushroom cloud forming the image of a woman in a bikini, with the words *Operation Bikini, 1946–1958: A Light Not of This World.*

We slide into a booth, and Dad and I order Double Atomics with crispy fries, and Siouxsie a green-chile Neutron with cinnamon taco chips. Dad orders three bottles of Dos Equis beer — "for lubricational purposes" — to be delivered "ice cold, twelve minutes apart." Siouxsie and I go with cherry-limes.

"Put your hearing aids in, Siouxsie," Dad says.

She plugs in the tiny fortune cookies. For some reason, we're getting along. We even mention Mom — how she made burgers with sautéed onions and pecan barbecue sauce. The way we talk, it's like she's still alive, back home in Clay waiting for us. Dad uses the present tense: "You know how Mom cooks onions . . ."

On the wall above our table is a picture of Neil Armstrong. He's in his space suit, helmet off, smiling at the camera. The caption reads *One giant leap for mankind.* Next to this is a photo of Buzz Aldrin shaking his eighty-year-old ass on *Dancing with the Stars.* Somebody has scratched out the caption and written *Infinite tiny steps for his sponsors.*

What really catches my eye, though, is a small, framed newspaper article. It's on the wall above the booth next to ours. All I can read is the one-word headline:

T-FOG.

I stand on my seat to read the rest:

While in Otero County, be sure to visit the John G. Magee, Jr., Monument and Memorial Chapel.

Pilot Officer John Gillespie Magee, Jr., was killed in December 1941 when his plane collided with an Airspeed Oxford trainer over Lincolnshire, England. He was nineteen years old. Three months before his death, he wrote the poem "High Flight" —

"Siddown!" Dad barks. "Show these Alamogordo-ites you're a well-bred pony."

I sit.

The waitress comes by with our drinks. "We sure like it when you notice our history," she says to me. "Lonnie's in the kitchen. He's our assistant chef and curator. He's crazy about space and rockets. If you want, I'll send him over."

"Yeah, definitely," I say.

"Fine," Dad says. "But first we'd like a few minutes alone with our burgers, if you don't mind."

"Assistant chef!" Siouxsie says, after the waitress has gone. "Doesn't she mean 'assistant cook'?"

The greasy-fryin' smells from the kitchen awaken me to the fact that I'm starved. It's been a long day. When our platters arrive, I dive into my Double Atomic. Dad stares at his in awe.

"Note how the UFO-shaped bun hovers over a bed of crispy fries," he says. "And note how the tarry sauce and layered mushrooms resemble the singe line left by a departed alien craft. Good God! I wouldn't dare put ketchup on this."

He chomps down, wagging a finger at the newspaper scattered on the next table. I lean over and scoop it up.

We munch, slurp, and read the *Alamogordo Daily News,* greasily swapping the sections. Mom would never have allowed reading during a meal. Eye contact was important. Posture was important. Talking about each other's day was important.

"Two-four-six-eight — *communicate!*"

That was one of her favorite sayings.

Dad's scanning the TV listings. "Hey," he says, draining Dos Equis bottle number one. "Check this out — *Battleground.* Would you guys mind if I caught a late movie on TV?"

"I'd definitely mind," I say. "Got a big day tomorrow. Gotta rest up."

"It's a World War II tank-and-grenade epic," Dad says, like he didn't hear me. "Great action sequences. Saw it when I was about your age, Arlo, at the Raton drive-in."

"A war movie!" Siouxsie says. "I thought you were a pacifist."

"I *am* a pacifist," Dad says. "War movies don't count."

"Nuh-uh," Siouxsie says. "Arlo needs a good night's sleep."

Dad folds the TV page. "You're absolutely right." He toggles his empty bottle at the waitress. "We all need our sleep."

I'm polishing my platter with the last of my crispy fries, and Dad's nursing his third Dos Equis, when Lonnie swings out of the kitchen in his grease-splattered apron. The waitress points to our table. Lonnie shambles over.

"Hiya, folks, where you from?"

"Clay Allison," I say.

"Outlaws!" He aims a finger at us. "Bang, bang!"

None of us even fakes a smile. How could we?

"I hear you're interested in our space and aviation collection," Lonnie says.

I point to the framed article hanging above the next booth. "What's T-FOG all about?"

Lonnie looks surprised. "Nobody ever asks about that one," he says, "though they should. John Magee, he was the original T-FOGGER. Wrote the most beautiful poem, 'High Flight.'"

"Hold on, give me a sec," Dad says. He presses the beer bottle to his forehead, closes his eyes, and recites:

"Oh, I have slipped the surly bonds of earth,
And danced the skies on laughter-silvered wings."

"Yes, sir," Lonnie says. "You hear that poem about every time you go to a funeral around here. There's a theory that he composed it in a state of hypoxia."

"Hypoxia?" Siouxsie asks.

"Oxygen deprivation," Lonnie says. "Magee flew so high in an unpressurized plane — a Spitfire, I think — that he probably got stoned for lack of oxygen and started hallucinating. That's how he came up with those wild images."

Dad lifts the bottle to his forehead again, recites:

". . . wheeled and soared and swung,
High in the sunlit silence."

Lonnie nods. "Images like that. It was either hypoxia or . . ."

"Or what?" I ask.

"Or he had a breakthrough."

"Like a religious breakthrough?" Siouxsie asks.

"Not exactly," Lonnie says. "T-FOG — Touch the Face of God — doesn't necessarily mean in a religious way. It just means to connect."

"Connect to what?" I ask.

Lonnie opens his arms. "To every molecule in the universe."

"Sounds Zen-y," Siouxsie says.

"It does sound Zen-y," Lonnie says. "But there's a bunch of scientific reports that say some pilots — when they get up high in the atmosphere, or go into space — become hyperaware and experience a 'transmolecular epiphany.'"

"Hey, go easy on the English language," Dad says.

"Put it this way," Lonnie says. "They see themselves as part of the universal family of planets and stars. The astronaut Edgar Mitchell T-FOGGED all the way back from the moon, just gazing out the window."

"And I T-FOG every time I down a Dos Equis," Dad says, hoisting his bottle. "Same result at a reduced cost."

Lonnie says, "We are all children of the universe."

"Too bad he had to die so young," Siouxsie says.

Lonnie shrugs. "War is war."

Dad points to a portrait across the room. "Tell me, Lonnie, why is Julius Caesar in your collection?"

"Sir, that's not Caesar, it's Aeschylus, the Greek playwright. According to legend, an eagle mistook his bald head for a rock and dropped a tortoise on it. That's how he died."

Lonnie points out a bunch of other stuff in the collection. He's proudest of the spare tire from the Lunar Roving Vehicle — the "moon buggy" — hanging on a nail above the hostess station.

"That's really the crown jewel in our collection," he says.

"Say, isn't that Raquel Welch in the bikini poster?" Dad asks.

"No, sir, that's a generic voluptuous woman."

"Speaking of transmolecular," Dad says, "could we possibly mingle some of our molecules with a parfait?"

"Yes, sir. I'll bring you a dessert menu."

CHAPTER 18

WE STOP FOR GAS ON the way back to the Travelodge. Dad ducks into the minimart and comes out with a six-pack of Dos Equis.

Siouxsie goes silent.

It worries me, too.

By the time we get to our room, I can barely keep my eyes open. I brush my teeth, peel to my boxers, and fold into the queen-size bed I share with Dad.

Falling asleep is like stepping off a ledge. Mom takes my hand to guide me. I could think of a thousand things, but when I close my eyes, I think of only one.

We're on Burro Mesa, walking on the north rim. On the horizon is the Front Range of the Rockies. Just a few feet away is that sheer drop to the dusty floor of Colorado.

The whole view is like one gigantic IMAX screen. The wind whips Mom's hair. When we stop and look down, I'm asleep.

Nothing can wake me tonight, except maybe a bomb. And that's exactly what happens. I jerk awake at the sound of explosions. Dad's sitting at the foot of our bed, sipping a beer and watching *Battleground.*

"C'mon, man," I groan. "Turn it off."

He grabs the remote and lowers the volume. "Sorry, must be all those pineapples. You know what a pineapples is?"

"Grenade," I say. "Now turn it off."

"Just one more minute," Dad says. "There's a great scene coming up."

I crush a couple of pillows against my ears and try to will myself back to Burro Mesa, but the ongoing barrage of pineapples makes sleep impossible. So I give up and open my eyes on a snow-covered forest.

Dad glances back. "Let me catch you up," he says. "Battle of the Bulge. Winter of '44–'45. Pivotal time for the allies. What a great cast! See that dog face — the guy playing Pop? — Wait, here comes the scene."

The GIs are chipping foxholes in the ice. One thing about World War II soldiers, they were baggier, grimier, and less ripped than soldiers of today — the guys out in the hardscrabble hills and war holes of the world, like the Swat Valley. But maybe that's because I'm looking at actors of long ago — who went home to swimming pools and barbecues. No wonder they're so chubby.

The GIs curl up in their foxholes and fall asleep. How they can do this is beyond me. I can't even fall asleep in my Travelodge bed.

Now it's the darkest hour. A Nazi patrol creeps through the trees in crunchless snow. It's a scene of stealth and fog. And no music — just silence and *rat-a-tat-a-tat*. One GI rolls out of his foxhole and flanks around to the back. Another joins him, and together they mow down or capture all the Nazis.

"Hey, it's been a lot more than a minute," I say.

"Hold on," Dad says. "This isn't just about you. I'm entitled to some R and R."

I hammer my pillow.

Now it's daytime, and the GIs are marching down a road. The glare off the snow lights up their smudged faces. It flickers brightly in our room. I glance over at Siouxsie.

"*Psst!* Dad, turn it off."

I ram a foot against him. He scowls over his shoulder. But when I point out Siouxsie—at the buried-in-blankets-sobbing mound she has become—he gets up, goes over, and sits on the edge of her bed.

"Siouxsie. Ah, poor Siouxsie," he says, slurring his words. "You've gone through so much. More than anybody. What can I . . . ? How can I—?"

She flings off the blankets and glares at him, her face soaked with tears.

"You can't!" she cries. "You don't know how!"

Dad reaches out to her, but she slaps his arm away. Then she goes at him, pounding her fists against his chest and shoulders like a maniac. Dad does nothing to defend himself, so I jump up, grab her, and toss her to the far side of the bed.

"Turn that damn thing off!" I say to Dad.

He just sits there, the movie flickering on his face—shadow . . . light . . . shadow . . . light.

I grab the remote and snap off the TV.

Dad stumbles in the dark to the foot of our bed and lowers himself to the floor. I fling a blanket and pillow at him.

For a while, Siouxsie sniffles from the depths of her covers. Dad begins to snore.

Me, I can't sleep. A foxhole would be more comfortable than this place.

I finally drift off around five a.m.

CHAPTER 19

AT SEVEN-THIRTY A.M., Kenya Man raps me awake.

I'm used to feeling sleep deprived, but not like this.

Maximum Efficiency. I roll to my feet. *It has to be ME today.*

I glance at the comatose form of Dad curled on the floor and count six empty beer bottles.

All I can see of Siouxsie is her hair mopped across her pillow.

I crank out a shower. Get dressed and slip into the hall, easing the door shut.

At the free-breakfast counter, I grab a dinky blueberry muffin and a Styrofoam cup of coffee. Stir in lots of sugar and powdered cream. I'm just dozing off in the lobby when Mullins pulls up in his flatbed. It's one minute to eight. I refill my coffee and go outside.

"Mornin', ace," he says, cheerfully.

"Mornin'," I mumble.

"Day two, Arlo. Not many people make it this far. What I hear is, only you and one other."

"Nah, man, don't mess with me," I say, and climb into the flatbed.

Mullins gets behind the wheel and fires her up. "Guess you sang on key yesterday. You don't look too happy about it."

"Just trying to wake up," I say.

We pull out of the Travelodge parking lot and lurch along the boulevard until it smoothes into Highway 70. I sip my coffee, remembering yesterday and last night—white sand and glaring snow, drones and pineapples. It all gloms together like the glue in my cup—the glue in my belly. I welcome Mullins's yammer.

"Disgust and gratitude, Arlo," he's telling me. "That's how I feel about the United States military. I enlisted because I wanted to specialize in helicopter mechanics. I'm a damn good mechanic. I would say great, but, hey, I'm modest. My recruiter says, 'Sure, you can be all that and more.' Beware of recruiters, Arlo. I was willing to go to a war zone. But they sent me here—to Toe Suck, Egypt—instead. To drive a flatbed truck. Go figure."

"What about the gratitude part?" I ask, egging him on. It's easier not to talk.

Mullins shrugs. "Pays the bills. The benefits are good too. And the bonuses, oh, man—"

"Bonuses?"

"The looks you get when you wear this uniform. Just walking down the street. Or inside Safeway. Or at the ballpark. Or the airport. That's real respect, man. Last year, I flew to San Antonio, and this guy in first class swapped seats with me. This uniform means something to people. They see me, and they think of their grandpa at Khe Sanh. Or their great-grandpa at Omaha Beach. I'm part of something big. Driving a flatbed? Hey, somebody's gotta be low man on the totem pole. Just ask that guy." He points to a coyote trotting across the scrub about two hundred yards on our left.

I'm tempted to tell him about yesterday — how I hitched a ride on his flatbed out to the Organ Mountains, then fired up, tilted my wing, and caught the updraft. I want to thank him. He saved my ass. But cool can be cruel. Plus, I probably shouldn't have taken those pictures of him napping.

I let it go.

We drive onto the post and park outside the Skunkworks. Mullins guides me to a small room. The sign on the door says GROUND CONTROL.

"Short day today, Arlo. You'll be done at two-thirty. I'll be waiting right here. On the dot. And don't forget, when you're up there —"

"Yeah, yeah," I say. "T-FOG for you."

"T-FOG for both of us, Arlo."

"Do my best," I say.

"I know you will."

We bump fist, and I go into Ground Control.

Like yesterday, Major Anderson is standing behind a tinted-glass wall.

"Good morning, Arlo," he says through the mike. "Take a seat and log on — you know the password."

I drop into a leather armchair and face a bank of flatscreens. Punch in *swatvalley*. The sign above my station reads:

WARNING! RESTRICTED AREA.

USE OF DEADLY FORCE AUTHORIZED.

I'm messing around, tinkering and customizing, when one of the pilots from yesterday walks in. I've been wondering who it will be, hoping it won't be him. But damn, it is — the officer with the bulging eyes of a Gila monster. Lipless. Desert-faced. Bald. He sits at the station one row ahead of mine, one to the left. I have a clear view of his screens, and he knows it.

Major Anderson mikes in:

"Gentlemen, yesterday was mainly about approach and reconnaissance. Today is about the hit. You will be flying an MQ-1 Predator in a video-simulated environment. The Predator is a true alpha MALE — Medium Altitude Long Endurance. It's an extremely lethal weapons system. Whether you shoot skeet, squirrel, man, or MiG, the principles are the same. We will throw targets at you. Some will sit still. Some will move. And some will move so fast you won't see them. Conditions may be that a target's shadow looks more real than the target itself. We will blind you with sun, and we will blind you with rain. Your job is easy — just track, lock, and fire. Do not attempt to think with your head. This game will outfly your head every time. Think with your gut. Questions?"

Gila shakes his head.

I shake mine.

"Game on," Major Anderson says. "Launch at will."

I take a deep breath and rally all the molecules I can. They feel heavy and slow today. It's going to be a long one.

I thumb my button and am gone.

Into the blue of the Swat Valley. Spruce forest. Granite cliffs. Arghandab River. I can practically smell the trout. Man, it's pretty country. Everything looks like the river canyons of western Orphan County. Like the Front Range of the Rockies.

Lewis and Clark would've felt at home here. Kit Carson too. And probably Clay Allison himself.

We blast out of the Swat into the broken desert. Standing on the horizon are the Hindu Kush mountains — the snowy humps of the world. It feels right. It feels good. I'm waking up.

Gila fires a missile. I track his POV camera and watch a military truck levitate. Crystallize. Shower down.

Perfect strike.

Gila doesn't flinch.

Never waste a motion — that's what he's about. And he's right. You can be wasteful in your ground life, litter it up — just like my room at home. But in the air it's different. You can't be messy. Every millisecond, you're either going to live or die. So you've got to keep it clean.

An arsenal of crates appears. I track, lock, and fire.

A missile arches up. Fades into the sun. I track, lock, and fire.

Gila and I go on like this for half an hour. Pulverizing everything. He scores the points. He does not miss. I'm sure he knows that I'm aware of this.

I score the points too. My gut tells me not quite as many, but close.

After a while, my eyelids get heavy.

I wiggle my toes, scratch my face, clench my sphincter. Do anything I can to stay awake. But the whole environment inside Ground Control conspires against me. The whirs, hums, and pings soothe like a lullaby. My leather seat molds to me like the softest bed.

My eyelids droop.

I track, lock, and fire.

Track, lock, and fire.

« « « » » »

DURING A PISS BREAK, Gila and I stand at the urinals. I'm hoping he'll say something to humanize himself, but he pisses like a statue.

At the sink, splashing water on my face, I look up and see him staring at me in the mirror.

"Do you know who I am?" his reflected self says.

A shudder goes through me. "Yeah — I mean, yes. Sort of."

"Let me tell you," the reflection says. "I was flying interceptors before you were *born!* I've flown eighty-one combat missions. Look here." He taps a patch on his shoulder. "This is for conspicuous gallantry. Do you have the slightest idea what that means?"

My reflection does not answer.

"It means I've risked my life for my country," he says, stepping beside me in the mirror. "Gone above and beyond the call of duty. Lost good men along the way. Do the words *gallantry, duty,* or *sacrifice* mean anything to you?"

I turn and face him. Stare into those bulging eyes. "The last one does," I say.

Gila rips a paper towel from the dispenser. Places it on the counter. Pulls out a pen and does a quick drawing.

"See here," he says, flapping the drawing in my face. "This is a flight pyramid. I'm here." He points to the top. "You're there." He jabs the bottom. "And why you're even there is beyond me. It's insanity that you're here to begin with. What the hell are they thinking? Go home and play with your damn Xbox . . . or Tonka toys . . . or whatever it is you play with. Or just go suck on your mommy's tits."

He crushes the paper towel and flings it in my face.

I blink, and he's gone.

Track, lock, and fire.

Perfect hit.

Now when I sit at my station in Ground Control, I'm not drowsy.

Not one bit.

CHAPTER 20

DAD AND I ARE SITTING at a table in the Tularosa Café, a few miles north of Alamogordo. The waitress sets a platter of hot churros between us. And little bowls of chocolate and raspberry dipping sauce, plus cinnamon dust.

We should be moaning in ecstasy — the churros are that good. But we dip, dust, and chomp in silence.

Dad tilts his head toward the window. We can see Siouxsie sitting in the pickup, slumped against the door. She's hasn't spoken all day.

"God, what a fool I was," he says, chewing sullenly. "Wish I could do last night all over again."

"Wish we could do the last six months all over again," I say, crunching into my churro.

"You and me both, Arlo."

We glance out at the pickup.

"It's a lot harder for her," Dad says. "She's fighting two battles — your mother's death and Huntington's. You and I, we're just fighting one."

A car pulls into the parking lot, blocking our view of the

pickup. It's a shiny black Crown Victoria LX, government plates. The back door opens and Colonel Kincaid steps out.

"*Whoa!*" I say.

"You got that right," Dad says.

Colonel Kincaid strides into the café, spots us, signals a waitress, barks "Coffee!" and pulls up a chair.

"Hello, Arlo. Hello, Hector."

"Hey, sir," I say.

"How'd you find us?" Dad asks.

Colonel Kincaid launches an index finger. "One of your little friends, Arlo."

"You mean —"

"Exactly," he says. "A Red Dart 200. Our eye in the sky."

Dad and I lean against the window and peer up. All I see are dirty clouds.

"So much for the Bill of Rights," Dad mumbles.

The waitress sets a mug of coffee in front of the colonel.

"I'll get right to the point," he says. "Arlo, you are hot shit." He looks at Dad. "Hector, your son is *the* drone pilot. What he did yesterday was pure rapture."

Dad looks puzzled. "What did he do?"

"Loaves and fishes, Hector," the colonel says, sipping his coffee. "He turned scarcity into plentitude."

Dad lifts an eyebrow.

"And today," Colonel Kincaid goes on, "he hit every target. The twelves, the thirteens — and he annihilated the fourteen. That's deadeye." He smacks the table. "Arlo, this weekend you outflew and outgutted some of the best combat pilots in the country.

Others were good here and there, but you were good everywhere. Nobody topped you."

"Not anybody?" I ask.

The colonel shakes his head. "Not even close."

Relief glows inside me.

Dad looks impressed. "How did you do all this, Arlo?"

"Luck, I guess."

"Hell no!" the colonel says. "Arlo, have you ever taken an IQ test?"

"Not that I know of," I say.

"Definitely not," Dad says. "My kids don't take IQ tests. They're the intellectual equivalent of taxidermy. They do not represent the heart, guts, or spirit of a person. I've written that editorial a dozen times."

"How about psychological tests?" the colonel asks. "Ever taken one of those?"

"Pretty sure I haven't," I say.

"That would be correct," Dad says.

Colonel Kincaid settles back in his chair. "Arlo, you have two advantages over the others. First, your primary language is drones; theirs is jet fighters. Second, you have outstanding situational awareness."

"Situational awareness?" Dad asks.

"Yes," the colonel says. "Arlo sees things sooner. As a result, he comprehends them more quickly. Therefore, he's able to act more decisively. And more precisely. Most of our top pilots possess superior situational awareness. But Arlo is off the charts."

The colonel locks on me.

"Arlo, you're the one I'm looking for. The whole package."

I reel from the praise. "Yeah, but—"

He cuts me off.

"Arlo, you can't build a bridge with 'but.' And you sure as hell can't win a war. Stop thinking 'but' and start thinking 'and.'"

"Hold on," Dad says. "'But' can be useful to convey dissent and opposition."

Dad and the colonel go eye to eye, 'nad to 'nad. The colonel blinks first.

"Bottom line, Hector, Arlo can help us. And we can help you."

He slips an envelope from inside his jacket, places it between the bowls of dipping sauce. Dad's eyes drift out the window.

"One thing, Carl," Dad says. "We've had violence in our lives. Violence changes you. You can't be who you were before."

The colonel shrugs. "The world is a violent place, Hector."

"Yes," Dad says. "*But* Arlo is not a violent person."

"Oh, really!" the colonel says. "He sure proved himself capable yesterday."

"Hold up!" I say. "Yesterday was just games and simulations. If it's real, forget it. I'm not gonna take anybody out. That's totally not who I am."

The colonel skews his head and studies me. "Who are you, Arlo?"

"Dunno," I say. "Does anybody ever?"

Colonel Kincaid leans across the churros.

"Let me tell you who you are," he says. "You're our drone pilot.

You'll get up close — closer than anybody else can — and you'll see. You'll be our eagle eyes. We will plan and execute based upon the information — the *intelligence* — you bring back. At all times, you'll be ten thousand miles from harm's way. You'll launch from our airbase in Pakistan, but in point of fact, you'll be safe and *remote* in a soft chair in White Sands, New Mexico. Doing what you do best — flying drone."

He pushes away from the table and stands. "Now I'm going to step outside and make a phone call. When I come back, I want an answer: do you want to fly with us or not? If you need help deciding . . ." He taps the envelope.

After he's gone, I reach for the envelope and start to tear it open. Dad snatches it away.

"Hey, don't you want to see how much it is?"

"No, Arlo," Dad says. "I want to talk it over."

"What's to talk over? You don't have a job."

"Excuse me!" Dad says. "I have a job."

"The Snack Shack? C'mon, how can we take care of Siouxsie on that? We need this."

"We need something," Dad says. "I'm not sure it's this."

"But I'm good at *this,*" I say. "Didn't you hear him? I beat out some of the best combat pilots in the country."

"Oh, I heard him, all right," Dad says. "He said your primary language is 'drone.' And all these years I thought it was English."

We go on like this, but Dad doesn't have a case, and he knows it.

When the colonel returns, Dad signals for me to do the talking.

"I'll be your drone pilot," I say. "But on one condition."

"Let's hear it," the colonel says.

What I'm about to tell him has been rolling across my mind since Mom died, a distant wave that finally pounds the beach.

"I won't take anybody out," I say. "I'll do the advance work, the reconnaissance. I'll get in as close as you want me to. But I won't push that button. Because you never take out just one person. You do more damage than that. And I'm no killer. So I won't. I just won't."

"You won't have to, Arlo," Colonel Kincaid says. "Your role will be purely recon. We will never ask you to do anything lethal."

"Gotta be that way," I say.

Dad nods. "Yes, it absolutely must be that way."

"It will," the colonel says.

"He's seventeen years old, Carl."

Dad's eyes fill with tears. Tears are like prayers, and you don't talk when somebody is praying. You don't touch your fork or coffee mug. The most you do is glance at your phone. Or read the road signs across the street.

I'm feeling a bit funny, because recon is the first step to lethal — it's all tied together. It's not like I don't know that.

Colonel Kincaid taps the envelope. "What! You haven't opened this? Well, I'll sum it up for you. Go on with your lives. Keep quiet. Whistle to the bank. Arlo, this takes priority over everything else. When you get a call, stop what you're doing. I don't care if you're taking a damn SAT or rolling in the hay with a rodeo princess. When you get the call, haul your ass down to White Sands. Is that clear?"

"Yes, sir," I say.

"I'm old-fashioned," Dad says, thrusting a hand across the table. "Let's shake on it."

We shake all around. Kincaid is a bone crusher.

"Arlo, I will message you on a need-to-know basis," he says. "The fact is, you need to know very little. Most of the content you receive will be redacted. Do you know what that means?"

"Blacked out," I say.

"Right."

Colonel Kincaid signals for the check. "You will say nothing about this to anyone. A breach — even the merest — is grounds for termination. Is that clear?"

"Yes, sir," I say.

Dad looks away.

Colonel Kincaid gives me a final, assessing look. "I wish to hell you were five years older, Arlo. I'm going way outside of channel with you. I'm doing it for one reason — because you have an aptitude that cannot be denied. You fly drone like nobody else, and by God you know the Frontier. Still, it's a risk. Don't let me down."

"I won't, sir."

Colonel Kincaid opens his wallet and plants some cash on the table — stirs a hand to tell us it covers all the churros and coffee.

"Oh, I almost forgot . . ." He reaches into his coat and pulls out a copy of *Imperial Rider* magazine. The motorcycle on the cover is a Ducati Monster 1100 EVO. Diamond black. A rocket of the open road. Rigged to draw you into a curve at an insane angle.

If Arnold Schwarzenegger in his prime had been a motorcycle, he would've been a Ducati Monster 1100 EVO. Not the biggest on the stage, but the shiniest and most ripped.

Colonel Kincaid hands me the magazine.

"Just a little reading material for the ride home," he says.

CHAPTER 21

GREEN SIGNS FLASH US NORTH—Los Lunas . . . Santa Fe . . . Wagon Mound.

Dad doesn't say a word. And Siouxsie hasn't spoken all day. So I celebrate alone, the fireworks limited to the space within my skull.

Springer . . . Maxwell . . . Clay Allison.

When we turn in at our mailbox, the house looks more than dark. It looks deserted. Not two days deserted. Five months deserted.

El Guapo materializes in the window, a fuzzy ghost. All those hours of waiting—he's not going to let us off the hook. Because he's a very sociable dog. He hates to be left alone. His idea of paradise is a big party featuring dogs, ducks, and beautiful women—the kind that wag with him. ("Oh, aren't you a nice dog—yes, yes, yes!")

I open the pickup door and turn to Siouxsie. "Want some help?"

Her head jerks no.

We leave her sitting in the pickup. Dad unlocks the back door. Turns on the porch and kitchen lights.

I grab a tennis ball from the kitchen closet, go out onto the porch, and pitch it into the driveway. Guapo's off like rabbit. He returns with the ball and the hint of a wag in his tail. I pitch another and another until he's his old self, wagging and grinning. All is forgiven. All is forgotten. Dogs are easy that way. If only people could forget.

Every couple of minutes, Dad goes to the kitchen window. "She's just stubborn," he says. "She'll come in when she gets tired."

"Or cold," I say.

I go out to the barn to check on the mares. Water, oats, alfalfa — Cam and Lobo have done a good job. The floor is swept. The pucky piled. Cam and Lobo may be absent-minded about some things, but you can count on them in a barn. Life is here, and babies are on the way.

The mares cling to the quiet of night. We'll talk in the morning.

On my way back to the house, I rap on the pickup.

"Hey, wanna blanket?"

Siouxsie's on her cell phone.

"Who you talkin' to?"

She turns her back on me.

Hell. I go up to bed, and even though I'm totally dog-assed, I can't fall asleep. I conjure Mom on the mesa. Today she's wearing her jeans jacket — the one embroidered with sunflowers and bachelor buttons, a gift from an old boyfriend. Mom and I go along, ponder-walking through the eyelash grass, never getting near the rim but extremely aware of it — that sheer edge. That clean fall.

I'm just drifting off when I hear tires crunch up the drive. I get up and go into the hall. Dad's already there, standing at the window.

We watch Lupita and Lee Fields walk over to the pickup. Lupita gets inside with Siouxsie. Lee stands by the truck, the barn light shawling over her, shadow and gold.

"You goin' down?" I ask Dad.

He shakes his head.

"Well, I am."

Dad snorts. "Don't blame you, Arlo."

"What's that supposed to mean?" I ask.

"Like you don't know," he says.

Damn! Is it that obvious?

I go down to the kitchen, toss Dad's duster over my boxers, and step into a pair of muck boots. Normally I wouldn't go outside like this—half naked. But time is ticking. Opportunity is knocking.

I open the door and shamble forth into the night.

"Nice raincoat," Lee says as I walk up.

"Naw, don't call it that," I say. "This is a tin-cloth duster. A real, old West longcoat. Jesse James wore one. So did Clay Allison. And Clint Eastwood in some of his movies."

Lee cuts me a smile. "Well, Jesse James, your sister's having a hard time."

The door of the pickup opens. "Evening, Arlo," Lupita says, getting out. "You look like the cowpoke who scraped down the trellis."

"Evening, Lupita," I say.

"We're going to borrow your sister for a while," Lupita says, helping Siouxsie out. "She needs a little girl time."

"Girl time?" I say, something creeping into my tone that probably shouldn't.

Siouxsie glares at me. "Yes, girl time. I sure don't need any more time with you. All you ever do is ride your dirt bike and play Drone Pilot." She thumps her chest. "You can't get away from what happened, Arlo. 'When in doubt, talk it out.' That's what Mom always said. Well, you don't ever talk it out. That's the problem. You and Dad — you're clueless as cows."

"C'mon, Siouxsie," Lupita says, walking her to the Dodge.

"And don't think I'm coming back," Siouxsie says, over her shoulder. "I'm staying with Lupita and Lee from now on. May your days be merry and bright. And may all your Christmases be white."

Lee brushes up against me as she passes. "And may your Rice Krispies go snap-crackle-POP!" she says, the last syllable bursting breathily in my ear.

Before she gets in, Lupita spots Dad in the upstairs window. Something in her eye sparks. If I had to guess, I'd say it meant "Don't worry, we'll take care of her." But it could also mean "You bastard!"

They pull out, and I go inside and find Dad staring into the fridge.

"To hell with it," he says, reaching for a beer. "Let her go."

"Wow, really!" I say. "Just drink a beer and let her go. Is that all you can do?"

I bound upstairs and burrow under my covers, hoping sleep will get me through the night. But all this excitement has El Guapo in one of his moods. He jumps onto the bed and starts to hump me. I push him away. When he tries again, I shove him, and he lands on the floor on skittery toenails.

He jumps up and curls beside me, defeated. What must it be like — to want to hump a world that does not want to be humped? It saddens me to think of it.

But not for long. Because with Guapo, when you shut off one quirk another starts up. Now he begins to lick the air, his tongue moving in and out.

Thup-thup-thup.

Thup-thup-thup.

I clamp my hand on his snout.

Silence.

Release my hand.

Thup-thup-thup.

On and on.

What the hell. Just live with it.

He was Mom's dog; now he's mine. I didn't choose him. He chose me. There's honor in that, I guess.

Every ten minutes or so, Dad pops open another beer, adding a *tssst* and a *chink* to the *thupping* soundtrack.

And just a few hours ago, life was looking up.

I wonder, is there something in the universe — some teeter-totter — that automatically kicks in when things start looking up and starts them looking down again?

Teeter up.

Teeter down.

Never in balance.

I think about Siouxsie. Two years ago versus today. Teeter down. Way down.

I think about Lee, how she bumped against me and murmured "snap-crackle-POP!" — the "POP" tickling my ear.

How the barn light reflected shadow and gold in her hair.

Teeter up.

Teeter way up.

Teeter so damn far up that I better call the fire department, because somebody's got a seven-alarm inferno in his boxers.

There's only one thing to do.

But it's tricky, with El Guapo curled beside me.

Plus, the guilt. I don't want to think about Lee this way.

So I hit the remote button in my mind and switch to a memory of Dolores de la Cruz. One night last summer walking up to me all wine-happy and sparkly at the Orphan County Fair. Bustin' out of her peppermint tank top.

She asks for a ride on my 250. When she's saddled behind me, she reaches out to grip my waist and misses by about a foot. We go straight to the river park—to the cottonwood shadows. Just enough light to see lace on skin. Plenty of dark to taste wine on tongue.

Dolores isn't even on my radar. But that night—and right now:

Oh my God.

Oh . . . My . . . God!

CHAPTER 22

I CAN'T SLEEP. SO I roll out of bed and fire up Drone Pilot.

For the next couple of hours, I go and go, blowing away attackers, pulverizing targets, lost in the Zone yet aware of the beauty around me — the geometric orchards, the rushing Arghandab River, the rugged-brown hills, and on the horizon the Hindu Kush mountains, spiked like a picket fence.

Sometime long after midnight, my laptop pings. What the —? It's Colonel Kincaid.

Arlo, please see the attached memo. It contains a reference to you.

I open the memo. This time, it's not quite so redacted. I can actually see some content, though not much:

To: Mideast High Command and Coalition UAV Strategic Units
RE: Operation Brave Panther

Embedded between blacked-out chunks of text is this unredacted paragraph:

In all exercises, the pilot has handled difficult weather and limited resources effectively. It may well be that his lack of formal training is to our advantage. He is forced to solve problems in real time without the knowledge of our step-by-step or legacy procedures. In every case, his solutions were solid or superior.

Teeter up.

And then this:

Tuesday's strike on the known hub of militant activity killed six enemy soldiers.
Our attack Thursday on the suspected militant safe house resulted in eight enemy killed.

Then this:

The attack resulted in sixteen civilian and three friendly fire deaths.

Two things stand out to me. First, the drone strikes killed more friends than enemies. Second, the information looks backward at what's already happened. Nothing talks about what's planned for the future.

The exception is a single sentence near the end of the document. I wonder if Colonel Kincaid wants me to see this — or did he just forget to redact it?

Every day he lives is a day of victory for the enemy.

CHAPTER 23

"YOU DON'T HAVE TO BE Superman to see with x-ray eyes," Uncle Sal says.

We're sitting in the den at Two Hole, Uncle Sal's ranch. The real name is *La Paloma Verde* — Green Dove. But everybody calls it Two Hole because of the outhouse out back, under the elm. Lobo's Great-Aunt Portia still uses it. God knows why. They have plenty of bathrooms at Two Hole.

"X-ray eyes," Uncle Sal says, tapping his eye bags. "Or as they say at the Harvard Business School: creative visualization."

Cam, Lobo, Lee, and I sprawl on his big Denver Broncos couch, taking it in.

"Let's use our x-ray eyes right now to see Rio Loco Field," Uncle Sal says. "It's homecoming Friday. A mere eleven days away. Halftime. Packed house. The band wraps up and files into the bleachers, piccolos to tubas.

"Now it's your turn, Arlo. You mount up and rip that throttle. I want to hear you way up in the high seats. Every damn cc. Can you see it? Can you hear it?"

"Pretty much," I say.

My real focus is on my shoulder pressing against Lee's. If I add a bit more pressure, will she do the same? I lean against her. She edges away.

"Arlo, are you listening?" Uncle Sal asks.

"Yeah," I say, snapping back. "But hey, won't the refs and officials chase me off the field if I ride my bike on it?"

"Arlo, you're a headline entertainer now," Uncle Sal says. "You have new rights and privileges. No one's going to chase you off the field. I'll see to that. I want you to ride out there, front and center. Preen a little. Do a wheelie. Knees to the breeze. Warm up the crowd. Prime them for your jump."

"Where will you be?" I ask.

"Up in the announcer's booth introducing you. Now, remember, I want to hear every damn cc. You're a chainsaw. Got it?"

"Got it," I say.

Well, sort of. Because x-ray vision is a personal thing. Like art. You got your Norman Rockwells, and you got your Picassos. Norman Rockwell is like looking through window glass. Picasso is like looking through a Coke bottle.

Uncle Sal sees it more like Norman Rockwell.

I see it more like Picasso.

As I visualize, my eyes drift to the wall behind Uncle Sal. It's filled with photos tracing the history of the Focazios in America, from the immigrant coal miner brothers to the official army portrait of Lobo's dead brother, Davy, to the many aunts, uncles, and cousins in between.

Uncle Sal is the Pied Piper of the family, leading it out of the coal mines in one generation. He stands tall and barrel-chested at the center of most photos: grinning in his army paratrooper fatigues; rodeo clowning; flipping pancakes at a Kiwanis breakfast; rockin' a bolero jacket on Cinco de Mayo. On and on.

Plus a photo of him and Alex Trebek standing on the *Jeopardy!* soundstage in Culver City, California. This was taken long ago, during their mustache phase.

"Now, listen!" Uncle Sal says, snapping me back again. "I've lined up Wingo Lumber and Hurtado Toyota. Masterson Electric should pony up too. They better — they owe me. That's three sponsors. By local standards, we're a success. But I'm not interested in local standards. And this team sure as hell is not a local team. Arlo, remember what I said about changing your name — to something you can write sideways on a scorecard?"

"Yeah, I remember."

"How do you like the sound of Jett Spence?"

"Jett Spence?" I say. "How come? Everybody knows who I am."

"Do they really," Uncle Sal says. "Last week, they thought you were Scooper. Is that who you are?"

"Nah, not at all," I say.

"The 'Jett' part is obvious," Uncle Sal goes on. "We'll spell it with two *t*'s, for effect. And 'Spence' picks up on your Grandpa Spencer's name. Don't worry. You're Arlo Santiago to us, and always will be. But for promotional purposes, you'll be Jett Spence."

Lobo pumps a fist. "Go, Jett!"

"Wait!" Lee says. "'Jett Spence' is totally fake."

Uncle Sal looks at her for a while, like he's trying to weigh her allegiance, because most people don't question him. "You're right, Lee," he says at last. "'Jett Spence' *is* totally fake. The whole

Jeopardy! thing was totally fake too. But look what happened when we changed the name. Sulphur Springs, New Mexico, was dying on the vine. Today, Jeopardy, New Mexico, is thriving. The vine is producing succulent grapes. So what's in a name? I'll tell you what's in a name—*cha-CHING!*"

He reaches into his pocket for his money clip. Peels off a one-hundred-dollar bill.

"Jett, go online and buy yourself a jumpsuit for the big night—something . . . Elvis-y. Something that says 'I love America.'"

"I can help with that," Lee says. "But to be totally honest, a hundred bucks isn't enough. If we're really serious, we'll need at least two hundred."

Uncle Sal goes cold. We suck in. Because you don't question if Uncle Sal is serious. And you definitely don't ask for more money. Not if you value your *cojones.* You take what he gives you, then figure it out. Even if it means reconstituting one of his yellow smokejumper suits hanging in the barn.

Finally, he cracks a grin. "Well, well. Jett, it looks like you've got yourself a personal manager here." He peels off another Benjamin. "Get a jumpsuit with gauntlets."

Lobo looks shocked. I'm feeling it too.

Uncle Sal shakes a finger at Cam. "Make sure Arlo's bike is primed. I want it to both purr *and* roar. Here's an idea—fill the tank with jet fuel. Maybe that can be part of our campaign."

"Nah," Cam says. "Jet fuel's basically kerosene. It'd burn up the valves."

"I'm okay with regular unleaded," I say.

Uncle Sal shrugs. "If you boys can get high performance out

of low octane, so be it. But Arlo . . . *Jett!* . . . remember, your good name is better than the best cologne. If you want it back, nail the jump."

"Try my best," I say.

"Don't try," Uncle Sal says. "There's no such thing as 'try' — only 'do.'"

"Hey!" Lobo says. "You just quoted Yoda. 'Do or do not. There is no try.'"

Aunt Portia waddles in carrying a tray of foaming glasses. We all stand. In Lobo's family, you stand for anybody of that generation, man or woman. Portia's the last. She's Uncle Sal's aunt, Lobo's great-aunt. She's a scrawny five-foot tower of Italian peasant royalty.

Aunt Portia beams at Lee. "The secret —"

Cam and Lobo chorus, "The yeast, the yeast."

"That's right," Aunt Portia says to Lee. "The secret is in the yeast."

Cam rescues the tray, and we each grab a glass of Aunt Portia's world-famous *hoja santa.* Everybody takes a sip except Lee.

Uncle Sal gasps. *"Man-o-man!"*

"*Mmm* — excellent batch!" Cam says.

Lobo wipes an arm across his foam mustache.

Aunt Portia says to Lee, "Mix the sarsaparilla and licorice roots. Add just a pinch of *hoja santa.* And remember to mix the yeast grains evenly with the sugar."

"I will," Lee says.

Aunt Portia waits for Lee to take a sip. She finally does.

"It . . . tastes . . . *um* . . . like root beer, only . . . only . . . "

Only hell! Aunt Portia's *hoja santa* has blow-your-brains-out carbonation, plus a tart acidity that makes your spine shudder and vertebrae fall into place. Plus Aztecan medicinal qualities. Plus something of the Italian earth.

A mellow buzz sets in. Aunt Portia insists it's not alcoholic, but I've drunk real beer that's a lot weaker. We're always different after we drink her *hoja santa.*

Humbler. Calmer. Wiser.

I nudge Lee. "Hey, you ever go skydiving?"

"No, why do you ask?"

Before I can tell her, Aunt Portia plants her face in mine. "Arlo, introduce me to your girlfriend."

"I'm not his girlfriend," Lee says.

Aunt Portia makes to swat me. "Arlo, what's wrong with you! You ain't brought a girl like her around since—"

"Since ever," Lobo says.

Aunt Portia swings around and makes to swat Lobo. "You should see the girls *he* brings over. *Ugh!* Half their buttons never been used. At least Arlo has standards."

"Hey, I got standards too," Lobo says.

"No, Lobo, you do not have standards," Aunt Portia says.

Lee holds out her hand. "I'm Lee Fields."

Aunt Portia takes her hand and caresses it. "I'd know you anywhere. Your Aunt Lupita used to come to our Christmas parties. She and your mother, Arlo, were the two prettiest girls in the county. Lupita played piano. And, Arlo, your mom played the concertina."

"Accordion," I say.

Aunt Portia still has Lee's hand. "I'm so glad you know my boys. Arlo and Cam practically grew up with us. They helped with the expansion after we got the *Jeopardy!* money. And they built the airstrip all by themselves — cleared and rolled it. They even moved my privy. That reminds me —"

"Oh, yes!" Lobo says. "Tell her!"

I shudder. "Definitely do *not* tell her."

"Lee, you must hear this," Uncle Sal says. "It's one of Portia's Top Forty."

Lee laughs. "I'd love to hear it."

"Well," Aunt Portia says, smoothing a hand down her skirt, "I call Arlo my Little Craphouse Compadre —"

"Aie-eeeeeee!" Lobo shrieks.

"Hush, Lobo! Let me tell it," Aunt Portia says. "Well, one morning when Arlo was four or five years old, I was . . . *ahem!* . . . in the privy. The latch turns, and in steps little Arlo. He drops his pants and sits beside me on the next hole. 'Good morning, Aunt Portia. How are you today? Isn't it a beautiful morning?' He goes on like this, and we have a wonderful conversation. Just like we're snapping peas on the porch. Even as a little boy, Arlo had nice manners. He could talk like a book. He was an old soul. After a time, he finished his business, buckled up, and said, 'Nice speaking to you, Aunt Portia,' and then he slipped out. He even remembered to pull the door closed. So many children would have forgotten, but not Arlo. It just tickled me. Ever since, I've called him my little Craphouse Compadre."

Lee looks at me and laughs. I want to crawl under the couch.

"Little Arlo sounds like quite a character," Lee says.

"Character is forever," Lobo says.

"See what I mean? Top Forty," Uncle Sal says.

He swivels around, pulls back the curtain, and inspects the sky.

"Magic hour, kids."

CHAPTER 24

WE BANG OUT THE BACK door into the emptiness of late afternoon. Tangerine sun. Fingernail moon. Twink of Venus. It's all here. All boring and amazing at the same time. The day is dying. The year is dying. It truly is magic hour. A time to live, because death feels so close.

"What do you know about flying?" Uncle Sal asks Lee.

"Nothing."

"Perfect. Come with me."

They march across the landing strip to the hangar. Cam, Lobo, and I go to the barn and pole down two parachutes. Lobo takes the table, and Cam spreads out on the floor. Their fingers go to work.

A pecking order exists here, too. I'm top QA: quality assurance. Uncle Sal won't let Lobo be QA. Just Cam and me, and I beat him by a year.

I watch as they clear their shroud lines, check for snags, square their canopies, and fold from the bottom up, as Uncle Sal taught us. Lobo gets a bit sloppy with his static lines, so I rewrap them around the metal loop. I help him with his pilot chute. Then I pole down my chute. Cam QAs.

"Packing is prayer," Uncle Sal likes to say.

We zip into the yellow smokejumper suits Uncle Sal bought on surplus, complete with fluorescent cuffs, radio pockets, and shovel straps. We each carry a cell phone, flashlight, and hook knife. Lobo has been known to carry something to smoke after landing. Me, I'm not into that. It defeats the purpose.

We shoulder into our rigs and head outside. We can hear Uncle Sal and Lee powering up in the hangar. Uncle Sal's a fanatic about his checklist.

Pretty soon, the *Hi-O Silver* rolls out and noses into the wind. Not many people go up with us at this point. They talk like they will, but when they peer into the cabin and see that Uncle Sal has stripped it for skydiving, and all that's left is a pilot seat and a butt-hard floor, plus an open hole where the door should be, they chicken out.

"Got ourselves a passenger," Uncle Sal says.

"Way to go, Lee!" Lobo says.

She scoots in back and folds up her knees. I get in next, then Cam. Lobo wedges himself up front by Uncle Sal, back against the dash.

"Lobo, move your ass six inches to the left," Uncle Sal says.

The *Hi-O Silver* is designed to carry four people, and we are five. So Uncle Sal takes care to distribute our weight. We all shift a few inches.

I press up against Lee. Lobo winks.

"Pass this back," Uncle Sal says.

We hand Lee a barf bag.

"Will there be much turbulence?" she asks.

"It's not the turb I'm worried about," Uncle Sal says.

He pulls out a Cupido cigar and stuffs it in his mouth. "Relax, I won't light up till after they've jumped."

Uncle Sal mumbles his mantra — "Fuel. Throttle. Magneto. Ammeter." — and cranks to 1,000 rpm. Guns it to 1,800. The propeller blades strobe into a single line and then disappear.

We go. Build past the hangar, the junked generations of trucks and tractors. Blast down the airstrip. Aunt Portia comes out and waves. We lift off and whine into the sky.

We fly west toward Kit Carson Mesa and the flattening sun. Make a sweet chandelle turn and begin to climb. To the north, Zuni Mesa looks like an aircraft carrier. To the northeast, Burro Mesa, where the dust of Mom lies — where Dad has marked a square of earth for her monument — looks like a fortress on fire. As we fly over, I lean out the door.

Lee gasps.

"Aw, don't worry about him," Lobo yells over the engine noise. "He always does that. Arlo lives on the edge."

I pull Lee beside me and throw an arm around her. Because all first-timers need to see this: God's IMAX. Especially at magic hour. Fear and wonder shine in her eyes.

"Just lean with me," I say into her ear.

She tucks against me but keeps a hand on the wall grip. "I'm not into heights," she yells.

"It's not a height anymore," I say. "We're way too high for that. Think of it as a front-row seat." I point to Burro Mesa. A couple dozen browns are scattered across the flat top, little specks, grazing. "That's the highest mesa in the whole damn state and my favorite place in the world. See how the north rim breaks sheer and clean?"

Lee leans with me, looks down.

"Yes, I see it."

"That break, that's the border where New Mexico ends and Colorado begins. And up there, those are the—"

"Spanish Peaks," Lee says.

"Yup. And those in the far distance—"

"The Rockies."

"Yeah, well, everything's the Rockies," I say. "Those are what we call the Front Range. That peak in the middle—the whale back—way, way up—"

"Pike's Peak," Lee says.

I squeeze her shoulder. "You got it."

"Will we fly over my aunt's place?"

"Yeah."

We climb in a miles-wide spiral. Soon we're over Chicorica Canyon, looking down on the whole of Lupita's ranch—some seven thousand acres—from the high rim rocks to the cattle-specked valley. It's the country Lupita and Mom used to ride.

"Oh my God!" Lee says. "It looks so dry."

"Bone-ass," I say.

She points to the dam. "All because of that."

From up here, it's easy to see how the dam divides Lupita's land into bright green and tinder brown sections. The majority is tinder brown.

"Too bad this plane isn't a Predator drone," I say. "We could fix the whole mess right now."

"Lee," Uncle Sal shouts over the engine. "Everything sounds cheap up here. Even Johnny Cash. The exception is Italian opera. I hope you're a fan of the Lone Ranger."

"I'm not *not* a fan," Lee says, and we move back into our places.

Uncle Sal switches on the sound system. A lone cello cuts through the rpm.

"This is the *William Tell* overture," he shouts. "It's better known as the *Lone Ranger* theme. Composed by Rossini. It's the greatest skydiving tune ever written."

We listen to the drum growl and the flutes tiptoe. Then the whole orchestra slams in, and Uncle Sal begins to conduct with his unlit Cupido. Just when you think something's going to break, maybe even the wings, the music tapers into a sweet, fluty sunrise.

Kenya Man is way more my style, but up here, when you look down on lonesome infinities, your pores open up, and Rossini soaks into you.

We're approaching our drop zone—a stump- and gully-free field a mile and a half up the highway from Two Hole.

"You're on, Camerado," Uncle Sal says.

Cam scoots to the open door, reaches for the wing strut, plants his foot on the step, and swings outside the plane. He holds and waits as Lobo crowds onto the step beside him. Now they are four white knuckles gripping the wing strut.

"Queuing up," Uncle Sal says. "Lee, you're gonna love this." He cranks the volume. You can hear French horns riding to the rescue. Uncle Sal launches into his spiel:

"Who is that masked man who rides the range and fights injustice?"

Cam, Lobo, and I shout: "The Lone Ranger!"

Uncle Sal recites the Lone Ranger's creed:

"God gave us firewood, but we must gather the light ourselves."

"Amen!" we shout.

"To have a friend, a man must be one."

"Amen!" we shout.

"Everyone has within himself the power to—"

Before he can finish the creed, the French horns gallop up. Uncle Sal shouts:

"Hi-o, Silver, awayyyyyyyy!"

"Awwayyyyyyyyy!" Lobo screams, and he and Cam tumble back into the sky.

Now it's my turn.

ME—maximum efficiency. Slide to the door. Feet on step. Hands on strut. Hold. One . . . two . . .

And my own creed:

Yea, though I fly through the valley of the shadow . . .

Lee touches my shoulder. Never do that. Never cloud my mind when I'm about to jump. I brush her hand off.

"Hi-o, Silver, awayyyyyyyy!" Uncle Sal shouts.

I let go.

Flip into the sky.

Ball up.

One . . . two . . . three . . . four . . .

Cam and Lobo wait for me to join them—if you can call falling spread-eagled at 160 miles an hour waiting.

I close in, pop out of my tuck, reach, and catch Cam's hand. Then Lobo's. We snap into a circle. We would never hold hands like this on the ground. But in the air, brotherhood is natural.

« « « » » »

TWILIGHT AND BURNING VENUS.

Dusk in the purple west.

I land on soft earth.

Cam touches down easy too.

Lobo skates to a stop on his knees. Farts majestically. "Oh hell, *yes!*" he cries. We gather in our chutes.

As we tramp up the shoulder of the Clayton highway, approaching cars ignite us like matchsticks. They slow down to check us out. Our fluorescent cuffs glow radioactively.

"Escaped from Pluto!" Lobo shouts at one car.

It's dark when we reach Two Hole. We hang our chutes in the barn. Peel out of our smokejumpers. Go to the house. Uncle Sal is sitting in his armchair, reading the *Albuquerque Journal.* He's smoked the Cupido down to a stub.

"Sadly, Lee was a casualty," he says, tapping his ash into the cup of a golf trophy. "Maybe if I'd smoked a Tiparillo instead. This crafted Cuban can really turn the stomach."

"That barf bag didn't work?" Cam asks.

"Barf bags only work when you barf into them," Uncle Sal says.

"That's true," Lobo says.

We go into the kitchen and hydrate ourselves under the faucet. Then we dehydrate ourselves with some super chunky peanut butter on Cabaret crackers.

We come back into the living room and flop on the couch. Lobo clicks on the TV. It's news hour, but he flips to *Family Guy.* Overhead, the floorboards creak.

Lee and Aunt Portia start down the stairs. When Aunt Portia sees us, she grabs Lee's shoulders and plants her on a middle step.

"Hey, you boys, turn down that trash!" she cries.

Lobo thumbs the volume.

"Stand up!"

We stand and face the stairs. Uncle Sal lowers the *Journal.*

"Take a look — *huh!*" Aunt Portia says. "Because this is what a *real* girl looks like."

Lee's wearing a dress pulled from some immigrant trunk or mothball closet. A wine-colored dress. Simple as Cinderella. The most skin you can see is her collarbone, and it doesn't exactly cling.

She's holding a plastic shopping bag—kind of hiding it behind her.

"Guess, I wasn't born with an iron stomach," she says.

Lobo snickers. "Guess not."

"Hey-hey-hey!" Aunt Portia snaps. "You listen to me, you boys. You can go all over the world — Timbuktu to China — but you'll never see so plain as you're seeing now a beautiful girl. Look at her! *Mio dio!* Lobo, if you make another face, I swear —"

Uncle Sal flourishes his cigar. "A moment of silence — for beauty."

Lee reddens. "Oh my God, I'm not —"

"Oh my God," Lobo mimics. "Yes, you are."

Cam bumps me. "Dude, stop drooling."

I'm not exactly drooling, at least not literally.

"Arlo, this is the girl for you," Aunt Portia says. "The one to take to the opera."

"No, not the opera!" Lobo says. "Anything but the opera."

"The opera!" Aunt Portia insists.

"She's right, of course," Uncle Sal says.

"And not just any opera," Aunt Portia goes on. "You take her to the one in Rome."

"Rome, Italy?" I say. "Or Rhome, Texas?"

But what I think is,

Oh my God, yes, you are.

« « « » » »

TEN MINUTES LATER, I'M CRUISING down the Clayton highway on my 250 — the white line spinning my eyeballs into visions of Lee — when Kenya Man barks:

L.A. . . . L.A. . . . L.A.
Gonna get my junk in play
At the corner of Sunset and La Brea.

I dig my phone out of my jacket and pry it under my helmet — not easy when you're bombing on a dirt bike.

It's Dad, breaking my spell.

"Tie up your nag!" he shouts, then hangs up.

How can I tie up my nag when I'm riding it? My other nag, my Yamaha YZ 125, is already tied up — cozy in the shed beside Dad's dinosaurs.

He must've drained a can or two. Or three. Or four. Or six.

When I get home, I tie up my 250 and go into the kitchen. Dad's sitting at the table, glasses perched low on his nose, mumbling over his manuscript. He looks like he's had a marathon session of novel writing. I glance around for empties but don't see any.

"Go tie up your nag," he growls.

"Hey, already did," I say, a little pissed.

He pushes his chair back, gives me a tough look. But there's a glint in his eye. "I beg to differ — follow me."

He flips on the driveway lights, and I follow him out. Parked off the drive is an extremely ripped and shiny motorcycle. A diamond black Ducati Monster 1100 EVO. Naked and muscular. Exhaust pipes aimed like twin silencers.

"*Whoa!*" I say. "Where did *that* come from?"

"Compliments of the United States of America," Dad says.

"But why? I haven't done anything yet."

"Get used to it, Arlo," he says, handing me the keys. "You're a government employee now."

I go over and check it out. The Ducati is one bulging engine. Even parked and keyed off, you can almost hear it pulsing.

"Guess I better try it out," I say.

"No you don't," Dad says. "Dinner first. C'mon, I've cooked us some glorious empanadas."

« « « » » »

I WOLF MY GLORIOUS EMPANADAS and then take the Ducati Monster 1100 EVO for a test drive. I ease along the access road. All the cutoffs that tempt me on my dirt bikes do not tempt me now. The Ducati smells one road only: Interstate 25.

At the Shell station, I ramp on and aim south. Gradually, I give it teeth — seventy miles per hour. Eighty. Ninety. But the Monster snoozes on. Just south of Maxwell, the interstate straightens into a black arrow. Smack smooth. Famously unguarded.

I wake up the Monster.

CHAPTER 25

IT'S AFTER MIDNIGHT. I'M DRIFTING off—about to plunge into the REM trench—when my laptop pings. I rub my face and sit up.

It's another e-mail from Colonel Kincaid. He can't seem to he keep normal business hours.

Arlo, what do you know about the mountain lions of Asia?

Say what?

Specifically, what do you know about the Caracal? For instance, did you know that this big cat survives through clandestine movement and the ability to vanish into the rugged high terrain of its native land?

Think about it.

He signs off as simply, "Kincaid."

What the hell! Is he drunk?

I could kick his ass for waking me up.

But he's the reason I'll be getting the paychecks. And the reason there's a Ducati 1100 EVO Monster parked in our shed tonight.

So I forgive him — just this once — and go back to sleep.

CHAPTER 26

"THREE DAYS," DAD SAYS. "I give your sister three days. Fish and guests spoil in three days, as Ben Franklin liked to say."

We're driving into Chicorica Canyon. The sign at the hairpin — 10 MPH — is blistered with gunshot. We cross the creek. Only there's no creek anymore. Just gully and goo.

"Ben must've got it wrong," I say. "'Cuz it's already been four days."

"Has it?" Dad looks out at the country.

At every other turn, we see the pipeline. It runs downhill, trestling over pines, chaparral, and arroyos. When it hits the bottom of the canyon, it points like a ruled line to the town reservoir six miles to the west.

It's been almost a year since they finished construction on the dam and pipeline, but the copper glistens like it was yesterday.

We bounce over the cattle guard, grind past the barn, and pull up outside Lupita Fields's house. Through the cottonwoods, I can see the Punch Bowl — the deep-wide part of the creek where Siouxsie and I used to splash around. Now it's a scum-green bog. The irrigation canals are dry. Lupita's ranch looks, feels, and smells like thirst.

"Go raise some hell, Guapie," Dad says, opening the door. El Guapo is off like a jackrabbit — down the hill, across the pasture, to the town where the prairie dogs live, to do just that.

"A happy poodle is a joy forever," Dad says.

The screen door slaps, and there's Lupita, looking summer tanned, even though it's pale October.

"Been a long time, Hec," she says.

"Yes, it sure has," Dad says, grabbing Siouxsie's suitcase from the back of the pickup. "Unless you count me staring down at you from an upstairs window."

"I don't count that," Lupita says.

She's wearing a turquoise tank top and a green Western shirt, with a bit of silver in her belt — about as much as she has in her hair, which is twisted up in a clip with falling coiled tendrils. Dad sneaks a hand behind his back and tucks his shirt in.

"Hey, you!" Lupita says to me. "Come here, handsome boy."

I go up the steps, and she engulfs me in her arms. Everything about her is a ten-thousand-dollar saddle. I can feel her softness, strength, and sorrow — sorrow not for herself, because many women down in Clay would gladly trade places with her, despite her solitary ways and drought problems, but for us.

Lupita Fields is full of grit, with no patience for shit — that's how she is.

"You plan on breakin' your neck while you're up here?" she asks, nodding toward my YZ 125, which I've tied down in the back of the pickup.

"Something like that," I say.

She lifts her voice. "You guys are staying for dinner. Guess who's cooking?"

"I don't believe it," Dad says.

Turns out Siouxsie's not really cooking. She's sitting at the kitchen counter rolling pie dough. A colander of apples stands beside her.

"Jonathans?" Dad asks, as if nothing happened four nights ago.

"Jono*golds,*" Siouxsie says, not looking up.

"Mmm-mmh!" Dad says. "Apple pie is God's own comfort food."

"I sure hope so," Lupita says. "Because our main course might not be all too comforting."

"Lee's making tofu," Siouxsie says, leaning heavily on the rolling pin.

"Imagine that," Lupita says. "Four generations in the beef cattle business, and I'm serving tofu to my guests. That is the impact of my niece."

"Hey, where is she?" I ask.

"Glued to the news," Siouxsie says, rolling the pin with extreme care, even though it's just flat pie dough. Dad notices too.

"That's right," Lupita says. "We aren't likely to see Lee until after the *BBC World Update.* The girls' room is command central these days. You'd think Pakistan was next door in Colfax County."

"Lee's obsessed with the *BBC World Update,*" Siouxsie says.

"Who isn't?" Dad says. "All those dapper British broadcasters. They sure know how to enunciate. We Americans just hem and haw—*yup, y'know, uh-huh.* We take a dull ax to the old Anglo Sax. Lupita, isn't your brother stationed over there?"

Lupita sighs. "Yes, he is. Lee's dad's in that hellhole up on the border. Scares me too."

"Go on down, Slim," Siouxsie tells me. "She's been working on your project."

"Slim!" Lupita chuckles. "Your mother used to call you that — Little Texas Slim. You were so skinny. And proud of your boots."

Siouxsie leans over to check out my scuffed Gringos. "Not anymore."

I pick up the suitcase and go down the hall to Lee's room, which Siouxsie now shares. I stop in the doorway.

Lee's doing some kind of yoga pose in front of a wide-screen TV. She's wearing a powder-blue T-shirt, cropped high, and white yoga pants, cut low. The pose looks like one of those sun-salutation-*chakra* types, the kind you see flipping across cable. She has that just-showered look — sleek, damp, and shiny, her hair towel-fluffed. Only problem is, it's so long it's hiding her butt. Her legs are toned and tight. A silver ring shimmers on the second toe of her left foot.

I mean, *damn!*

I rap on the doorjamb. "They tell me this is command central."

Lee flashes me a smile. It's one of those pasted-on ones, the price I must pay for my bad joke. But was it really that bad?

"I've marked some jumpsuits," she says, holding her pose. "Go ahead and have a look." Her head tilts toward the laptop on her desk. "Just don't talk to me — the war segment's coming up. Siouxsie's had to learn the hard way."

"Yes, ma'am," I say, scooping up her laptop.

I drop onto the couch and inhale her post-shower, pear-dipped-in-honey essence.

I'm buzzed. A slave. Willingly.

But the moment I embrace this thought, I reject it. Man is not born for slavery, as the Declaration of Independence states. I'm sure the hell not.

On TV, the anchorwoman says:

"We go now to Pakistan's North-West Frontier, where correspondent Ethan Shackleton has filed this report."

Lee unpretzels herself and comes over to the couch, sits at the far end, and folds up her knees. She gazes at Ethan Shackleton. He definitely has her attention.

"This . . . is a broken country. A land of gnarled hills, craggy canyons, and scarce rain — until today, when it rained death . . ."

"Rained death," I echo. "Nice one, Ethan."

Lee cuts me a look.

"Today's air offensive overshot its intended target and struck an allied convoy, reportedly killing four U.S. and seven Pakistani soldiers. The number of civilian casualties is still unknown."

The camera pans down a road to a smoking bus.

"This is the fourth attack gone tragically wrong in the past two months. A warning, these images are not for the faint of heart."

The camera zooms in on charred bodies.

"'Spotty, at best' is how one high-level official today described the coalition's aerial campaign against the insurgency. 'An outright failure' is the consensus of many leading opinion makers.'"

"'Spotty, at best'! C'mon, Ethan. You can do better than that."

The camera lingers on the crumpled body of a soldier. We see the American flag patch on his uniform.

"One more down," I mumble.

"That's it," Lee says, thrusting her arm toward the door. "Get out, Arlo!"

I slide lower in my seat. "Don't get bogged down in all this," I say.

Lee's eyes spark. "Bogged down! That soldier had breakfast this morning. He had a future this morning. Now it's gone. Why? Do you understand why? I sincerely doubt it. So how can you sit there and say 'Don't get bogged down in all this'?"

"Yeah, well . . ." I say, and leave it at that.

What I don't say is, I've thought a lot about this — how death goes down in our society, our world. What I've come to realize is that for your sanity's sake, you've got to draw a line. Because the world loves death — or, to be fair, loves images of death. They are everywhere: in the ABC-BBC war holes, in the fictional slime of prime time, in the splattery world of movies and video games — especially video games. I should know.

My advice: Do not grieve. Cut yourself off from all that. Because one real death is all a body can take. Real grief chews you up, sucks you dry, and spits you out.

But I don't say this to Lee.

Her dad's over there.

I open the laptop. She's bookmarked "Motorcycle Jumpsuits." Uncle Sal wants me to get "something Elvis-y" — or something that says "I love America."

Lee has marked:

> The "Jeweled Elvis (glasses included)."
> The "Elvis Zombie Mechanic (new with tags)."
> The "Elvis Fountain Jumper."

Elvis — come on. Didn't he die on a toilet?

And do I really love America?

I love the sky over America. I love the mesas. Especially Burro Mesa. The north rim is my favorite place on earth. If that's America, then hell, yes! I love it.

Lee's also marked some non-Elvis-y jumpsuits:

> The "General George Armstrong Custer, complete with gauntlets."

The “Evel Knievel, with ‘EK’ embroidered on the waistband.”

The “Robbie Knievel, with ‘Live Life at Full Throttle’ blazed on the back.”

The “Elton John.”

I scroll through page after page of “Motorcycle Jumpsuits,” sure that Uncle Sal would love the flame-colored suit with the huge wrestler’s belt or the American flag suit with tire treads up the back.

But I can’t. I just can’t.

Finally, “Motorcycle Jumpsuits” ends. I’m about to close the laptop when my eye catches something on the next page under “Specialty Flight Clothing.”

The headline reads:

Flying Wingsuit
For the Hard-Core Insane.
*Bargain of a F***ing Lifetime!*

I pop the link and read:

My beautiful new wife does not think it healthy for me to base jump, bridge jump, or cliff surf anymore. So I guess I’m going to take up golf instead. If you’re into extreme sh*t — and want to know what it feels like to truly soar — then this suit is for you. She’s a veteran of Royal Gorge and Devil’s Tower. I will profoundly miss the ‘Old Flying Squirrel.’ Awesome airfoil. Excellent condition. Bid now.”

"Got it," I say.

Lee stays fixated on Ethan Shackleton. Stunned into submission, you might say.

"In the last year alone, the United States has launched scores of drones against insurgent strongholds in the Swat Valley."

I set the laptop between us and lean toward the TV.

"Unmanned aerial vehicles of varying sizes and purposes prowl the skies of the North-West Frontier twenty-four hours a day, three hundred sixty-five days a year."

Images of various drones pop up. I'm extremely familiar with most of them — the hunter-killers like the Predator and Reaper. And the hunter-gatherers like the Firefly and Hummingbird.

For sheer shock and awe, I prefer a hunter-killer. But the fact is, I never met a drone I didn't like.

"Indispensable in aerial imaging and lethal in attack — when they hit their targets — drones represent the West's best hope to defang the tiger of terror."

"Tiger of terror." I almost compliment Ethan on that one. He really does have a way with words. But I hold my tongue.

"This is Ethan Shackleton, BBC World Update, *reporting from Pakistan's North-West Frontier."*

Lee turns down the audio. "Okay, Arlo. What do you got?"

She grabs the laptop, perches it on her knees, and stares at the "Flying Wingsuit."

"Hey, this isn't what Uncle Sal—"

"Bid everything," I say. "All two hundred bucks."

CHAPTER 27

"KNOCK, KNOCK."

Lupita's leaning in the doorway, arms folded. "Hope I'm not interrupting any important military business."

Lee closes her laptop. "No, we were just—"

"I'll bet you were." Then to me, "Hey, Slim, your dad and I are going for a drive. You tag along. We need to talk."

"And, darlin'," she says to Lee. "Tear yourself away from Pakistan and go help Siouxsie with her schoolwork. In about forty-five minutes, I want you to start on that famous *to-FU* of yours."

"All right," Lee says.

Five minutes later, Lupita, Dad, and I are grinding into the canyon in her Dodge "longbox." Dad cranks down his window and inhales the crisp, piney, lonesome, delicious October twilight. "My God," he sighs.

We stop below the dam that holds back Chicorica Creek. The creek used to run fast here. Thin-fast in the winter, fat-fast in the spring. Now a trickle drips out of a pipe into the mucky bed.

Lupita kills the engine and pulls the hand brake. We stare at the dam—a wall of concrete about eighteen feet high and a hundred feet wide. This is the first time I've seen it up close.

A sign reads:

NO TRESPASSING.

PROPERTY OF THE TOWN OF CLAY ALLISON, NEW MEXICO.

"Well, that's progress for you," Lupita says. "God put my water up there, and gravity pulls it to me. Been that way since the dawn of time, or at least since the last ice age. Until the town council decided to play God and dam my creek."

"Goddamn town council," Dad grumbles.

Dad and the *Orphan County Gazette* fought building the dam.

"Tell me again," I say. "Why did they do it?"

"For the so-called greater good," Dad says. "The needs of the community exceeded the needs of the individual. It's called eminent domain."

"Nah, it's called stealing," I say.

Lupita pats my knee. "Slim, I've never heard it summed up so neatly."

I point to a ridge above the dam. "Hey, didn't we used to go up there a long time ago?"

"Yes, we did, Slim," Lupita says. "Picnicked right up there, where the water gushes out of the ground, a natural aquifer. Your mom was pregnant with Siouxsie. Speaking of whom . . ." She looks at Dad. "Siouxsie should stay with us for now."

Dad sets his face like stone. "Not gonna happen."

"You got a lot on your plate, Hec."

"I don't have a damn thing on my plate, Lupita. It's licked clean."

"You're in mourning," Lupita says. "Mourning goes on for a long time. It can be a full-time job."

"Is that what I'm in?" Dad ducks an eye and starts tracking a hawk. "I don't know anymore."

Lupita leans across me and grabs his arm. "Yes, Hec, that's what you're in." She lets go and sits back. "The girls get along. They have something in common, if you count the fact that Lee's mother is absent too. The main thing is, Siouxsie *wants* to be with us now. She doesn't want to be at home. Probably too much of a reminder. And, Hec, she needs regular medical care."

Dad scoffs. "Hell, I know that."

"Obviously, you don't," Lupita says. "Since she hasn't seen a doctor in two months."

"It hasn't been two months," Dad says.

"Yeah, it has," I say.

Dad keeps tracking that hawk.

"She'll need a wheelchair," Lupita says.

"Not yet, she won't," Dad says.

Lupita leans on the wheel. "Look at me, Hec."

Dad turns and looks at her.

"Your daughter needs your full attention. And until you're ready to give it to her, she's staying with me."

"Like hell," Dad says.

"You heard me," Lupita says. "And I'm taking her up to Colorado Springs in the morning to see that neurologist, Dr. Navarro, like you should've done."

Dad shakes his head. "I owe him. Plenty."

"Don't you worry about that," Lupita says. "I'll cover you for now."

Dad jerks open the door, gets out, and slams it. We watch him kick through the grass.

"Way too proud," I say.

"Don't you know it," Lupita says. "Well, there's nothing we can do but let him ride that bull."

We watch Dad cross the creek, stepping from rock to rock to avoid the muck. He stops at the No Trespassing sign and stares at the wall of concrete.

Lupita slides an arm around me. "The good part is, I got you all to myself now." She gives me a long look. "I hear Uncle Sal's enlisted you in one of his schemes. You really going to jump your motorcycle at the homecoming game?"

"Got to," I say. "Scooper's gonna stick if I don't."

"Nothin' wrong with a nickname," Lupita says.

"Lot wrong with Scooper," I say.

She nods. "So you plan on cleaning your boots with one little jump?"

"One or two," I say.

We watch Dad walk along the pipeline. He picks up a rock and raps it against the copper. We hear a puny *thunk-thunk*.

"Still the journalist, isn't he."

"Yeah, sure is," I say.

Dad ducks under the trestle where the ground dips and begins to climb the slope above the pipe.

"That niece of mine," Lupita says. "Is she showing you all the respect you deserve?"

"Not hardly," I say.

Lupita smiles, slyly. "But you gotta admit, she's easy to look at."

"Totally," I say. "She's extremely easy to look at."

Lupita laughs. "Too bad she's so vegetarian, antiwar, and all. I have nothing against any of her positions, but it's not necessary to plant your flag every half mile. Must be all that liberal rain up in Seattle. I'll tell you what she needs, Slim. A strong cowboy type. Somebody to pull her off that high horse and loosen her up. You know anybody like that?"

"Nah," I say. "But I'll tell you what she really needs — to get on a dirt bike and ride some high country. That'll loosen her up. Maybe she won't plant that flag so often."

Lupita ruffles my hair. "Let's call it a plan," she says.

We watch Dad scramble onto a flat rock above the dam. He gazes downhill, toward the pipeline, all six miles of it, linking canyon and town.

"He's taking some kind of measure," Lupita says. "He misses that old newspaper. And he misses her."

"You got that right," I say.

Lupita slides a hand behind my back, finds a knot, and goes to work kneading it out. "Catch me up on those brood mares."

"Gettin' fatter by the day," I say. "We're looking at mid- to late January. Or possibly early February."

"Winter babies," Lupita says. "You going to birth them all by yourself?"

"No way. Mr. Wasserman's got Charlie Ferguson lined up."

"Charlie Ferguson!" Lupita stops rubbing. "Hell, I taught that man everything he knows."

"I wanna be there, though," I say. "I wanna help."

"You should be there, baby," Lupita says. "Just remember, a horse is like you or anybody else, sturdy and delicate at the same time. Respect both parts of that equation. Tell you what, when the time comes, leave Charlie Ferguson out of it. Call me instead. We'll birth 'em together."

"Hey, thanks."

Lupita gives me a peck on the cheek.

When you're not supposed to think a thought, maybe that's the best time to think it. Right now, I think about kissing Lupita. Damn, what's wrong with me? Twenty minutes ago, it was Lee. Now I want to kiss her aunt, my mom's best friend. A beautiful woman — but still . . .

My heart's a traitor. Hell, it's not my heart. "A man's kickstand has no conscience," Dad likes to say.

My kickstand sure doesn't. Because all I can think about now is being alone with Lupita in some faraway place, like a cabin on the Colorado, where she could teach me everything — *everything!* I'd a million times rather get my wisdom from her than from some professor or scoutmaster.

It's a sinful thought. A joyride. I hold on for about eight seconds, then let go.

Lupita points up the canyon. "Hey, Slim, let me share a little secret with you. See way up there, that sandstone slab up in the rim rocks, the one with the vertical fissure?"

I spot the rock, cold pink in the sinking sun.

"Yeah, I see it."

"Your mother was always getting me to go places I didn't think wise to go and then later was glad I went."

"Makes two of us," I say.

She smiles. "Bet it does. Well, one day when we were about your age, we came up here on horseback. Your mom kept staring at that rock. God knows why. We'd ridden up the canyon a thousand times, and never once had she mentioned it. You can't tell from here, but that slab stands more than a hundred feet tall.

And the fissure's gotta be ten feet wide. Trouble is, to get there you got to climb the hill, and then scramble up that steep talus slope."

"Or go around back up the ridgeline," I say.

Lupita nods. "Anyway, that rock was just calling to her. I thought it was a reckless idea but agreed because—"

"Because you always agreed," I say.

"That's right, Slim. With your mom you always agreed. We tied up our horses and clawed our way up, pretty sure we were the first humans ever to set foot up there."

"You probably were," I say.

Lupita shakes her head. "That's just it. That slab of rock—the outer wall, but mostly the inside walls—was just covered with art."

"Art?" I say.

"That's right," Lupita says. "Very old art."

"You mean, like petroglyphs and stuff?"

"Exactly, like petroglyphs and stuff. Images of bear, deer, wolves, lizards—you name it. A whole mural of running buffalo. Scratched or carved right into the rock. Pictures of humans, too. A man playing a flute. A woman large with child. We guessed they were Navajo, maybe a couple of hundred years old. Then we did our research. They're Anasazi. They date back a thousand years or more."

"So what did you do?" I ask.

"Next day, we brought my father up for a look. 'Don't breathe a word,' he said. 'As soon as you start talking, people get stupid. We're gonna let this stay lost.' So that's what we did. We let it stay lost. I don't want to broadcast this, Slim. Don't want curiosity seekers coming up. And sure as hell don't want a TV crew. This is my land. My water. But that art up there, I can't claim it. Someday, somebody will find it and make a circus of it. But not in my lifetime."

"So who knows about it now?"

"Hmm," Lupita says. "Let me count. One . . . two . . ." She bumps me. "Guess just you and me."

"Not even Lee?"

"Not even Lee."

"So how come you're telling me?"

She searches my eyes. "Because you're your mother's son."

Dad crosses the dry bed and ambles back to the truck. He looks more like himself now. Like he's done riding that bull.

He gets into the Dodge. Eases the door closed. Lowers his head. We wait for him to speak.

"It's been a helluva year," he says finally.

"Yes, it sure has," Lupita says.

"Rock bottom."

"Rock bottom's a good place to build on," Lupita says.

Dad meets her eye. "Lupita, if you're going to cover me on this doctor visit, I want you to know something. Arlo and I have embarked on a little enterprise. If it pans out, we can pay you back pretty quick."

I give Dad a jab. He's not supposed to talk about my job at White Sands, and he knows it.

"You robbin' banks?" Lupita asks.

"Not quite," Dad says. "It's government work."

"What kind of government work?"

"Contracts," Dad says.

"What kind of contracts?"

"Quiet ones," Dad says.

"Well, then," Lupita whispers. "We better keep it quiet."

She fires up the Dodge, and we lurch down the canyon. At the water tank, she hits the brakes. "Look there," she says, pointing at the herd. "How did that sheep get in with my cows?"

"That's not a sheep," I say.

"It sure the hell isn't," Dad says. "That's a pure junkyard poodle."

We roll closer and watch El Guapo stalk a calf. He tries to mount her, but the calf skitters away.

Lupita says, "He's not much for long courtships, is he?"

"No," Dad says. "Guapo's all about direct action. His gear has never been in reverse."

"There's nothin' wrong with that," Lupita says.

CHAPTER 28

WE'RE SEATED AT THE LONG table in Lupita's dining room—the only room left of the original log and adobe hacienda. The rest of the house is about five generations newer.

Lee's tofu tastes like lard encased in teriyaki-flavored axle grease. I shove it around my plate and hide it under my salad. Dad munches hungrily.

"Only one thing could improve this meal," Dad says. "A good pinot or Chardonnay. Wish I'd brought a bottle."

"I don't drink anymore, " Lupita says.

Dad looks up. "Oh? When did this happen?"

"Nine years ago," Lupita says.

"Nine years!"

Siouxsie snorts. "Your head's been stuck in the sand, Dad."

"A mile deep," I mumble.

"You ought to give it a try," Lupita says.

Dad shudders. "Me, give up the juice of the grape, the harvest of the grain? Think what might happen. My sweat might start tasting like Evian water."

Lupita laughs. "Best thing I ever did."

"Well, good for you, Lupita. I truly mean it."

Dad's eyes wander about the room — to the smoke-blackened pothooks in the fireplace, the Spanish beams in the ceiling, the muzzleloader hanging over the mantel.

"You can hear whispers of old Mexico in here," Dad says. "You've had governors at this table, have you not?"

"Yes, and a hundred sweaty cowhands," Lupita says.

I nod toward the west wall. "What happened to all your stuffed animal heads — the bobcat, antelope, all those guys?"

"I'll let Lee answer that," Lupita says.

"I took them down," Lee says.

"How come?" I say. "They were the best part of the room."

"The symbolism," Lee says.

"That's right," Lupita says. "Lee wouldn't eat a morsel in here until those critters were out of sight."

"Lee's antimeat and antiwar," Siouxsie says. "Nobody else I know is both of those. Just her. She actually *thinks* about all this."

"If you really want to see those stuffed animal heads," Lee says, "they're out in the barn."

Lupita's corn pudding and green salad are good, but Siouxsie's apple pie — from Mom's old recipe — is the high point of the meal. The atoms of sugar and cinnamon levitate to the underside of my skull, then drift down and illuminate my toes. I eat two massive slices. What's left of the pie, about an eighth, gets covered in tinfoil and set aside for me to take home.

Dad volunteers us for dish duty. He stations Siouxsie at the kitchen table to dry, and me at the sink to rinse. He stands beside me scraping and scrubbing.

"It would please my ears greatly, Lupita," he says over his shoulder, "if you would tickle the ivories while we work the suds."

"Happy to," Lupita says.

She goes into the living room and starts to mess around on the piano. Then she plays "On the Bayou." Dad hums along, mumbling about gumbo, crawfish pie, and *"Me oh my oh!"*

"Hey, Dad," Siouxsie says when "On the Bayou" ends. "What're you gonna do when I die?"

Dad stops scrubbing and stares into the soapy water. "Not tonight, Siouxsie," he says.

"I just wanna be sure you get it," Siouxsie says, polishing a plate. "Because not everybody lives to be old."

"We get it," I say.

"Yes, we get it," Dad says.

"Okay, so what're you gonna do with the rest of your life after I'm gone? Be like you are now?"

Dad flicks the water off his hands and faces her. "What's wrong with the way I am now?"

"You're miserable," Siouxsie says, stacking a plate.

Dad looks puzzled. "How can you say that? I'm with my kids. Surrounded by friends. I just had a great meal. I'm a happy man."

Siouxsie grabs another plate and goes to work. "Hate to break it to you, Dad, but you're not."

I aim the spray hose at her and let her see my finger twitch. We all go back to work—especially Dad, who muscles into a frying pan with the scraper.

"So I was just thinking," Siouxsie says, interrupting again. "Maybe that's your way of crying."

Dad's hands freeze in the soapy water. "What are you talking about, Siouxsie?"

"I mean, sticking your head in the sand. Maybe that's how you cry. So maybe it's okay."

He thinks about this, then nods. "Good theory. We'll go with it."

We finish the dishes, dry our hands, and wander into the living room. Now Lupita's playing some blues tune with a country-western tinge. Lee's stretched out on the couch reading a *National Geographic*.

"Lupita," Dad says in a big voice, "may I please request my all-time favorite, 'Wichita Lineman'?"

"Only if you'll sing along."

"Me, sing? I haven't sung in years."

"What key?"

"Key! Are you kidding?"

Lupita finds Dad's key, and he sings the entire song, even the second verse, reaching up to cradle that final phrase, "Still on the *lliiiiiiiiiiiiinnne.*"

"My God!" he says when the last chord fades. "I felt like I was there. High up on that power pole in the middle of the Kansas grasslands, pining for my baby."

Lupita smiles. "You were."

We grab our coats and the leftover pie and go out onto the porch.

"Just inhale this cricket night," Dad says. "This Milky Way bright, this magnificent splatter of stars. Look at the Big Dipper. Doesn't that make you thirsty for good well water? And check out Orion the Hunter — dressed in all his finery — belt, sword, boots 'n' spurs."

Lupita chuckles. "Hec, you shovel a fine grade."

Dad grabs Siouxsie by the shoulders. Pecks her on the forehead. "This is just for now, young lady."

"Everything's just for now, Dad," Siouxsie says.

"Hold up," I say.

I go down to the pickup, pop the tailgate, and roll out my YZ 125. Plant it at the bottom of the porch steps. Toe the kickstand. "It's all yours, Siouxsie."

Everybody stares at me like I just told a bad joke.

"I can't drive that, and you know it," Siouxsie says.

"I want you to have it," I say. "And when you're ready for it, it'll be ready for you."

"Ready for it! I'll never be ready for it."

Lupita wraps an arm around her. "I think it's a beautiful gesture," she says.

I pat the seat. "Just honor the spirit. She was born to grind, so don't park her in mothballs. Or let her clutch go dry. I was thinking, maybe Lee could drive it, just to keep it running strong."

"Wait!" Siouxsie says. "Are you giving it to her, or to me?"

"He's giving it to you," Lee says.

"Sure doesn't sound like it," Siouxsie grumbles.

If you can love a machine, I love this one. A nothing bike, if you don't know her. But if you do, you know this: she has shredded it all — the hills and mesas, the meandering arroyos and lone goat trails. She's flown off a million humps and bumps. She's never hurt me. Only protected me.

On a great bike, you don't break your neck. You save your neck.

I'm definitely giving it to Siouxsie.

"It's kind of an insult," Siouxsie says. "But you don't mean it to be. So I'll take it."

CHAPTER 29

I'M DEAD TO THE WORLD—deep-Delta comatose—when:

L.A. . . . L.A. . . . L.A.
Gonna get my junk in play . . .

I shove El Guapo off me, find my phone—dog-butt incubated—and gasp into the receiver: "*Whaaa!*"

"Arlo, this is Major Anderson."

"*Huh?* What time is it?"

"Zero-hundred hours."

I open my eyes in pitch-darkness.

"Zero hun . . . ?

"It's midnight, Arlo. We launch in six hours. Saddle up that Ducati and get down here."

Click!

In the battle between awake and sleep, sleep is Goliath, a thousand times stronger, but the loser.

I swing my feet over the side of the bed. The floor is ice cold. I shiver into my clothes, stamp into my Gringos, shamble downstairs, and slip out into the frozen night. Scurry to the shed and roll out the Ducati.

On the back porch, I glance at the thermometer: eighteen degrees Fahrenheit.

Factor in wind chill.

Then factor in chill when I hit speed.

In the kitchen, I slip on Dad's down parka and duster. Dig through a drawer and find ski gloves and a wool mask. It's a pretty uncool getup, but it'll keep me warm.

Dad's baked a drawerful of corn dodgers for just such a night. I stuff a couple handfuls in my pocket. Guapo suddenly appears, and I toss him one. He gulps the little corncake. Sits in tail-twitching humility staring at my pocket.

"Greedy bum," I say, and toss him another.

I jot a note: *Gone to White Sands, 12:15 a.m.*

I remember the mares and add: *Don't forget to water and feed—*

But you can't get this wrong. You can't forget. Babies are on the way. If Dad wakes up on the novel-writing side of his brain, those horses won't get fed till noon, or maybe not at all.

So I scratch out this line and instead write: *Already fed and watered the mares.*

I stick the note on the fridge and head to the barn.

Queen Zenobia is awake in her stall, watching over her sleeping sisters. She stares at me, a pretty liver chestnut with flaxen mane and black eyes. Her ears prick forward.

You can tell how old a horse is by looking at its teeth, how it feels by looking at its ears, and how it thinks by looking into its eyes. A horse says a lot with its eyes. Right now, Queen Z is saying,

"Whatever brings you here at midnight, I support you one hundred percent."

In some ways, being trusted by the mares is the most important thing in my life.

I fill their oat bins, fork alfalfa, and top off the water buckets. I do this with Maximum Efficiency and stealth.

Then I rub Z's neck, because she doesn't like to be patted. Breathe her good, warm smell.

You can lean against an old tree, or against a pregnant mare, and feel the same thing: life beyond life.

"Headed down to White Sands," I tell her. "Can't say more — top-secret. Plus, you wouldn't understand."

Fact is, she does understand.

« « « » » »

I SLIP ON MY HELMET and push the Ducati up the drive — far enough so there's a chance I won't wake Dad when I fire her up.

Guapo's tagged along. "I'm placing you in command of the fort, Guapie." He stares at my pocket. "Okay, okay, you bum!" I flip him one last corn dodger.

I throw my leg over the saddle — choke up, clutch in — and heave into the air. On the third try, the Monster sparks to life.

Full of growl.

Capable of 160 miles per hour.

But still half asleep.

As I ease onto the access road, Guapo trots along beside me. When I add a click, he fades back. Compared to my dirt bikes, this is like floating. A few minutes later, I bend through a pond of Shell-station glare onto I-25.

Add a few more clicks.

Damn, it's cold!

Just south of the city, the interstate opens up flat, straight, and unguarded.

Stars rain down the sky.

I wake up the fire-breathing Monster.

CHAPTER 30

MAJOR ANDERSON ASSIGNS ME a small reconnaissance drone called a ScanHawk. Length: five feet, three inches. Wingspan: twelve feet, seven inches. Maximum endurance: five and a half hours. Maximum speed: one hundred five knots. Cruising speed: sixty-eight knots.

He's equipped me with two cameras: a belly-mount forward-looking infrared stop-action; and a gimbal-mount video, with extreme telephoto. I can zoom in on tonsils, even in the dark.

Day is breaking in New Mexico. But on the far side of the world — Pakistan's Swat Valley — it's getting dark. No moon tonight.

I log in and launch. Soon I'm skitting across the face of the valley, so close I can feel my updraft.

"Pull out, Arlo!" Major Anderson barks through the mike. "Don't get fancy on us."

I pull out, even though I wasn't being all that fancy.

Mullins plants a cup of coffee at my side. "Don't forget to T-FOG," he says.

I spend the morning — the night — capturing images of

Compounds 52 and 117. After about five hours in the air, I return to point of origin—a dirt landing strip just off the Arghandab River, no more than one hundred yards from the flatbed catapult where I launched.

Major Anderson swings through the glass door. "Good sortie today, Arlo. We're filling in that map." He hands me an envelope. "Why don't you grab a cot next door and catch a few winks."

"Nah, I'll be fine," I say.

I'm dog-assed from lack of sleep and flying drone, but I know the Monster will keep me on my toes.

Five minutes later I'm decked out in my road clothes straddling the machine.

Twenty minutes later, I'm on a flat, empty stretch, making the needle bounce off the bar. In the heart of speed lies stillness. In the heart of a Monster's roar, silence.

It's a good place to relax.

A good place to think.

« « « » » »

WHEN I GET HOME THERE'S a message waiting for me on my laptop:

Arlo, congratulations on your successful flight today. Please read the following memo carefully, as it pertains to you and your mission. Kincaid.

This time, the memo is completely unredacted. Not a single blacked-out sentence. I wonder why. Is he getting lazy? Does he trust me more? But I don't think about it too long.

Memo for Record

To: Mideast High Command and Coalition UAV strategic units
From: Col. (Ret.) Carl Kincaid, ARI
RE: Operation Brave Panther
Type of aircraft: ScanHawk
Purpose: Persistent intelligence and surveillance
Pilot: Rope Thrower
Duration: Five hours, seven minutes

Summary: Last month, we identified for observation Compounds 52 and 117 in the Swat Valley of northwest Pakistan. From this mountainous position, insurgent forces have repeatedly launched attacks against our military personnel, resulting in heavy losses. More than one dozen previous attempts to photograph and map Compounds 52 and 117 have failed owing to weather or pilot error. Two of our UAVs were shot down.

On today's mission, our new pilot (hereafter Rope Thrower) was able to capture excellent photo and video intelligence at both sites. Results confirm diverse arsenals, from variants on the old Kalashnikov assault rifle to sophisticated shoulder-launch missiles and armor-piercing explosives.

Rope Thrower's images do NOT, however, confirm the presence of Caracal inside either compound.

It is my belief that Caracal moves stealthily between Compounds 52 and 117, meticulously concealing himself against external observation.

We will continue to analyze real-time imagery of the compounds. And we will continue to use Rope Thrower's images to build the "human map."

Kincaid

CHAPTER 31

NEXT DAY IS HOMECOMING FRIDAY.

When I roll up after school, Dad's packing the pickup. He's got on his Snack Shack ball cap. He studies his clipboard.

"Doritos, bunny grahams . . . Arlo, a box arrived for you . . . Skittles, Gummi Bears . . . It's on the porch . . . Styrofoam cups, napkins . . . From Estes, Colorado. . . tamales, hot dogs . . . Who do you know in Estes?"

"Nobody," I say.

I tie up my nag and find the box on the porch. It's lighter than it looks. I carry it upstairs to my room, grab some scissors, and cut the tape.

Inside is this note:

Dear Arlo,
Congratulations on your winning bid. The Flying Squirrel is now yours. Someday, I hope to look up from a golf tee and see you soaring overhead. But I must warn you, this is extreme. If you haven't already, I STRONGLY advise that you get training from a qualified wingsuit instructor.

Take care — and I mean TAKE CARE!
Yours truly,
Wade Jackson
Estes, CO

The Flying Squirrel is made of a tan, silky material with lots of snaps, straps, and zippers. Plus rigid wingtip grips. A pocket on the lower leg contains a hook knife — a bonus gift from Wade.

I strip to my boxers and zip in. The suit clings to me like skin.

I close my eyes and step to the mirror.

Spread my arms and legs.

Open my eyes.

Oh my God!

It's obvious why Wade calls this the Flying Squirrel.

I repack the wingsuit and carry it out to the truck. A dark cloud hangs over Tinaja Mesa.

Cam shows up on his Kawasaki KLX, and we roll out my 250.

Cam — all six-pack and ponytail — has always tinkered with motors. He was raised on the scrapyard outskirts of Clay Allison, where the Cimarron River trickles talc-y and snaky into the wider, faster Rio Loco. He can run a bike off the whiff of an oily rag.

He's been priming my 250 all week. Changed the sparks, oil, and filter. Cleaned the exhaust. Installed an almost-new drive chain.

I had two requests:

1. Add handlebar extensions.

2. Replace my old shocks with the best frickin' shocks in the world.

He has achieved both. The handlebar extensions will let me lie low and spread my arms like wings. The new shocks mean I won't crush my landing.

Cam's not about "before-market" or "after-market" prices, he's about "free." Cruise the junkyard, not the auto-parts store.

And — like me — he's about customizing.

Customizing gives you that extra foot of altitude. That extra click of speed.

Customizing is also how you blow a cylinder. Crack a tire. Or break your neck.

There's always that tradeoff. Real gambling doesn't happen when you go to Vegas. It happens when you customize.

He peels off his jacket, spreads it on the ground, leather side up, and dumps the contents of his tool bag on top. We hunker down and get to work tweaking and testing the handlebars to my specifications.

Dad walks over. "Hey, Camerado, whatcha reading these days?"

"Oh, hey, Mr. Santiago," Cam says. "Kawasaki's just come out with a new parts catalog."

"You ever read that Steinbeck I gave you?"

"Nah, not yet."

"Well, add this to your list." Dad pitches an old paperback. Cam catches it. Stares blankly at the cover. Mumbles, "*Lady . . . Windermere's . . . Fan.*"

"Nobody beats Oscar Wilde for sheer satire and social commentary," Dad says. "Everybody should read at least one of his plays. Should be the law of the land. Fact, I think I'll write a couple of legislators in Santa Fe tomorrow."

He tosses Cam a bag of Skittles. "Tell me, Camerado, what do you think about Arlo's big jump tonight?"

Cam grins. "Gonna be epic."

"Think so?"

"Yeah, if he hits it right."

"What if he doesn't?"

"He will," Cam says. "Arlo always hits it right."

"Nobody always hits it right," Dad says.

They both look at me, and I can feel them pondering the possibility of a disaster. I turn and focus my wrench on the handlebars.

"Think about it, Cam," Dad goes on. "Arlo's riding against a crowd and bright lights. He's not used to any of that, are you, Arlo?"

"Nope," I say, loosening a screw.

"And there's no denying," Dad says, "it's one helluva leap."

"Sure is," Cam says. "I couldn't do it."

"That's because you have too much sense to try," Dad says.

"Too much fear, you mean," Cam says.

"And suppose it rains," Dad says.

"Hey, it ain't gonna rain," Cam says. "It already rained this month."

Dad points toward Tinaja Mesa. We all gaze at the black stovepipe cloud hovering there, leaching into the yellow horizon.

"Looks like a good night to fly a kite," Dad says. "If your name is Ben Franklin."

"*Jeeeez!*" Cam mumbles. "Of all nights."

I truly want Dad to go away—because he's not helping me, he's depressing me. Instead, he steps up and pats the seat of my 250.

"I used to ride with my buddies too," he says. "My first bike was a Desert Phantom. She was all the vacation I ever needed. Good thing, because we were scratch-ass poor. But I never did what you boys do—the crotch-rocket stuff. Never risked like that. Never saw the point."

He pulls off his Snack Shack cap and looks inside it, as if it holds an answer. "What befuddles me, Camerado, is that I don't stop Arlo from doing this. I could and should, but I don't. What does that tell you about me? Am I a bad father?"

"You're here, aren't you?" Cam says.

"Oh, I'm here, all right," Dad says. "But my compass is broken. I just go round and round the mulberry bush."

"Maybe your compass ain't broke, Mr. Santiago," Cam says. "Maybe the reason you don't stop Arlo is because you know he has to do it. It's an honor thing. Like a knight riding out to reclaim his good name."

"Thank you!" I say. "'Bout time somebody mentioned honor."

Dad shakes his head. "The sad fact is, many a knight who rode out never returned."

He checks his watch.

"Ten minutes, Arlo."

« « « » » »

WE WIPE DOWN THE BIKE and pack up the tools. Cam rips open the Skittles, pours half in my hand, and drains the rest.

Then he slips on his jacket, stuffs *Lady Windermere's Fan* in a pocket, and mounts his Kawasaki. He kicks it, grinds some pepper, lowers it to a sputter.

"Dude, your dad was all over your grill tonight."

"Yeah, pretty much," I say.

"All these books he gives me . . . I've never read a single one."

"Nobody ever does," I say.

"You do."

"Sometimes."

I hand him the tool bag, which he zips, like it's a puppy, inside his jacket.

"Hey, man, just to be honest, this jump is the biggest thing in your life. You scared?"

Fear has never been a problem for me when it comes to jumping my bike. But this is no ordinary jump.

"Guess so," I say. "All those people watching. It's just not natural."

"Forget them," Cam says. "Just do like you do on Little Piñon when you hit Davy. Nobody in the world, just you. The whole run-up, just you. Remember, nobody can fly like you. Shut us out. Slam the door. Shred the sky. Hey, you're not thinking about a girl? You better not be. 'Cuz if you're thinkin' about her—"

"I'm not thinkin' about anybody," I say.

Cam peers into my eyes. "I sort of believe you," he says. "And I sort of don't." He grinds the throttle. "See you at Rio Loco."

We bump fist, and he is gone.

CHAPTER 32

WHEN DAD AND I DRIVE up to the Snack Shack, the marching band is out on the field rehearsing "Mighty Trucks of Midnight."

"Make it *shimmer!*" bandleader Bernie Kohler shouts through his bullhorn. "Rub some Brasso into that brass."

Dad notices a banner stretched across the front of the announcer's box:

WINGO LUMBER,
OFFICIAL SPONSOR OF JETT SPENCE

"Who the hell is Jett Spence?" Dad asks.

Then he sees the second banner — this one vertical — hanging above the entrance to the pedestrian tunnel. It's a picture of me flying off a mound on my Yam 125, catching serious air. Uncle Sal took it the summer before last, with his telephoto lens. Dad published it in the *Gunslinger.* My shirt's off, hair's flyin', and I'm lookin' ripped, if I say so myself. I got a lot of good feedback on that picture. Uncle Sal hung a copy in the game corner at Tunza-Funza.

Dad reads aloud the words on the banner:

HURTADO TOYOTA
PROUD SPONSOR OF MOTORCYCLE
DAREDEVIL JETT SPENCE.

"Tell me — Jett," Dad says. "What's the average lifespan of a motorcycle daredevil?"

"Don't ask me."

"Well then, answer me this: What happens when the daredevil breaks his neck — and his father has no medical insurance? Who pays the bills for that daredevil, now a quadriplegic?"

"How should I know?"

"Arlo, you're putting the whole family at risk. Just so you can grandstand and prance about on your motorcycle."

"It's just another jump," I say. "I do it all the time."

"Not like this, you don't," Dad says. He points to the bluff. "What do you call that cancer growth up there, where you plan to do the deed?"

"The Lips," I say.

Dad scoffs. "Arlo, I know this much about motorcycles: Mother Earth can come at you hard and fast. So tell me the gut truth: why are you doing this? I hope it's not because of this Scooper nonsense."

"That's part of it," I say.

Dad rolls his eyes. "The last thing I need is more ashes to scatter. So the rest better be good."

The marching band swings by again, this time rubbing more

Brasso into "Mighty Trucks of Midnight." It pivots and angles away.

I shrug. "You know that monument you want to build to Mom up on Burro Mesa?"

"Yes, what about it?"

"Maybe this is *my* monument."

Dad grits his teeth, thrusts a finger in my face. "Just don't make a mess of it, Arlo. Do *not* make a mess of it."

"Hey, don't worry," I say.

« « « » » »

DAD SETS UP THE GRILLS. I roll down my Yam 250. Tuck the box containing the Flying Squirrel in the back of the Snack Shack. Drape Dad's duster over it.

Dad measures the Folgers and Swiss Miss. I fill the grills with hot dogs — twenty-four per grill. Hit the buttons, and the rollers start to roll.

"Best move the truck now," Dad says, tossing me the keys.

I drive the pickup over to the parking lot, park, and walk back through the pedestrian tunnel. Two weeks ago, I chased a dog through this tunnel, on my way to fame and glory. Now it's just me and my boots. Guaranteed applause: *clap . . . clap . . . clap . . . clap.*

Every step gets darker.

I'm about to do what I never do — perform in front of a crowd. Just the thought makes my guts yo-yo.

I think about what Dad said about grandstanding and prancing.

All the ego stuff.

Maybe he's right. Maybe that's the real reason I'm doing this.

Don't go there!

What if I mess up and make a bigger fool of myself?

Focus!

What if it rains?

Focus!

What if I break my neck?

FOCUS!

Whenever I hit the bumps on Little Piñon, nobody's watching but Cam and Lobo — and maybe Uncle Sal down below, sitting in a camp chair with his Cupido and Chianti.

But tonight, half of Orphan County will be watching.

All the Neanderthals and nobodies.

But also people I've known all my life who treat me like a human.

Do I care what they think?

Damn right, I care.

Don't think about them.

Lee Fields?

Definitely do NOT think about her.

FOCUS!

Focus is everything.

About halfway into the tunnel, I notice a moth latched to a glass light bulb cover. I stop and peer at the insect. A thousand people could walk by and never see this moth. It looks like every splotch on the wall.

But I see it.

I envy it.

The thing about jumping a bike — or, for that matter, flying an MQ-1 Predator drone — is, it's all about performing, nothing else.

If you try to grandstand, you're dead.

The moment you start thinking *me*, stop everything. Crank a one-eighty and blast out of there. Go to that place inside you where you can't tell the difference between jumping a Yam 250 and flying a Predator drone.

Because they are the same machine.

Don't let *me* tempt you.

Squash the ego.

Go with your gut.

Like Cam said — shut 'em out, slam the door, shred the sky.

Pretty much, that's all there is to it.

I've known it all along.

But I almost forgot.

Up close, the moth is a work of art, its wings a canvas of dusky patterns and muted colors. I reach out and nudge it. The moth seems dead. Then it flutters away.

Joy tingles in my fingers.

I can't wait to get on my bike.

« « « » » »

FOR THE NEXT HOUR, PEOPLE pack into the bleachers. The line outside the Snack Shack snakes all the way to the instant replay booth. I shift into ME — Maximum Efficiency. Do my hot -dog dance:

Tong it,
bun it,

drop it in a trough.
Ring it.
Ching it!
"Mustard on your left."

Lots of people call me Scooper — grandparents, parents, and even little kids.

That ain't gonna last.

« « « » » »

AT KICKOFF, EVERYBODY'S PRIMED ON beer, sodium nitrates, glucose, cleavage, and patriotism. The average IQ drops fifty points.

Tonight it's Clay Allison (the Outlaws, 9-0-1) vs. Raton (the Tigers, 4-5-1). The rivalry between Clay and Raton ceased to exist about the time Bill Clinton was president. But it feels like the Super Bowl.

The cheerleaders shake their star-spangled asses. The stadium swells with testosterone. The crowd roars at two-yard gains.

A couple of minutes into the first quarter, the Outlaws trigger a long bomb and snap to a 7 to 0 lead. A few plays later, we intercept and lead 14 to 0. The stadium sighs, and business picks up again at the Snack Shack.

Early in the second quarter, Lobo drops by. He leans over the counter and snatches the tongs out of my hand.

"Damn, dude! What're you still doin' here?"

He ducks under the counter and shoos me away. "Go suit up! Get on that bike! Stay vertical. Go ugly. Full nutsack balls to the wall. C'mon, go!"

Dad won't even look at me.

I grab the box and Dad's duster and go out behind the Snack Shack. Cam's there, sitting on my Yam 250, hair unbraided and loose, looking like Chief Sitting Bull. He lets go of the grips and his arms float up, palms to the sky.

"Feel that?" he says.

I hold out my hand and catch some drizzle.

"Your ol' man was right," Cam says.

"Yeah maybe," I say. "But hey, we gotta change something up."

"Change?" Cam says. "Isn't it too late for that?"

"Nah, here's what—"

Before I can tell him, Uncle Sal walks over, looking all hefty in his fur-collared overcoat and tiny Frank Sinatra hat.

"Jett! Where's your Elvis jumpsuit?"

I pat the box.

"Good," he says. "Now, listen. See those two trucks out there?" He points to a shadowy area about a hundred yards from the end zone. "That little pickup is our film crew—we'll be chronicling this for posterity and promotional purposes. The bigger truck, that's Henry Gomez. He's our power grid tonight. He's positioned spotlights there . . . and there." Uncle Sal points to the base of the bluff and to a notch near the top. "Our tracking spotlight is right there."

He points to a saucer-shaped light mounted on top of the cable truck. "Arlo, listen carefully. Those two stationary lights intersect at the Lower Lip. The tracking spot will find you on the field and follow you up the hill. When you lift off, the tracker will stick with you and cradle you as you go high. Got it?"

"Yeah," I say. "But we need to change something."

Uncle Sal gives me look. "*Change* is not a word I welcome right now," he says. "What's the problem?"

"Henry Gomez," I say. "Maybe he knows how to shine a light, but he doesn't know me."

"Sure he does," Uncle Sal says. "He's known you all your life."

"But he doesn't *know* me. So I think Cam should take over. He should run the tracking spot."

"Me!" Cam looks shocked. "I'm no light man."

"Maybe not," I say. "But you know how I ride."

"You ride like a freak from hell," Cam says.

"Exactly," I say.

"Good point," Uncle Sal says. "Cam, as of now, you're our tracker. When I say the words you fire that light at Arlo. Hold on to him. Never lose him."

"What're the words?" Cam asks.

"*Land of bright* mañana," Uncle Sal says. "When you hear me say that phrase, blast Arlo with everything you've got. Wherever he goes, track him. Down the field, across the turf, up the slope. When he sticks the jump, stick with him. Shower him with light. Do not lose him, even for one second. Repeat after me: I will not lose him."

"I . . . will . . . not . . . lose . . . him," Cam says, zombielike.

Uncle Sal turns to me. "Arlo, when you're up there in the air, spread your arms like this, like Jesus—because . . . because . . . Why, hello, Lee."

Lee walks up. Just the sight of her makes me feel better.

Uncle Sal says, "I was telling Jett here to spread his arms like Jesus."

"Like when he was crucified?" Lee asks.

"No, like the Sermon on the Mount," Uncle Sal says. "'And seeing the multitudes, he went up on a mountain.' People love an iconic pose. It's how the mind remembers."

"It's raining," Lee says.

We look up into the field lights. A silver vapor clouds over them.

"Lee, you're still new here, so let me educate you," Uncle Sal says. "This is not rain. It's Orphan County mist. You know how you can tell? The ground is so dry it scares the drops away."

"I'm pretty sure I know what rain is," Lee says.

Uncle Sal leans close to her. "Did you hear the one about the girl in the boys' locker room?"

Lee shakes her head.

"Everybody wanted her to go," Uncle Sal says. "Everybody wanted her to stay."

Lobo busts out laughing. He's the only one.

"Well, I want her to stay," I say. "And she's right, it *is* raining. In fact, it's getting tarrier every second we stand here. So either let's do this or go home."

"Let's do it!" Uncle Sal says, with a handclap. "Lee, you help Jett get his Elvis on. Cam, you join Henry Gomez. Remember, when I say '*Land of bright* mañana,' fire up that light—and hold on to Arlo for dear life. Me, I'm going to cut my speech in half." He reaches into his coat, pulls out two pages of text, and tears one up. "C'mon, kids, let's get this thing off the ground."

Uncle Sal grabs my shoulders. Looks like he's going to kiss me. And then he does. Godfather-style, on both cheeks.

"Arlo-Arlo-Arlo. You are a diamond—uncut—but a diamond. I've always seen it. I've always known it. It's been an honor to watch you grow up. But something makes me ache."

"What would that be?" I say.

His eyes brim. "The fact that you are oblivious."

"Oblivious?"

Uncle Sal nods. "Beautifully oblivious. You simply don't know how good you are. Destiny is a huntress, and she's hunted you down."

He pats my cheek.

"*Defecare due volte,* my friend. Wipe Scooper off the map. *Be* Jett Spence."

CHAPTER 33

NOW IT'S JUST LEE AND me behind the Snack Shack. Nobody can see us. Well, almost nobody. A slice of the bleachers — from about the Clay twenty to the end zone — *can* see us, if they look.

Mostly, though, they're watching the marching band. Sixty plume-topped military shirts rubbing Brasso into "Mighty Trucks of Midnight."

Mighty trucks of midnight
Movin' on.

Nobody actually sings these words, but we can all hear them in our head. At least, I can. Because, hey, I'm movin' on too.

"I'm gonna need some privacy," I say, tossing Lee the duster.

She shakes it open and holds it like a curtain. I yank off my Gringos. Leave on my socks. Peel off my flannel. Leave on my T-shirts, because it's so frickin' breath-cloudy cold.

And drizzly wet.

"Okay, I'm gonna drop my pants. So hold on to that coat. I don't want any of those perverts over in the bleachers watching."

"Nobody's watching, Arlo."

"You can."

"No thanks."

I unbuckle and shuck my pants. Reach into the box for the Flying Squirrel. Stretch one foot, then the other, through the ankle grips into the padded boots.

"Last chance to check out the scrawniest ass in the county," I say. "Don't believe me, have a look."

Lee says, "I don't want to check out your scrawny ass, Arlo."

"Your loss," I say, zipping into the Flying Squirrel.

The loudspeakers crackle.

"Ah, ladies and gentlemen. It's my honor to hand over the microphone to one of the foremost citizens of our county, your uncle and mine. Let's hear it for Salvatore Focazio — Uncle Sal."

Everybody knows Uncle Sal, so Rio Loco Stadium pretty much crumbles.

"Hey, look," I say as the applause goes on.

Lee lowers the coat, and I snap open my wings.

The sight of me startles her. Then she smiles.

"You're crazy, Arlo Santiago."

"Yeah, well —"

"Good evening," Uncle Sal reverbs through the loudspeakers. *"My favorite word in English is* homecoming. *Let me define* homecoming. *It means . . . 'coming home.'"*

I slide on my helmet, swing a leg over the bike.

Lee steps up. Kisses me. On the lips. Turns and walks away.

I watch her red-gold hair sway back and forth.

Damn! That was exactly what I didn't need.

I slam down on the starter. My 250 kicks right in.

"Some of us here tonight root for Raton. Some root for Clay Allison. But all of us root for New Mexico. Our shared home. Our Land of Enchantment."

I jerk my wrist and burst down the sideline, brake, and catch Lee by the arm. Pull her to me. Kiss her. Peach soft. Taste the shiny insides of her mouth. Plum sweet.

"Are we not the 'state of esperanza*'?"*

A crazy joy floods through me.

"Are we not the 'land of bright mañana*'?"*

The spotlights blink on. Cam's tracker rushes down the field, flares across us. Lee brushes a hand on my cheek. Throws back her head and laughs. Steps away just as the tracking spot slams into me.

Now I'm blindingly bright.

"Ladies and gentlemen, please welcome Orphan County's homegrown daredevil — Jett Spence."

I click the throttle and roll onto the field. Into a sea of choppy sounds — clapping, cackling, hooting, "Scoopers," and even unflattering references to El Guapo. It's nothing like the huge roar that greeted Uncle Sal.

I anchor at the fifty-yard line — the heart/soul/Ground Zero of Orphan County. Stare at the Lips. Zoom in on the Lower Lip.

I think about the moth. That humble splotch on the wall.

Just be like that.

I grind the throttle.

GRIND!

So loud my mind goes silent.

I jerk my wrist and loft into a wheelie.

The ten-yard lines strobe beneath me. I flash across the end zone and bump onto hardpack. Open the throttle. Float toward the bluff.

Go fast enough and anything can fly. But a Yam 250 can truly soar.

I hit the base and swoop like a yo-yo up a string. Only tonight, the string is greasy and wet. On the steepest part of the hill, my tires spin. I reach out and brace with my feet. That one little move clips my wings. I lose speed — and the power to fly.

When I hit the Lower Lip, instead of shooting into the air, I pop maybe five feet.

Land with barely a bounce.

Brake to a stop in the timid dark.

Cam's spotlight leaps after me but falls short.

I yank off my helmet. Hear the raw voice of Rio Loco — the cackling Neanderthals.

When you fill a stadium with humans, that's what you get. Reverse evolution.

The rain on my neck feels like spit.

How can I go back down to that?

I won't. I'll stay up here forever.

White-dark sky. Cold-soft rain.

Closer to heaven. Closer to Mom.

Or maybe sneak down the back side and go — just *go!*

Get the hell out of Orphan County, New Mexico.

Head out to L.A. . . . L.A. . . . L.A. . . . and get my junk in play.

Anyplace but here.

Riding away would be so easy.

Cam's spotlight skips across the chaparral, searching for me. It illuminates broken bottles, a sagging fence, a rusted barrel.

Cam knows how I think. Probably more than anybody else in the world.

He knows I'm hiding.

He swings the light around. Levels it at the Lips. They glisten and pout.

He's waiting for me.

Thinking the same thought.

I slide on my helmet. Click the throttle. Spin and face the Lips.

They are the edge of the world—and the edge looks like a darkened movie screen filled with falling diamonds.

I clasp my fingers around the extension grips. Flatten my body against the bike.

All the alarms are blaring inside me—all the evolved, life-saving "no's" and "don'ts."

I jam them off.

Go silent.

Grind into the zone.

One last breath.

Yea, though I fly through the valley of the shadow . . .

I jerk my wrist and blast into diamond darkness.

CHAPTER 34

LOBO GETS TO ME FIRST. Eyes bugged out and chest heaving, he drops to his knees and crosses himself.

"Dude, don't die on me! Please, do not die on me!"

Referee Ray Sandoval rushes up. "Don't even think about moving, Arlo!"

Then Dad's here. Eyes so fragile I think they'll break.

"Did you see him?" Lobo says to someone. "Lit up like a struck match. Those wings — he just flew!"

"Shut up, Lobo!" Dad says.

The paramedics slide a spine board under me. Lobo trundles alongside as they carry me off. "Listen to that!" he rasps.

I can barely hold on.

"They love you, man. C'mon, give 'em something to let 'em know you're alive."

I try to lift my arm.

"Hey, you can do better than that!" Lobo says into my ear.

I manage to lift my arm in the air. Even clamp my fist.

You'd think I'd fired a cannon.

Man, do I hear it.

I'm pretty sure they hear it in Mexico, too. Maybe even the Incas down in Peru.

The stadium roars.

« « « » » »

"DON'T TRY TO COUNT the stitches, Arlo."

It's Dad. Somewhere off to the side. I can't move my head to see him.

I watch anonymous fingers thread a needle through the purple-jagged skin of my left arm. The gash begins to close in a long, even seam.

Dad's right. Don't count the stitches. It's depressing.

I fade out.

Next, I'm inside a machine. Crammed like a corpse. The machine goes *chuffa-chuffa-chuffa*. I freak. They slide me out. A tech in mirrored glasses puts a towel over my eyes and tells me to imagine paradise. They send me back into the coffin. I imagine Burro Mesa.

I fade again and wake in a darkened room. Dad is snoring in the corner. It feels like everyone in the world is asleep. I watch rain slither down the windowpane.

Now I sink deep. People come and go. Touch me. Say my name. But I'm far away on Burro Mesa. Anchor of earth, spiral of sky.

Mom stands on the north rim, wind whipping her hair. She looks out toward the mountains. I stand beside her, looking down at that sheer drop.

It would be so easy to step off.

Instead, I step back. Onto safe ground.

Then a baseball bat smashes the piñata that is my head. I gasp and scream. Dad calls a nurse. They drip painkillers into me. The piñata slowly pieces together.

A doctor comes in. She bends all my extremities, down to the pinkies. "Can you feel this? Do you have any sensation here?"

I say "Yes" over and over, and Dad whispers "Thank God!" each time. And finally to her, "Thank you, Doctor."

She tells him she's not a doctor but a medical student. Born in the Philippines. Dad reads aloud her name tag: "Student Dr. Malea Santos."

"Do you mind if I lift your shirt and palpate your chest?" she asks me.

"Hell, no, he doesn't mind!" Dad says.

The closer Student Dr. Santos's fingers get to my collarbone, the more I want to puke. And then I do. Dad lunges for a towel and catches the dregs.

Later, my primary-care physician, Dr. Henry Akeem, comes in.

"May I shake the hand of a celebrity?"

We shake. And even though his clasp is light, I wince.

"You were all over the Action Seven News, Jett," he says. "I saw it twice, once in slow motion. Looked to me like you were going to fly over the moon."

"Arlo, not Jett," I mumble.

Dr. Akeem and Miss Santos huddle over their laptops murmuring medical-speak — "MRI," "hematoma," stuff like that.

"Arlo," Dr. Akeem says, looking up. "While you were missing in action, we did a number of tests. Are you ready to hear the results?"

"Guess so," I say.

He tells me that I have:

> A concussion.
> A punctured lung.
> A broken clavicle. ("The clavicle is your collarbone," he says.)
> Two cracked ribs.
> An ugly-as-hell gash on my left arm.
> And a hundred hell-a deep bruises.

"No single one of these is life-threatening," Dr. Akeem says. "But taken as a whole, it's serious. Still, you could've been paralyzed. Or worse yet, killed. All in all, I'd say you were very lucky."

Dad lets out a long whistle.

"That scar's going to last," Dr. Akeem says. "Think of it as a reminder."

"Of what?" I ask.

"Of what happens when you make stupid decisions," Dad says.

Student Dr. Santos adjusts her glasses. "There's a sticking point, Arlo. We don't understand why you did this — why you chose to jump your motorcycle off such a steep height. Can you tell us why?"

"Nah," I say.

"Give it a try," Dr. Akeem says.

I try to focus my memory. I go back to the bluff, the rain, the Lips.

"All those hoots," I say, my voice slurry, "how do you go back down to that? The spotlight came around and caught the rain. It was beautiful. Like it was calling to me. So I thought, *Here's my chance.* Maybe you get only a few chances like that in your life. Do you go or stay? The time you have to decide is a split second. Green light or red."

"And it was green?" Miss Santos asks.

"Yeah, green," I say.

Dad frowns.

"Arlo," Dr. Akeem says, "you're alive and in one piece for three reasons. First, you were healthy and fit to begin with. Second, you wore a helmet. Third, you're lucky."

"And fourth," I say, "my shocks. Don't forget them. They deserve some of the credit."

"I'm glad you brought that up," Dr. Akeem says. "I'd like you to shockproof your home environment. The whole Arlosphere."

"How do I do that?"

"By taking it extremely easy for the next few weeks," he says. "Concussions and bones need time to heal. Tissue needs time to grow. Slow way down, Arlo. Pretend you're walking on the moon. Can you do that?"

"Moonwalk? Yeah, sure. But can you do something for me?"

"I'll try. What is it?"

"Hospitals are expensive," I say. "So I was wondering, since I'm not too bad off, can you let me out of here? Because every day costs like five thousand bucks, and we're already deep in the hole."

Dad winces. "Damn it, Arlo!"

He and Dr. Akeem go out into the corridor and powwow. While they're gone, Miss Santos fits me with a sling to protect my collarbone.

"You've suffered a lot of trauma, Arlo," she says. "If it were me, I'd keep you here for a week, just for observation."

Dr. Akeem tells me that I might be able to go home a day early — but only if I show steady progress and promise to get lots of rest, moonwalk, and take my meds religiously.

"I'll see to it that he joins a monastery," Dad says.

"In the meantime," Dr. Akeem says, "I want you to meet with Dr. Cynthia Andrews. She's our mental health specialist. I've asked her to drop by. And one more thing: stay off that motorcycle."

"For how long?" I ask.

"Four weeks," Dr. Akeem says.

Dad frowns. "Forty years is more like it," he says.

« « « » » »

"HOW SHOULD WE PASS the time, Arlo?"

Dad's seated in the armchair beside my bed, his face slack with tiredness.

"You tell me," I say.

"Well, I can read to you. Or we can watch TV. Or we can play 'Who Am I?' But let me propose something more practical. We Americans get two hours less sleep each night than did our forebears a century ago. Therefore, it behooves us — as patriotic citizens — to help pay down the National Sleep Debt."

We sleep all afternoon — at least, as much as you can in a hospital with all the interruptions.

Later, Dad calls Major Anderson and tells him about my little "event" at Rio Loco. Major Anderson says he'll notify Colonel Kincaid.

After dinner, we watch *The Shawshank Redemption,* which is a good movie to watch in a hospital bed, because when the escapee Andy Dufresne gets it all — money, freedom, a reunion with his friend, and a great beach to live on — you truly feel better, even though you hurt in a hundred places.

I drift off just as Dad starts on a grainy Humphrey Bogart movie.

During the next two days, I spend most of my time paying down the National Sleep Debt. Visitors come and go without me even knowing or wanting to know. Dad is with me, day and night.

On the morning of my third day in the hospital, Student Dr. Malea Santos slips some treaded socks on my feet, and Dad and I go moonwalking up and down the corridor. In reality, I go slower than Neil Armstrong padding across the Sea of Tranquility. I hurt everywhere, but it's sharpest in my chest. My lungs crackle. It takes a long time to walk to the end of the corridor.

On the way back, we pass Miss Santos standing at a workstation. Dad checks out her legs. Gives me a sly look.

"*Whew!* That Malea!"

"Hey, man, show some respect," I say. "She's in medical school."

"Point taken, Arlo. I shouldn't be dragging my knuckles at a time like this."

"Ask her out," I say. "'Bout time you did something."

Dad shakes his head. "Too soon, Arlo. I'm still on the charred side of the burn line. Besides, I'm way too old for her. She's closer to your age."

"C'mon, man, she's like twenty-five. Plus . . ."

"Plus what?"

"Plus nothin'."

« « « » » »

THAT AFTERNOON, DR. CYNTHIA ANDREWS stops by my room. She's a nicely dressed woman with dyed-brown hair pulled into a tight bun in the back, and a serious but not unkind face. Dad offers her his chair and slips into the corridor. She sits down and opens her notebook.

"Arlo, you sustained a concussion, so I'd like to begin with a memory exercise. Just to see where we stand."

She asks me some basic questions, starting with "What is your name?" followed by "Who is the president?" followed by "Can you count backward from twenty?" On and on, until she asks:

"In what year did World War I begin?"

"Depends," I say. "If you mean in Europe, 1914. If you mean, when did the United States join in, 1917."

She jots something in her notebook.

"Arlo, let's talk about that motorcycle stunt. What was that all about?"

"Just seemed like the thing to do," I say.

She makes a note.

"Were you trying to take your life?"

"What!"

"Is that what you had in mind?"

"No, not at all."

More notes. The fact is, her question has blindsided me.

"Was this the first time you've engaged in such extreme behavior?"

"It's not extreme behavior to me," I say.

"What would you call it?"

"Extreme beauty."

She jots more notes. I know she's trying to help me, but she's also closing doors.

"Arlo, sometimes there's a connection between excitement-seeking and wishing to harm oneself. I'm not saying that's true here. But let me ask, do you have any unresolved feelings about your mother or the violent circumstances surrounding her death?"

"Look, no offense," I say. "But this is starting to feel like trespassing."

"Arlo, I don't want to trespass on your feelings. But the facts are public information. Your father's own newspaper reported them."

"Hey, I know the facts," I say. "But that doesn't mean I want to talk about them."

"Talking about them can be good for you, Arlo. Getting them out in the open is a big part of the healing process."

"Nah, the healing process is way different," I say.

"How would you describe it?"

"Blasting my bike into the light. That was healing."

"Did it work?" Dr. Andrews asks.

"You mean, am I healed? Not yet."

"Meaning what?"

"Meaning . . . I dunno."

It goes downhill after this. As far as I'm concerned, she's closed all the doors. Still, I get where she's coming from. What kind of normal person would ride his bike off an edge like that?

But no matter how many notes she makes, I doubt she'll ever get the point. Namely, that just because something doesn't make sense — or seems extreme — doesn't make it wrong.

She closes her notebook and flashes a tired smile. "There's lots to talk about, Arlo. This is merely the tip of the iceberg."

"I'm pretty sure it's the whole iceberg," I say.

After she goes, Dad comes back in and tosses me a little bag of SunChips.

"What's the verdict?" he asks.

My hands are too shaky to open the bag. Dad opens it for me.

"Hey, do you think I'm suicidal?"

"No, Arlo, I don't."

I crunch down on a chip. "What about crazy, do you think I'm that?"

He ponders this — too long, if you ask me.

"Not slipped-a-gasket crazy," he says finally. "Just young-and-stupid crazy. But I'll tell you something, Arlo. When I saw you come off that hill, it about killed me. Don't ever do anything like that again. I want you to promise me."

He looks at me hard and hurt.

"Yeah, promise," I say. "Never again."

CHAPTER 35

I'M IN THE HOSPITAL for five days. When I get home, I do a lot of moonwalking. Pop a lot of pills. The big ones are called Oxy blues, and they do more than kill pain. They gauze my mind. It's not a bad feeling. It's not a good feeling. It's a personal-vacation-from-self feeling. Destination Siberia.

One thing the Oxy blues don't gauze is my memory of Lee. How when I kissed her, she brushed a hand on my cheek, threw back her head, and laughed.

I know she saw me all beat-up at the hospital. Dad said so. I don't remember any of that. I don't want to see or call her now. Fact is, I don't want to see or call anybody.

During the next few days, I rack up some of my highest scores on Drone Pilot. My left arm may be in a sling to protect my clavicle, and my mind may be in Siberia, but my fingers haven't forgotten. No offense to SergeiTashkent and IpanemaGirl, but all they can do is eat my dust.

When I'm not playing Drone Pilot, I'm paying down the National Sleep Debt. The best place for this is the barn. I shove some bales into a square and layer the base with an old mattress and a couple of quilts.

I love the smell of hay and the closeness of horses. I'm less into kittens. But once those kittens take me for who I am, they help me to pay down the debt. We sleep under the caring eyes of the mares. No sweeter lullaby ever was sung than that by pregnant mares just breathing.

On my third night home, Dad finds an old recipe box in the pantry closet. Resurrects Linda Evans's *Dynasty* Corn Pudding—which we both agree is *muy delicioso.*

After dinner, he comes out of his study carrying a stack of books. "Hey, remember these, Arlo?" He plops down on the couch beside me.

"These" are books he read to me when I was a kid. Now he pages through them, reading aloud bits and pieces, holding each book like he's holding a crystal ball.

Until we come to the bottom of the stack.

A thin yellow book.

"Saved the best for last. Remember this one?"

"Yeah, sure do," I say.

He opens to the title page and gasps at the sight of Mom's handwriting:

For Arlo—our very own Curious George.
Love, Mommy and Daddy.

He starts to read:

"This is George. He lived in Africa. He was a good little monkey, and always very curious."

His throat clogs up. He takes off his glasses, drops his head, and pinches the bridge of his nose.

I put my arm around him — the only one I have left not in a sling.

CHAPTER 36

FOR A WEEK AND A HALF, Cam and Lobo take turns dropping off my homework. I make an effort to keep up, but it's pretty half-assed. One evening, I'm snoozing in my bed of hay and kittens when Kenya Man jolts me awake.

"Hello, Arlo. It's Colonel Kincaid."

I rub the sleep off my face. "Hey, sir."

"I saw the whole thing on YouTube," the colonel says. "Quite a stunt. Got banged up good, huh?"

"Yeah — yes, sir. But I'm better now."

"Well enough to fly drone?"

"Um . . . When would that be, sir?"

"Tonight, Arlo. We can't put this off any longer. We have a map to draw."

I peel a kitten off my chest and sit up, one degree at a time, so as not to awaken my clavicle.

Colonel Kincaid says, "What I need to know is, can you do it? Or has this knocked you out of the ring?"

I grab a post and pull myself to my feet. "There's nothing wrong with my head and hands," I say. "It's in between that's messed up. Only problem is, I'm not supposed to drive."

"Don't worry about that, Arlo. Just give me a straight answer: can you fly?"

"Yes, sir."

"Good," he says. "I'll have Major Anderson send up a transport. Be at the Shell station off the interstate in two hours — that's twenty hundred my time, eight o'clock your time. Don't be late."

Click.

I head over to the house and find Dad slouched at his computer staring at his novel. When I tell him the plan, he jerks.

"What! No. It's too soon."

"It's not too soon," I say. "All I need are my fingers. They're as good as ever. And, I don't have to drive; they're sending up a transport. Plus, it'll be another paycheck."

Dad glances at the clock. "You sure about this?"

"Yeah, I'm sure."

"Okay, then." He hoists himself out of his chair. "Better get dinner going."

He goes into the kitchen and starts banging around. I go into the bathroom and slap water on my face. Brush my teeth. Gargle Listerine. Pop two Oxy blues. Drop a half-dozen more in my pocket.

Hold my fists to the mirror, open and close them.

The thing about Oxy blues is, they reinforce how I see myself these days. Looking into the mirror, I see:

Dark lost eyes.

Dark lost mind.

Fact is, mirrors obstruct the view. They are like the shiny surface of the well you toss the coin into. The truth is what the coin sees as it sinks to the bottom.

Who am I?

"Dinner!" Dad shouts.

Who am I? I ask again.

"Drone pilot," I say to my reflection.

I grab my laptop and plant myself at the kitchen table. Over salsa scramble and pesto-slapped English muffins, I search for Colonel Kincaid's old e-mails and memos. The memos total a couple dozen pages. I cut and paste highlights of the unredacted text onto a blank page.

I'm trying to put all this information into some kind of logical order. To make the most sense of it. Pretty soon I have this:

TO: Mideast High Command and Coalition UAV Strategic Units
FROM: Col. (Ret.) Carl Kincaid, ARI
RE: Operation Brave Panther

I. Since last summer, the number of attacks on our personnel has sharply increased.

II. Insurgency forces have initiated attacks from steep outposts ringing the Swat Valley, the most dangerous being Compounds 52 and 117. Previous attempts to neutralize these outposts have failed.

III. Intelligence reports suggest that Caracal is masterminding these attacks. This is despite the fact that he was presumed dead following a drone strike last year outside Peshawar. The attacks contain his signature traits of surprise, boldness, and surgical precision.

IV. Caracal has always been externally focused. We must assume that his primary goal is strategic and that he plans to strike another heavy blow against our interests, most likely on the U.S. mainland, as soon as possible.

V. Setbacks involving civilian and friendly fire casualties have fueled cries in Washington, DC, and other world capitals for the termination of Brave Panther.

VI. We recently began looking beyond our traditional military sources for the best and brightest pilots.

VII. Recent gains can be attributed to the performance of one pilot in particular, Rope Thrower.

VIII. Rope Thrower possesses extensive knowledge of local terrain and exceptional flying ability. On three occasions he piloted a drone over Compounds 52 and 117 and gathered crucial photographic and video intelligence. He was able to commence mapping of human activities using real-time video imagery; commence tracking of courier travel patterns to, from, and between the compounds; and glide undetected throughout these missions.

IX. The success of Brave Panther depends upon consistent high-performance piloting. I believe we have found our pilot in Rope Thrower.

X. Next step: Escalate recon sorties to complete the mapping and tracking initiative in and around Compounds 52 and 117.

At the bottom of one of Colonel Kincaid's memos—at the end of a thick paragraph of blacked-out text—is a single sentence that boggles me. I'm pretty sure he meant to hide it. Then I wonder, maybe not.

It remains to be seen whether we can transition Rope Thrower from the role of forward observer to that of hangman.

I soak it all in.

Every last word.

CHAPTER 37

DAD AND I ARE PARKED behind the Shell station. Dad's tuned the radio to a blues channel out of Denver. Some guitar player is bustin' a slide called "Come Back, Little Mama." Dad's tapping in time on the wheel.

I watch cars rush up the interstate. I'm looking for a turn signal, but they all whoosh by. Then a light pricks the horizon and gets bright fast. Only it's not on the freeway.

"Jeez, Arlo," Dad says, "did they send a chopper for you? Are you *that* big a deal?"

A few minutes later, a helicopter lands in the field behind the Shell station. The door opens, and Specialist Mullins climbs out.

Dad and I bend into all that *whop-whop-whop.*

I bump fist with Specialist Mullins, and he salutes Dad.

"What happened to your flatbed?" I shout over the noise.

"What can I say, Arlo? I hang out with you and they treat me like a king. Ever fly in one of these?"

"Nah, never."

Dad starts to hug me, but my sling gets in the way, so he settles for a look—proud, sad, and "watch out."

"We'll have him back bright and early, sir," Mullins shouts to Dad.

I squeeze into a seat behind Mullins and the pilot. Strap in. All that rotor-turb makes it too loud to talk. As we lift off and fly south, I gaze down at the lone interstate travelers tunneling into the dark, and beyond into the blackness that veils New Mexico — the Navajo smoke and Kit Carson dreams.

Mullins hands me a pair of night-vision goggles. I put them on and the ground lights up like an x-ray. Now it's all boring scab-scarred plains and chunky hills. I take off the goggles. Better to see the darkness and the dream.

I want to be here, flying into the night.

I want to be heading somewhere, which is better than heading nowhere.

Heading *toward,* which is better than heading away.

« « « » » »

"WELCOME BACK, ARLO!"

Major Anderson waves from behind the glass wall inside the Skunkworks.

"How's your arm feeling?" he says through the mike.

"No problem," I say.

"That sling going to cramp your style?"

"Nah, my touch is pretty light."

"Good. Let's get started. You know the password."

I drop into the leather armchair and log on. Major Anderson opens the mike again.

"Tonight we'll continue mapping human activities in and around Compounds 52 and 117. You'll need to get in closer than last time. To see farther and deeper. Am I being too metaphysical for you?"

"No, sir," I say.

"Arlo, let's go over our mission. Can you explain it to me?"

I can't see Major Anderson all that clearly through the tinted glass. He's just a shadowy shape. I speak to it.

"Well," I say, "I'm looking for signs that somebody's hiding. Like maybe I see two people, and from how they stand I can tell there's a third person there, only I can't see him because he doesn't want to be seen. So I'm looking for, like, hints and traces, or reactions from others — stuff like that. 'Cuz that's all we'll ever see of him. 'Cuz he's aware. He's super aware. He's thinking about us the way we're thinking about him. He's safe as long as he doesn't make a mistake."

Major Anderson opens the mike. "Assuming he's there in the first place."

"Yeah, correct," I say. "Assuming that."

"What does your gut tell you, Arlo?"

"He's there," I say.

The mike clicks open. "It would be easy to drop Hellfires on these compounds, wouldn't it, Arlo?"

"Big mistake," I say.

"How so?"

"Because," I say, "if you're wrong about him being there, or if you miss, he'll just go into deeper hiding. And then you'll never find him. First, make sure he's there. Then once you're sure, hit him. But don't miss. You can't miss. You totally can't miss. And you can't hit anybody else, either. Believe me, I've done this before. It's how you score the big points."

"We're not scoring points here, Arlo."

"Yeah, sorry," I say. "Bad choice of words."

"Remember," Major Anderson says, "every action you take here causes a reaction twelve thousand miles away."

"Exactly," I say.

"Now let's get in tight and get those images."

Tonight I'm at the controls of a Mini-Shadow—just a bird, hardly bigger than a hawk.

Mullins slips in and places a cup of coffee beside me.

"Brought you three flavors of creamer, Arlo. Take your pick."

"All three," I say.

He winks. "Don't forget to T-FOG."

"Do my best," I say.

Major Anderson opens the mike. "Launch at will."

I launch from a catapult on a flatbed truck parked on a concrete slab twelve thousand miles from my cozy leather seat in White Sands, New Mexico.

It's nearly ten p.m. here at White Sands — nearly nine a.m. on Pakistan's North-West Frontier.

The Arghandab River shimmers in the distance. I glide over a village of stone huts. Look down on boys fishing from a bridge. Girls scrubbing clothes on the bank. Ponder their lives, which are so different from mine — no Safeway, no freeway, no Maytag, no Drone Pilot — though you can never be sure.

Still, I know what it's like, kind of. Cam, Lobo, and I have fished the Rio Loco, sitting on the Amtrak bridge. And on hot days, we've soaked our shirts in the river. Maybe it's a good life on the North-West Frontier, if you don't count the war. Maybe it's better than my life in New Mexico. I don't want to judge.

If they glanced up, they'd see me for who I am: an unmanned aerial vehicle — a drone. Property of the United States of America. Mission: covert tactical military reconnaissance.

I bank and throw my shadow downstream.

Flit across the Arghandab unseen.

Stretching before me are miles of orchards laid out in big squares. The valley breaks into foothills; the foothills split into canyons. Waterfalls slide down. I catch a thermal and ride it like an escalator.

Soon I'm high over the Swat Valley. On the horizon loom the Hindu Kush, the great frozen peaks of southern Asia. They look, as always, like the Front Range of the Rockies — the view you get from the north rim of Burro Mesa. That view from Burro is my all-time favorite on planet Earth.

Everything looks peaceful from up here. You'd never know there was a war.

Flying like this is easier than playing Drone Pilot. The game is relentless — constantly throwing ground flak and enemy fighters at you. Now it's just fly, stay out of sight, take pictures.

I dive and sweep toward Compound 117. See the sandbag walls getting larger. The camouflage nets, bunkers, and gun emplacements.

The dots are soldiers of the insurgency. They don't look too scary from up here. Sitting or standing at their stations. Probably grimy, itchy, cold, bored — who knows?

I aim my camera.

Zoom in on their tonsils.

CHAPTER 38

IT'S LATE AFTERNOON ON SATURDAY—two days after my trip to White Sands. We're sprawled on the Denver Broncos couch in Uncle Sal's den at Two Hole. Uncle Sal sits at his desk, swiveling meditatively. Out the window, the sun chills the mesa.

"Kids," Uncle Sal says, "the question before us today is, what's next for Jett Spence?"

Lee's the first to speak. "I for one don't think we should plan any next steps," she says. "Arlo's lucky to be alive."

I stretch my free arm behind her and rest it on the back of the couch.

Lobo says, "Lucky, plus—no offense, dude—you gotta be spooked after biting all that dust. Just sayin'."

"Any next step is up to Arlo," Cam says. "It's his life. Not yours or mine. I want what he wants."

Uncle Sal steeples his fingers. "Arlo, what *do* you want?"

I start to answer, but Uncle Sal throws up a hand.

"Before you tell us, I'd like everyone to listen—listen without prejudice or scorn—because opportunity has knocked on our door."

Uncle Sal raps his knuckles on his desk.

"Let's consider our achievements," he says. "One month ago, nobody outside this room had ever heard of Jett Spence. Today we are blessed with concentric circles of public awareness. First, the crowd at Rio Loco Field, which bore personal witness to Arlo's jump. Second, the TV viewers, locally and statewide, who saw our video on the news. And third, the Internet, which has spread awareness of Jett Spence from Podunk to Paraguay. Kids, what Arlo has achieved with one signature leap is — in terms of peddling our brand — the sanest form of genius."

"Wait — back up!" Lee says. "I can't believe we're having this discussion. Jett Spence doesn't even exist. Arlo is real. Haven't we learned anything? What's the point of peddling our brand if it means Arlo gets hurt or killed?"

"Exactly," I say, and my hand slips onto her shoulder.

"I don't disagree, Lee," Uncle Sal says. "However, what are we to do with our windfall of brand recognition? In the old days, you pressed a red-hot iron against the flank of a cow — that's how you got your brand out there. The cost was just cowboy wages. Today, you spend a fortune to advertise your brand. Arlo accomplished this with a single leap on his dirt bike. Didn't cost us a penny."

"Cost me a clavicle," I say.

"And a punctured lung," Cam adds.

"Two broken ribs," Lee says.

"That scar, dude," Lobo says.

"Yes," Uncle Sal says. "Arlo did pay a heavy price. And we need to take that under advisement. But let's face it, we've been handed a million dollars' worth of free publicity. What are we to do with it?"

Just then, Aunt Portia waddles into the study tilting a tray loaded with foaming glasses of *hoja santa.* Cam leaps up and rescues her. The rest of us stand.

"Look at you!" she says, handing Lee the first glass. "You could dance with a prince."

Lee blushes.

Everybody gets a glass, then Aunt Portia gives the order: "Drink up!"

We obey.

The *hoja santa* scalds my throat in the best way.

"Whaaaaaaaa!" Lobo gasps.

"Oh, yeah, great batch!" Cam says.

"Man-o-man!" Uncle Sal says, wiping his mouth.

"Drink up, dear," Aunt Portia says to Lee.

Lee gulps it down. Her face reddens.

"A pinch of this, a pinch that," Aunt Portia says. "*Hoja santa* is of the earth."

We drain our glasses and settle into the depths of the couch. Gravity pulls me toward Lee. Or maybe it's lust. All I know is, our bodies are pressed together. I feel drowsy, awake, wise, and stupid at the same time. I want to nestle my face in her neck. I want to inhale her hair. I want to kiss her.

Uncle Sal snaps his fingers. "Listen up, kids. Before we decide anything, I want to share an e-mail that I received yesterday. It's the main reason I called this summit."

He punches into his laptop and finds the e-mail. "This comes to us from Culver City, California — and as we all know Culver City is the hometown of —"

"*Jeopardy!*" Cam, Lobo, and I chorus.

Uncle Sal clucks. "Don'tcha just love coincidences."

He clears his throat. Reads aloud:

"Dear Mr. Focazio,

"Your name and contact information were provided to me by the Office of the Mayor of Clay Allison, N.M.

"I am the executive producer of the hit reality TV series CrazyDirty&Extreme (CD&E). We showcase individuals performing outrageous and awesome stunts in a variety of panoramic locations.

"I recently viewed a video of a young man named Jett Spence performing a top-level motorcycle stunt at a high school football game in your community. Although this stunt did not end happily for Jett, it did evoke the same spine-tingling, jaw-dropping thrill that we seek to provide our viewers with each week on our show.

"I was relieved to learn that Jett was not seriously injured. It is my hope that he will consider performing a similar stunt on CD&E as soon as he is able. We command a 35 percent market share in our time slot. This translates to twenty-one million viewers each week.

"We are proud of the fact that we pay our performers at the most competitive rate in the business. A top-flight stunt can result in a dizzying paycheck. Compensation is based on several factors, including level of risk, originality, and — most important — 'DOA (Degree of Awesome).'

"To ensure trust and integrity, all stunts are videotaped by a CD&E-authorized crew and witnessed by a neutral third-party representative from the Price Waterhouse Company.

"If you are interested in discussing this opportunity, I would welcome a call.

"Sincerely,

"Bill-William Cooper, Jr.

"Executive Producer

"CrazyDirty&Extreme"

"Aww, man, I know that show," Lobo says. "Half the time the last scenes are shot in the ER."

"Or the cemetery," Cam says.

Uncle Sal pulls a notepad out of his drawer. "I've done some research," he says. "Wanna know how much a 'dizzying paycheck' is?"

He jots something on the pad. Holds it up for us to see:

$100,000

Lobo gasps.

"Oops," Uncle Sal says. "Guess I forgot something." He clicks his pen and makes one little change on the notepad. He holds it up again:

$100,000+

"Slam!" Lobo says. "That's up in Hot Lotto country."

"Arlo, it's your turn to speak," Uncle Sal says.

I lean my head on Lee's shoulder. Thanks to the *hoja santa,* she seems just fine with that.

"Jett Spence is retired," I say.

Uncle Sal slaps his notepad on the desk. “That’s all I needed to hear. Let’s hang up those gauntlets and move on with our lives. See how painless that was?”

“Good call, dude,” Cam says.

“Yeah, who wants to be dead anyway,” Lobo says.

Uncle Sal swivels around and studies the pinkening sky.

“Magic hour, kids!”

CHAPTER 39

MOST PEOPLE WHO PLAY Drone Pilot think flying ability is the supreme skill.

But patience can be the greatest skill of all.

Spiders know this.

Pythons know it.

Learn to wait—patiently, with your eyes and pores open—and something happens.

The fly buzzes into the web.

The fawn wanders under the branch.

You start to see the unseen.

That's what happens during my next two chopper trips to White Sands. I map "human movement" in and around Compounds 52 and 117, tracking every insurgent soldier and even following the couriers as they beat a path by dirt bike along the steep mountain trails between the compounds.

I zoom close enough to see the brand on one courier's bike—Yamaha. Small world.

I map and track until my pores, if not my eyes, tell me he's there.

At least, somebody's there.

I can see his presence in little ways. How it quickens the soldiers' steps. Straightens their backs.

Some days this happens in Compound 52, some days in Compound 117.

On my second trip, flying over Compound 52, someone darts out of a bunker. I turn my belly-mount camera.

See a man in baggy pants, vest, and porkpie hat rush toward a sandbag wall.

Zoom in and see . . . not a man, a boy. Maybe eight or nine years old.

He peers over the wall — at that deep drop into the valley. I'm there with him — zoomed right up behind him. See him bend down and pick up a rock, pitch it over. He leans out to watch the rock plunge into the valley. For a moment, I feel that fall with him.

He's just about to turn and show me his face when a soldier grabs him and hustles him back into the bunker.

This all takes about fifteen seconds. Major Anderson opens the mike.

"Arlo?"

"Got it," I say.

"How much?"

"All of it."

When I log off after nearly five hours in the air, Major Anderson comes out from behind the glass wall. He's beaming.

"You sure earned this tonight," he says, handing me an envelope. "Go home. Rest up. See you next time."

I want to ask if that was Caracal's son, but I never caught his face. Never got that angle. So I'll never know.

Mullins joins me for the helicopter ride back to Orphan County. All that rotor-chop should make sleep impossible, but it lulls me like a baby. I sleep most of the way back, waking as the sun rises on the mesa breaks and torn shadows of northeast New Mexico, my home. A land so empty and aching that all I can do is stare in awe.

We skim low over Burro Mesa, right over the herd. A few cows cut and run. Then the grassy tableland slices off, and I'm staring down at that sheer drop to the dusty floor of Colorado.

That's when it hits me.

An idea so stupid it's brilliant.

A stunt so impossible it might even be easy.

Must be because I've just woken up in a helicopter at sunrise and opened my eyes on this patchwork of dazzling light and dusky shadow. Or maybe because my mother's ashes lie scattered below on the mesa. Or maybe because I'm still half dreaming.

But I can see it all.

And feel it.

My gut soars.

I shudder and shove the thought out of my mind.

We land five minutes later behind the Shell station. I fist-bump Mullins and the pilot and slide out of the chopper. Then they're off again. Quick as that. No snacks from the store. No piss break. Just up and gone.

Dad's waiting in the pickup. I get in, and he pours me a cup of coffee from his thermos. I hand him my paycheck. We watch the chopper get small.

"Arlo, you look like the cat spit you up. I better take you home to bed."

"Nah," I say as the caffeine kicks in. "Already slept. Just take me to school."

CHAPTER 40

"CLASS, WHO CAN DEFINE *OVERSOUL?*"

Mr. Martinez flips his necktie over his shoulder and scans the room. His glasses glint. "Arlo, please tell us what Ralph Waldo Emerson meant by *oversoul*?"

Damn! Dad was right — I should have gone home to bed. All that chopper adrenaline and caffeine has drained out of me. I can barely keep my eyes open.

Oversoul . . . oversoul . . .

From some smoky place, I cough up:

"Uh . . . it means . . . don't conform. 'Cuz when you don't conform and stay an individual, society as a whole benefits."

"Wrong essay," Mr. Martinez says. "That's Emerson's thinking on self-reliance, which we discussed last week." His eyes worry over me. Then he raises his voice. "Anybody?"

Everybody slouches and sucks in.

"You blocks, you stones," Mr. Martinez says, and thrusts his pointer at Lee. "Please enlighten your classmates, Miss Fields."

Lee doesn't talk much these days. Probably because it's embarrassing to always know the answer. Plus, being the shiniest spoon in the drawer doesn't sit well with everybody.

She hooks corn-silk hair behind her ear. "Um . . . Ralph Waldo Emerson believed . . . basically . . . that our individual souls are connected . . . and that . . . basically . . . they form a single soul, which he called the oversoul."

"Yes," Mr. Martinez says. "Now can you parse it down so that the livestock in the barn understand?"

"Um . . . it's like rivers," Lee says. "Each of us is a river. Like maybe I'm the Cimarron and Lobo's the Rio Loco and Arlo's the Rio Grande. We start out separately, but then we flow into the Gulf of Mexico and are no longer individuals. We're part of something bigger. That's like the oversoul."

Mr. Martinez thrusts his pointer at her again.

"And should we believe in this oversoul?"

"It's up to each of us, as individuals," Lee says. "But most people want some kind of proof."

"Ah, proof! There's the rub," Mr. Martinez says.

He taps his pointer against a sun-faded quote on the north wall. Without looking, he recites:

"'*We see the world piece by piece, as the sun, the moon, the animal, the tree; but the whole, of which these are shining parts, is the soul.*' Ralph Waldo Emerson."

He wanders over to my desk, leans down, and whispers, "You okay, son?"

"Yeah," I whisper back.

"You don't seem your usual upbeat self these days."

"Just tired is all."

He reaches into his pocket, shows me his phone. "Remember, if you ever need to talk . . ."

"Yeah, thanks."

He raises his voice. "Lee, close the circle for us. Can we apply the idea of an 'oversoul' to our daily lives? Or is all this just a useless academic rant passed down from one jaded English teacher to the next?"

"Useless academic rant," Vonz mumbles.

But Lee thinks about it. Finally, she says, "This morning on the news, I heard a report about another attack on the North-West Frontier. Something like a dozen Americans got killed. One was from here in Orphan County."

Mr. Martinez sets his face. "Carlos Johnson. He was a student of mine. Graduated three years ago. I know his family well."

Sharon Blossburg flaps a hand. "My cousin used to date him."

"I've been thinking about him all morning," Lee says. "All I can think is, he won't ever be able to do anything again. Not date anybody. Not dive into a swimming pool. Not smell ponderosa pine. Nothing."

Michelle Pappas snorts. "Girl, he's dead! Get over it. It's not like you knew him."

"Go on, Lee," Mr. Martinez says.

"Well, maybe," Lee says, "we should think of the oversoul as a strategy for living. I mean, we can choose to live connected — in our minds, bodies, and spirits — or not. The point is, we can, and Carlos Johnson can't. But I'm sure he'd give the world to be able to again. Not just breathe — but live — live to the fullest, in all his senses, connected in every way. Like the rivers are connected to the Gulf. If he were here right now, in this room, he'd say —"

"'Wake up, zombies!'" Lobo blurts.

Most of the class cracks up. But Lee looks serious. "Lobo's exactly right," she says. "He'd say, 'Wake up, zombies!'"

Mr. Martinez strolls to the front of the room. "Who here agrees with Lee?"

My hand shoots up, because everything she's said ties in with how I see it. The oversoul — that's just the Drone Zone.

A few other hands crawl into the air.

Mr. Martinez whacks his pointer on his desk.

"Everybody up there," he says, twirling the pointer to encompass all four walls, "from Harriet Tubman to Albert Einstein to John Lennon to Anonymous — tells us the same thing: Waste not the days, hours, or minutes. Dream big. Dream beautiful. Live — LIVE! For we know not when . . . we know not when. Give all!"

He beams at Lee.

"Young lady, that was one *helluva* speech!"

CHAPTER 41

THE EFFECTS OF MY BIKE stunt at Rio Loco linger worst in my chest, left shoulder, and left arm. But I'm getting better. I've gone from being barely able to lift my arm to being able to lift it, creak by creak, all the way up, and around.

It's a slow windmill. But a windmill's a windmill.

To reward myself, I throw away my sling and flush the Oxy blues down the toilet. For a day or two, pain floods back. Then it ebbs, slowly.

Over three weeks, I make five chopper trips to White Sands. Then I'm back on the Ducati, making the Monster roar. I'm not exactly a new man, but close enough.

One night, Major Anderson takes me to the back of the Skunkworks and shows me scale models of Compounds 52 and 117.

"We built these from your images, Arlo."

The desk-sized replicas are painted in the earth tones of the Swat and super detailed, with sandbag walls, gun emplacements, trees, crags, and sharp plummets.

"Extremely cool!" I say.

"Predictive analytics," Major Anderson says, "is the science of anticipating human activity based on routine patterns of behavior over an extended period of time."

He explains how he feeds all the data I give him — my video and still images — as well as other factors that he's constantly collecting — like weather, temperature, day of week — into a software utility that shows how people inside the compounds are likely to move around. Hour by hour. Minute by minute.

Just ask the utility to show you where anybody in the compound will be at any time of day or night, and it will. At least, it will predict it.

This is the "human map."

CHAPTER 42

"ARLO, WE NEED TO TALK."

It's five days later, and I'm back at White Sands again. Thursday night has bled into Friday morning. On the other side of the world, Friday morning has bled into Friday night.

Major Anderson's words could mean anything. But I have a good idea. I shudder.

We go through the glass door into the control room. Colonel Kincaid is here, sitting in the light of a thousand LED diodes, which illuminate the room to the brightness of a dim alley. His eye bags look pouchier than usual. He gestures for me to sit.

"Arlo, tonight we reached a milestone," Colonel Kincaid says. "We completed the surveillance phase of Brave Panther. We now have all our pieces in place. We can finish drawing the map."

"Hey, congratulations," I say, though I'm not feeling it.

"We took a risk bringing you on," Colonel Kincaid says. "We knew you could fly—you have all the instincts and reflexes of an elite pilot. What we didn't know was how well we would work together. So far, so good, don't you think?"

"Yeah—yes, sir," I say.

"We got this far, this fast because of you, Arlo. You caught all the images we needed. And you got one we never expected — the boy. That was fourteen carat. And you did it all with stealth. Not bad for a beginner."

"Hey, I'm not exactly a beginner," I say. "Not if you count the game."

"We don't count the game," Colonel Kincaid says. "You fly a real drone in real time. Never forget that."

"Sorry," I say.

Colonel Kincaid pinches some lint off his chinos, flicks it away.

"Arlo, it's time to begin the next phase of Brave Panther. If you've read my memos, you know what I'm talking about."

I look down at my boots.

"A single sting," Colonel Kincaid goes on. "Launched from one of our attackers. The kind you love to fly."

He waits for me to agree. I say nothing.

"Let me tell you about this man Caracal," he says. "He's not really interested in the day-to-day drudgery of killing GIs in the Swat Valley. That's just how he butters his toast. Caracal's a big-bang thinker. I'll tell you what he dreams about: our cities. Ever been to Chicago?"

"No, sir."

"How about Atlanta?"

"Uh-uh."

"L.A.?"

"I wish."

"Our cities, Arlo. That's what he's all about. Look at me."

I lift my eyes off the floor and look at him.

"We will be swift," he says. "One preemptive strike. Pinpoint and perfect. And you're going to do it."

"Not me," I say.

It comes out a whisper, but I'm definitely thinking it. Loudly.

Colonel Kincaid sighs. "Oh, yes. We had an agreement, didn't we. Nothing lethal. Wasn't that it?"

"It was more than an agreement," I say. "We shook on it."

"Yes, we shook on it. But this is war, Arlo. War changes everything."

"Not to me, it doesn't," I say.

He leans toward me, so close I catch a whiff of his aftershave — some kind of lemon-lime combination.

"Arlo, we have an opportunity here to do extreme and lasting good. The cost is cheap: one life — and hardly a life at that. A vicious killer. A monster. The payoff is monumental, saving countless lives."

"You don't know that," I say.

"We know enough," Colonel Kincaid says. "And this much we know for sure: we need our best drone pilot."

"Second best could do it," I say.

The colonel glares at me.

Major Anderson says, "Arlo, we're running the analytics now. We'll hit him in the dead of night, when he's moving between compounds. Everything is predictive. Nothing is guaranteed. So it's essential that we maneuver all the odds in our favor. That's why we need you."

I look down at my boots again — my Old Gringos, which Mom bought for me at Solano's in Raton. Unlike the officers' polished shoes, my Gringos do not reflect the diode light. They are scuffed and beaten. But they fit. Like molds.

I'm about to tell Colonel Kincaid and Major Anderson what they don't want to hear. Because once you go against your grain, you can't live with yourself. I sure can't.

Just as I open my mouth, Colonel Kincaid holds up a hand. "One more thing, Arlo."

One more thing! Why does there have to be one more thing?

"It's the best part," Colonel Kincaid says. "In return for doing extreme and lasting good for your country, your country will do extreme and lasting good for you."

"What's that supposed to mean?" I say.

"Arlo, what will happen to your sister?"

"My sister!" The thought of Siouxsie hits me like a jolt. "What's she got to do with this?"

"What's going to happen to her?"

Something spikes inside me. I clench my fist.

"Huntington's disease is a terrible road," Colonel Kincaid goes on. "Siouxsie will need lots of help. We can provide that help. We can take care of her."

"Shut the hell up!" I blurt out.

Kincaid doesn't even wince.

My mind tells me to get up and walk out, but I stay glued to my chair. Finally, I say, "How do you mean, 'take care of her'?"

"As time passes, she'll need more and more care," he says. "We'll be sure she gets it. We will help her. That's our pledge to you."

"Pledge!" I nearly spit the word. "You can't even keep a simple handshake promise."

"That's your view," Colonel Kincaid says. "Our view is different. We're warriors — as tough and adaptive as we need to be. But in this, we won't waver. You can count on it."

I plant my eyes square in his, matching him second for unblinking second.

"Exactly what will you do?" I say.

"Exactly this," Colonel Kincaid says. "We will make a heap of your father's debt. You know what I mean — everything that's delinquent and owed. Didn't he say he was sitting on a pile the size of Pike's Peak? Well, as soon as you complete the mission — successfully — we will liquidate."

"Liquidate?"

"Pay off everything he owes, Arlo. Level Pike's Peak."

The air sucks out of me. Everything I felt sure about a minute ago, I don't feel sure about now.

"You can do that?" I ask.

"Yes, we can do that," Colonel Kincaid says. "And furthermore, we will set in motion a process to ensure that Siouxsie gets the best medical care for the long haul."

I shiver. "'The long haul'?"

"The rest of her life," he says. "Many years, we hope. However, it could be merely a few."

I want to smash his face. I also want to climb into a hole and pull a boulder over me. Instead, I just sit there, paralyzed.

Something flickers on Colonel Kincaid's face — sadness, humanity, who knows.

"Arlo, I may seem to you like a hard-ass bastard, but I do this work because I believe in it. Wars don't just go away; they need to be stopped. It's a complex job — the math, the physics, the engineering. But the baseline is simple: You hit the opposing team to help the home team. You hit first, before they hit you. You hit below the belt, if you have to. And you don't miss. You hit the mark."

His mouth twitches. It's almost a smile. "You and I have something in common," he says. "We're both uniquely fitted to this work. Born for it, you might say. I don't know if that's a blessing or a curse. It's just the way it is."

"What if I say no?"

Colonel Kincaid shrugs. "If you decline, then your job here is done. You get on that big Ducati and roar back to Orphan County. You can keep the Ducati — you've earned it. Major Anderson will send you a final paycheck. You've got to admit, Arlo, these steady paychecks have been pretty nice compared to your Snack Shack revenue. Your last check should cover gas and groceries for several weeks."

"Arlo," Major Anderson cuts in. "We need to hit him before we lose him."

"When?" I ask.

"The analytics will tell us," Major Anderson says. "Just be ready for the call."

I shake my head. Shrug. Lost.

"So it boils down to this," Colonel Kincaid says. "You sacrifice for your country, and your country will sacrifice for you. Together we'll do extreme and lasting good for each other. Now go home, Arlo. You've got some thinking to do."

CHAPTER 43

IT'S JUST AFTER TWO A.M. when I pull out of White Sands. I'm heading north on Highway 54, fog rolling out of the Chihuahuan Desert, when I pass a sign I've never noticed before:

JOHN G. MAGEE, JR., MONUMENT AND MEMORIAL CHAPEL

NEXT RIGHT

I peel off the highway and cruise up a gravel road. The chapel, illuminated by garden spotlights, is perched on a hill. The roof is shaped like an airplane wing tilted into a chandelle turn.

As I coast into the parking lot, a shadow darts away. A garbage can rolls back and forth on its side.

I drop the stand on the Ducati, pick up the garbage can, and set it on its concrete base. Then I pick up the scattered crap — including a few half-eaten Happy Meals — and dunk it all back into the can. Jam on the lid and seal it tight.

Probably a coyote. Or possibly a raccoon or small bear. Caught him just tearing into those Happy Meals. If it's a coyote, I know he's watching me from under some mesquite bush. Coyotes persevere.

"Dude," I say into the darkness. "Pick up your own damn trash next time."

I go up the footpath to the chapel. The sign over the door reads DEDICATED TO THE MEMORY OF PILOT OFFICER JOHN G. MAGEE, JR., AND TO PILOTS EVERYWHERE MAIMED IN BODY OR SPIRIT. OPEN 24 HOURS A DAY.

The light inside casts a soft-yellow glow on the walls and pews. A marble plaque near the altar holds a large black-and-white photo of a pilot looking spit-shined in his uniform. Pencil-thin mustache. He stares at some horizon. The plaque reads:

> JOHN GILLESPIE MAGEE, JR.
> ROYAL CANADIAN AIR FORCE
> KILLED 11TH DECEMBER 1941
> AGE 19
> PILOT OFFICER MAGEE CRASHED TO HIS DEATH DURING TRAINING MANEUVERS IN THE SKIES OVER ENGLAND, JUST DAYS AFTER THE UNITED STATES ENTERED WORLD WAR II. THREE MONTHS EARLIER, HE COMPOSED A POEM THAT HAS BECOME THE AVIATOR'S ANTHEM AND EPITAPH.
> (PUSH BUTTON TO HEAR "HIGH FLIGHT")

I push the button and wander over to a pew. It's been a long day. I feel those miles. Just the thought of getting back on the road tonight — forget it.

Bagpipe music comes on. Then some overblown actor launches into the poem:

"Oh, I have slipped the surly bonds of earth,
And danced the skies on laughter-silvered wings . . ."

Dad recited these lines at the Atomic Burger in Alamogordo. He put a beer bottle to his forehead and remembered them.

"Sunward I've climbed and joined the tumbling mirth of sun-split clouds—
and done a hundred things
You have not dreamed of—"

My mind drifts to Colonel Kincaid's proposal. If the "human map" can find a target, I can hit it. And the payoff—leveling Pike's Peak and helping Siouxsie for "the long haul"—sounds like the best deal in history.

But if I do this, what happens? Because you don't take just one life. You take more than that. You kill something else. I know that for a fact.

"Up, up the long delirious burning blue
"I've topped the windswept heights with easy grace."

Was that Caracal's son running to the sandbag wall? What about his daughters—those little girls? Didn't they lose their mother like I lost mine? Why do I even care?

". . . and, while with silent, lifting mind I've trod
the high untrespassed sanctity of space . . ."

Fact is, I don't have anything against him personally. So what if he's an extremist. I'm an extremist. Colonel Kincaid says we need to prevent all those terroristic acts that he might do in the future. Not sure about that.

So why take him out?

To help my sister and father, that's why. I'd do anything to help them.

But what if the situation was reversed, and somebody took out my dad? How would that hit me?

". . . put out my hand and touched the face of God."

Damn! It's how I feel too.

I could never say it like John Gillespie Magee, Jr. His words are way too "delirious." But maybe we need to be delirious to get to the gut of how we feel.

It's why we ride the way we ride.

Fly the way we fly.

To feel something.

Let in life.

Hold back death.

Break through.

I get up and push the button again. Stretch out in the pew and plant a fat hymnal under my head.

Pull Dad's duster over me.

Close my eyes.

Wait for the last line.

Am asleep before it arrives.

« « « » » »

BANG! I'M AWAKE.

Dawn jitters through the cut-glass windows. I stand, stretch, and go outside.

Yup, there he is — damn coyote! Red-desert gray. Scrawny as hell. He's knocked over the garbage can again. I watch him paw the lid, circle the can. Sniff. Paw. He sits and contemplates his problem.

Never feed a scavenger, that's the rule. And coyotes are the worst. Better off shooting them.

I pick up a rock and pitch it — not to hit him, just to scare him off. He startles and bolts.

"Get outta here, you bum!"

He slows to a lope. Takes cover under a pine and watches me.

I go down the path and pick up the garbage can. Plant it square on its base. Brace the sides this time with flagstones from the garden.

"Hey, I got problems too," I grumble.

He stares at me with yellow eyes.

I pull off the lid, reach in for those Happy Meals, squat, and shake the contents of the bags onto the pavement. Make a heap of petrified fries and ragged burger remains. Perch the cold nuggets on top.

Then I seal the garbage can against all future coyote safecrackers — at least for a few hours.

I fire up the Ducati and rev all 1100 ccs. The coyote pricks up his ears, one growler respecting another.

Rolling out of the parking lot, I lift my voice and offer some advice:

"Watch out for those nitrates."

And I'm gone.

CHAPTER 44

WHEN IN DOUBT, *talk it out.*

Two-four-six-eight — communicate!

Two of Mom's favorite sayings.

They echo in my mind as I bomb north.

In Tularosa — the chocolate churro capital of New Mexico — I pull off and find a park bench. Dig out my phone. Call Mr. Martinez.

"Arlo! I'm just heading out." I hear a door bang, footsteps, jingling keys. "Will I see you at school?"

"Nah, gotta miss today."

I hear him get into his old Saturn and shut the door. He does not start the engine.

"Talk to me, son."

I tell Mr. Martinez the skeleton bones of my problem — leaving out the proper names and nouns out of respect for the confidential nature of Brave Panther.

"It sounds to me like you have a classic dilemma on your hands," he says. "That level of subtlety is above my pay grade."

I can hear his fingers drumming on something.

"Arlo," he says finally. "Of all the great men and women whose names grace the walls of our classroom, whom have we exalted to the highest rank, above all others?"

It's an easy question, because one name is written larger than any other on the wall.

"Anonymous," I say.

"Glad you remember, Arlo."

How could I forget. Mr. Martinez gives us his "Anonymous Speech" about once a month. It starts like this:

"'Anonymous' lived and died in obscurity. Was hoodwinked, vilified, exploited, enslaved, trampled, and ignored.

"Yet . . .

"'Anonymous' was wiser than Solomon, more eloquent than Shakespeare, braver than Joan of Arc.

"'Anonymous' sang the most beautiful songs, wrote the tenderest poems, built the loveliest cathedrals, fought the fiercest battles, painted the greatest frescoes."

On and on.

Mr. Martinez has been giving his "Anonymous Speech" for decades. Dad heard it in his day. Mom heard it in hers. It's kind of a local joke. I've heard people say: "Look at me, Mr. Martinez, I'm Anonymous." Meaning their lousy job, empty fridge, or depressing life.

Me, I like the speech, because it links me to all the nameless people in history who have helped me, like the pioneers, the GIs, and my ancestors.

"Arlo, most people don't get to drink from the cup of glory," Mr. Martinez says. "What matters more is, wherever you go and whatever you do — be sure it's you. Remember, you have a wise and loyal friend in yourself."

"Hope so," I say.

"Are you somewhere on your motorcycle, son?"

"Yeah, so happens."

"Stay focused. Drive safely."

"I will—thanks."

Next I call Lee. She's just pulling into the school parking lot. Tells me to hold on while she backs into a space. While I'm holding, I grab a stick and scrape about a hundred carmelized bugs off my headlight.

She picks up. "Hey, where are you?"

"Taking the day off," I say. "Probably take tomorrow off too."

"You're sure absent a lot lately."

"Yeah, well . . . I was wondering, you free Saturday?"

"Might be. Why?"

"'Cuz I want to show you some country. The real Land of Enchantment."

"Dirt bike show me?"

"Yeah, dirt bike," I say. "What other way is there?"

Lee laughs. "It's about time, Arlo."

"Just fuel up the 125," I say. "See you at the ranch Saturday morning. Early."

Click.

I blast another eighty miles up the pike. No cops out—just me and the desert.

Land so big, speed so pure it feels like I'm standing still.

Just hearing Lee's voice—it's like I've known her all my life. Fact is, I barely know her, and it's my own damn fault. *It's about time,* she said. And she's right. It *is* about time.

Siouxsie's always telling me that I get on my bike and ride away.

Why is that?

I don't know. It's beyond me. I'm my own mirage — the closer I get to myself, the more I recede.

Nah, that's a load of crap. I'm not a mirage — and it's not beyond me.

In the hills north of Santa Fe, I grind down and exit onto a rural road that squanders into dirt. Cruise over to a broken-vane windmill. Stop. Key off.

Now it's just me and the pine on the breeze. If Dad were here, he'd recite the names of the peaks to the north and the rift valley to the west. He'd talk about Navajos, Utes, and Kit Carson.

But he wouldn't talk about Mom. And he wouldn't talk about Siouxsie. Not in the way they need to be talked about.

I dig out my phone and call him.

"Mornin', Arlo," Dad mumbles from the depths of his pillow.

"Hey," I say. "Let's go up on the mesa today. We got some catchin' up to do."

CHAPTER 45

"THIS IS THE PRETTIEST PLACE on the earth, isn't it?" Dad says.

We're resting our asses on a hump of sandstone on the western edge of Burro Mesa. For the past couple hours, we've hauled, scythed, and shoveled. We've cut a black checker square of earth and spread sand. Because of my still-tender clavicle and arm, Dad's done most of the heavy lifting.

Just below wave the tendril tips of the pines and larches—those that cling to the west flank of the mesa. And far below in the meadow, tiny as a silver BB, sits a junked Airstream trailer. Some pacifist-hermit named Walter lived there during World War II. Nobody remembers anything more about him. He's basically Anonymous.

"Tell me one more time," I say. "Why do you want to mess all this up with a monument?"

"*Ughhh!*" Dad says. "That again." He goes over to the pickup, fishes in back for a couple of warm Sprites. Tosses me a can as he strides back.

"It's how I want to remember her, Arlo. Leave it at that."

"Not me," I say, popping the lid. "I want to remember her by leaving it all alone. Just let the grass grow green, the sky stay blue, and the wind keep on whippin'. That's who she was. That's the way she'd want it."

Dad settles beside me on the sandstone. "I'm old-fashioned. Just a few words in stone. Your mother will appreciate them."

"Who's gonna read 'em up here anyway?" I ask.

Dad shrugs. "You and me. Some occasional wrangler and literate coyote. Siouxsie, I hope. All those times I should've done something, said something. You know, all those little gestures. Life is about little gestures, Arlo. They ripple into waves, and the omission of them can flatten mountains. This is my little gesture. Long overdue."

"She wouldn't want it."

"Oh, yes she would!"

Dad points. El Guapo is sneaking up behind a calf.

"Here it comes," he says.

Guapo stands just outside of kicking range and starts to air hump. The calf glances back, bleats, and skitters away.

"Poor old Guapo," Dad says. "Helluva life. Got to hand it to him for trying. Perseverance — that's what it's all about."

"Plus, the weather's gonna fade it out," I say.

"Don't waste your breath, Arlo."

Dad looks over his shoulder at the black square of earth. Our afternoon's work.

"It's nice that it'll look down on your Grandpa Spencer's ranch," he says. "That'll be a comfort in the winter. But I'm still not sure this is the right spot. Seems a little crowded in here, among all this sandstone."

"You ever get that epitaph written?" I ask.

"Not yet."

"Shouldn't you write it before we do all this?"

"Words come when they come," Dad says.

"Just say 'Gone but not forgotten.'"

"Maybe I will," Dad says. "Hey, did I ever tell you about our first date?"

"Yeah, I'm sure you did."

Dad points. "See that switchback trail right there?"

I lean forward and peer over the edge at the western flank of the mesa.

"Yeah, I see it."

"We came up that trail on horseback, your mom on a mount called Pretty Boy, ornery as all hell. Your grandpa had warned her not to ride him—"

"Hey, you already told me this story."

"Well, Arlo, I'm gonna tell you again, because you need to hear it. It's who she was, and it's who you are. So just listen."

Dad sips his Sprite. Squints at the sky.

"All the way up the trail, Pretty Boy was docile as a buttercup. But when we got up here, and he saw this vast sea of sweet grama and alfalfa grass—good God, what horse wouldn't love all this?—he just bolted. Drew a line straight for the north rim."

We shift around and look north. It's a good run to the rim—more than a half mile.

"You ever look over that edge?"

"Plenty of times," I say.

"Just thinkin' about it spins my head," Dad says.

"Clears mine," I say.

"Sheer as a blade through cake," Dad says.

“Three thousand feet sheer,” I say. “That’s my guess.”

“Your mother knew that horse was just trying to con her — that he would never jump. He might have been ornery, but he wasn’t crazy. So she called his bluff. Gave him all the rein he wanted. I’m sitting up here on my mount watching your mom and Pretty Boy charge the rim at a full-tilt gallop. Not being much of a horseman, or well versed in horse psychology, I thought she was gone — this beautiful young lady, this rancher’s daughter, to whom I’d already lost my heart. As I watched, my whole future was galloping off into the clouds. It just about killed me, Arlo.”

Dad whistles. Shakes his head.

“Pretty Boy balked, of course. Reared up like a damn rodeo horse. Your mother wheeled him around, not five yards from the rim, and they came trotting back, sunny and peaceable. All those coiled muscles now loose. I’ll never forget the look on her face. She just glowed. She was the prettiest damn . . . You’re just like her, Arlo. You have that streak.”

“That would’ve been a good way to go,” I say.

“How do you mean?”

“Just gallop off into the clouds.”

Dad scoffs.

“I’m serious. A lot better than —”

Dad says, “Yeah, a lot better than that.”

“What happened with you and Mom? I mean, was it good being married?”

“Like I said, Arlo, little gestures — or the lack of them. The difference between men and women is, men are like folk tunes played simply, with two or three chords. ‘Red River Valley’ comes to mind. Or ‘Blowin’ in the Wind.’ Women are like Brahms concertos, full of nuances, depths, and complexities. In all future relationships, you will encounter this tension. A bad relationship shrivels you to less than nothing. A good one fills you out in every way. You become ten times who you were. 'Red River Valley' becomes, say, for the hell of it, 'Stairway to Heaven.' But the thing is, you've got to give to get. It's the law of opposites."

"So you didn't give enough?"

"Not nearly," Dad says.

The wind talks for a while. To the west, three ship shadows — the *Nina, Pinta,* and *Santa Maria* — sail across Zuni Mesa. They sail right off the edge.

"When I wake up from a nap these days," Dad says, "I lie there, and that's when I talk to God. Tell him how grateful I am, despite it all. Then I get down to business: 'Please keep an eye on Arlo and Siouxsie.'"

"Especially Siouxsie," I say.

Dad sinks into himself. He looks shot out. All that could happen to him seems to have happened.

I want to tell him about the "extreme and lasting good" that could turn us around. In fact, that's the main reason I wanted to come up here today.

But looking at him, I decide not to.

Why add my straw to his load?

Anyway, I know what I have to do. I've made up my mind. Being up here today has cleared things up.

Dad won't like it. He'll hate it.

I hoist my ass off the rock.

"Hey, let's put it over there instead," I say.

"What are you talking about, Arlo?"

I point north. "Mom's monument. Let's put it smack up against the rim — right where Pretty Boy balked."

Dad gets up and dusts himself. We ponder the north rim of Burro Mesa. That sheer line where grass meets sky. Beyond stand the Spanish Peaks. And far on the horizon, the broken jaw that is the Front Range of the Rocky Mountains.

All the beautiful, lonely bones of the world.

Dad drains his Sprite, crunches the can.

"Damn!" he says. "This was a wasted afternoon."

CHAPTER 46

NEXT MORNING, I RIDE OUT to Two Hole. Uncle Sal is seated at the dining room table eating silver-dollar pancakes and reading the *Albuquerque Journal.* The big headline on the front page says "Economic Doldrums."

"Mornin', Arlo!" he says, closing the paper. "How's my favorite diamond in the rough today?"

"Not too shiny," I say.

He signals for me to sit. I grab the chair across from him and eye his pancakes — a real breakfast. Drool-worthy.

"What's up?" he asks.

"Just wondering," I say. "Do you still have that e-mail from that *CrazyDirty&Extreme* guy?"

"Sure." He reaches for his phone and searches for the e-mail.

Aunt Portia comes in from the kitchen and beams at the sight of me. But when I stand, she frowns.

"Arlo, whatever you had for breakfast didn't work," she says. "I'm going to fatten you up."

"Please do," I say, and she goes right back into the kitchen.

"Here it is," Uncle Sal says. "His name is Bill-William Cooper, Jr. He's the executive producer. Why? What's on your mind?"

"Jett Spence," I say.

Uncle Sal spikes a couple of silver dollars and sponges up some syrup. "Last I heard, ol' Jett was out to pasture enjoying his retirement."

"Yeah, well, it might be time to un-retire him," I say.

Uncle Sal stuffs a forkful into his mouth and rolls a hand to get me talking.

I tell him my idea. By the time I'm done, he's eaten a half-dozen silver dollars, and his eyes are glistening. He grabs his napkin and wipes his mouth.

"You're joking, of course."

"Nah, I'm serious."

His face falls. "Good God, Arlo! Don't be ridiculous."

"Hey, you're the one who's always telling us to aim high. You know, *Defecare due volte* and all that?"

Uncle Sal rattles his head. "Yes, but this takes *defecare due volte* to a whole new level."

"Exactly," I say. "That's why they're gonna pay me maximal. Because this won't be any ol' jump into a dirt pile."

"The answer is no," Uncle Sal says. "Let me amend that—*hell* no!"

He picks up the newspaper and snaps it open, redacting me.

Aunt Portia comes in and sets a mug of coffee before me—"*Un caffe per Arlo*"—and a plate of silver-dollar pancakes. She's drawn a smiley face on the big pancake in the middle, using maple syrup. It even has a squiggle that's supposed to be hair.

"*Grazie,*" I say.

I take a bite, because Aunt Portia wants my verdict now.

"Mmmmmm. Super-*grazie.*"

"The secret is in the bread crumbs," she murmurs confidentially. "Add bread crumbs from a stale loaf to fatten your batter. Don't forget."

"I won't," I say. "Thanks."

When she's gone, Uncle Sal lowers the paper. "Let me get this straight. You're proposing to jump your Ducati motorcycle off the highest mesa in New Mexico. Do I have that right?"

"Hundred percent," I say. "But Burro's not just the highest mesa in New Mexico, it's also on the state line. So I'd be jumping from New Mexico into Colorado."

"What a relief," Uncle Sal says, rolling his eyes. "Listen, Arlo, I know something about risk. I've paved a highway to the bank with bricks made of pure, immaculate risk. But Sweet Mary from Tucumcari, this isn't risk, it's suicide."

"Nah, suicide's when you die," I say.

"Which almost happened at Rio Loco," Uncle Sal says.

"This'll be different," I say.

"How will it be different?"

"This time, I'll make it."

Uncle Sal shudders, raises the *Journal*, and walls me out again.

I bust through my pancakes. Drain my coffee. Mop up my plate. I want to lick it, but the standards at Two Hole are higher than at home.

"Hey, do me a favor," I say to the wall of newspaper. "Just read that e-mail from Bill-William what's-his-name. Out loud. Please."

"Fine," Uncle Sal says, folding the paper. "Makes no difference to me."

He opens the e-mail and starts to read aloud. His voice perks up at "thirty-five percent market share," "twenty-one million viewers," and "dizzying paycheck."

I hear his marketing mind clank into gear — and then skeptically unclank out of gear — about three times.

He finishes reading the e-mail and shrugs. "Happy now?" he says.

"So just thinkin'," I say. "If I did this — hypothetically, I mean — it would be a lot of fast money."

Uncle Sal nods. "If you did this — *if!* — and got away with it — bigger *if!* — it would be a windfall. You could skip the whole fried-chicken phase of your career and go straight to prime rib."

"I've been thinking of becoming a vegetarian," I say.

Uncle Sal flicks away the thought. "Arlo, tell me straight — nephew to uncle — why do you want to jump your Ducati off Burro Mesa?"

I point to the big headline in the *Albuquerque Journal.* "Economic doldrums," I say.

Uncle Sal broods on this. He knows where we stand at home — Dad's job status and all. And he knows about Siouxsie's health problems — not all the details, but enough to know that Huntington's is a bottomless pit.

"Where I come from, Arlo — going back a couple generations to old Italy, the port of Pescara — all our reasons for improving our lives came down to one word: *famiglia.*"

"Yeah, well, I must come from the port of Pescara too," I say.

His eyes glisten. "Arlo, I'm proud of you for wanting to help your family. But this idea of yours — I oppose it. Emphatically. Try it, and you'll break your neck."

"I'd break more than that," I say.

"Oh?"

"I'd break a promise."

"What promise is that?"

"To never never do anything like this again."

"Well, there you have it," Uncle Sal says. "Case closed."

I get up to go. At the front door, I turn and look back. I expect to see him walled behind the *Journal* again. Instead, he's staring at me.

"You may as well know," I say. "I'm gonna do it anyway. I'll call Bill-William Cooper myself. Just do me a favor, don't tell anybody. They'll only get gray hair. Especially don't tell Dad."

Uncle Sal looks at me like I'm already a ghost.

And maybe I am.

CHAPTER 47

IT'S SATURDAY. I'M UP EARLY—and I'm never up early on Saturday.

I wolf down a couple of sausages and roll out my Yam 250. Cam has wrenched and duct-taped it back to respectability after my little incident at Rio Loco Stadium. It's not in perfect shape, just like I'm not. But it's good enough to go.

I mount up and spin dust.

On the highway, I grind into silence. The scab plain—usually the blandest brown in the crayon box—is a hundred muted shades this morning. The road reeks of sage and creosote.

I wonder, how many more mornings like this do I have left? Because you never know your last. And not knowing—that's what makes it great. That's what makes this the Land of Enchantment.

I blast up the canyon, bump over the cattle guard, and pull up outside the barn. Lee's there tinkering on the YZ 125. She stands, flips back her hair, and gives me a smile.

I'm taking her into the high canyon today. If you can ride high country, and fit into it, everything and everybody is beautiful, not just the few.

Over at the house, the screen door slaps. Siouxsie rolls onto the porch in her new wheelchair. She doesn't really need the wheelchair yet. She's just messing around. And kind of messing with me.

"Hey, give me a minute," I say.

Lee glances at Siouxsie. "Take all the time you want," she says.

I cruise over to the porch and kill my engine. Pull off my helmet. Look up at my wheelchair-riding-but-not-yet-bound sister who stares at the rim rocks, a sulky sphinx. She is, however, wearing her hearing aids, and sphinxes don't do that.

If I had to guess her philosophy, I'd say it's this: life's a joke, but it hurts too much to laugh. And she would be right.

"Wish I could just go ridin' off," she grumbles.

"Soon enough," I say.

"Yeah, well, that's a lie."

She's wearing the headband Mom made for her — the one with the tie-dye shades of blue.

"Tell Lee to take care of my bike," she says to the rim rocks.

"Your bike'll be fine," I say. "It was born for today."

"Yeah, well, I sure wasn't."

Slam! There it is. The sphinx has spoken.

"And tell her to take care of you too, Texas Slim. You're not good for much except ridin' dirt bumps."

I let the words sink in. Because she's right. I'm not good for much when it comes to Siouxsie and all that clashes inside her. When I was twelve nothing clashed inside me — except whatever got between me, my bike, and the mesas.

"Where would you go?" I ask.

Siouxsie still hasn't looked at me. Just adjusted her sneer. "Huh?" she says.

"I mean, if you could go anywhere on the 125—*your* 125 . . . just hop on and blast off, where would you wanna go?"

"That's a stupid question," she says.

I toss my helmet in the air and catch it. Glance back at Lee, who's watching us.

"Hey, do you remember how you told Dad and me we all live on different sides of a mountain?"

Siouxsie twitches. "Yeah. So?"

"So I haven't been much of a brother. Not since Mom died."

Her shoulders jerk, like it's nothing.

"But I'm workin' on it. And if I don't make it . . ."

Her eyes cut to mine. "What do you mean, if you don't make it?"

I toss my helmet again and catch it. "Only . . . sometimes there's no right or wrong. Just half right or half wrong. Like, if you had to pick between stale or spoiled—"

"Stale, obviously," Siouxsie says.

"Well, this is harder than that."

Siouxsie pivots in her chair and rolls over to the top of the stairs. She peers down at me. "What on earth are you talking about, Arlo?"

"Nothin'," I say. "Only, maybe I've been living on the wrong side of the mountain. And I'm sorry."

She weighs my words. I can tell she senses there's more to them, but she doesn't ask me to elaborate, thank God. Because if she did, I might have to tell her that, if I were a better brother, I'd do everything I could to help her for the long haul.

I'm also thinking that someday I will ride away and one of us will be gone forever.

"Well, mountains have trails, you know," she says.

I get off my bike, climb the porch steps, go behind the wheelchair, and wrap my arms around her. Hold her close. Like I never have.

She sits there, not knowing what to make of me.

I'm her crazy brother.

I ride away.

I always ride away.

« « « » » »

LEE AND I FOLLOW the dry bed of Chicorica Creek, then cut through the cottonwoods and take an old road that runs through the Ponderosa. We climb a few miles through shade. To any distant ear, we must sound like obnoxious chainsaws. I pity the hibernating bear or sleeping cougar, but what the hell.

We break into a meadow. To the north, you can see all the way up Raton Pass, to the south all the way to the Capulin Volcano. East is an eyeful of mesa, traced with snow. West is filled with dam and pipeline. We don't look west.

I might not always like living in Clay Allison, New Mexico, but I always love the high country. It fills my eyes and lungs. Makes me feel punier and luckier.

Lee gets off her bike. Picks up a pinecone. Inhales it. Pockets it.

From here the ridgeline narrows up to the rim rocks. It's

the back way to the top of the canyon — also, come to think of it, to that vertical slab of rock that Lupita pointed out a while ago — the one blazed with "very old art" — the Indian petroglyphs.

I'm tempted to head up there to check out those ancient images. The high goat-trail aspects shouldn't be a problem for Lee. She's good on a bike — great balance, that's obvious.

What stops me is the secret — to respect the fact that nobody but Lupita and I knows about this place. Maybe she means to tell Lee herself. Maybe Lee already knows.

But I better not ask.

We better not go there.

Someday, maybe. Not today.

Never mess with a secret.

And never mess with a promise.

Unless your very life depended on it.

We cut down the meadow and hook on to an old mining road that leads to the ghost town of Sally Nickel. I signal Lee, and we stop at an overlook and ponder what's left of the town: the block foundations, slag heaps, and rusted metal. The ancient steam engine and busted coal carts. All the emptiness and ghostliness. The cabins, stores, and churches were torn down and hauled off long ago.

"What happened here?" Lee asks.

"Mines played out," I say. "She dried up some time after World War II. Don't know exactly when."

Lee points to the cemetery on the hill. "That might tell us something."

We cruise past the chimneys and coal ovens and take the cut up to the cemetery. Kill our engines and walk to the iron gate. Time has rubbed the headstones and even tilted a few. You can see where plastic flowers long ago bleached into the stone.

Lee wanders among the graves, reading the "Sleep My Beloveds" and "Rest in the Lords." She picks up a stick and scratches lichen off one faded name. I check out a few stones myself, then go over and sprawl in the grass. It's as high as wheat, a natural bed.

Pretty soon, she drops beside me. "Nineteen fifty-five. That's the most recent. But it doesn't mean anything. Somebody could've been buried here after the town dried up. You never know."

"You never do," I say. "Cemeteries are far from scientific."

Lee snaps off several stalks of grass. "Seems like half the people here died on the same day."

"Mine explosion," I say. "All these little towns were tragic."

She measures three stalks, and her fingers go to work twining them into a braid.

"I counted seven Espositos and five Papadopouloses," she says. "All died on May 5, 1948."

"Immigrants," I say. "One of my ancestors died in that explosion. On my mom's side."

"Tell me about your mom," Lee says. "What was she like?"

I shrug. "Like any mom."

"I've seen her picture, Arlo. And Lupita's told me about her. She wasn't like any mom."

I claw a hand into the earth, rip out a scalp-size chunk, and pitch it at the nearest headstone. It disintegrates in midair.

Lee says, "I hear she was good with horses."

"Extremely," I say. "She liked to ride bareback hell-bent. I've seen her do it a hundred times."

Lee chuckles. "I like her nickname for you, Little Texas Slim."

"Yeah, well, what can I say. Siouxsie won't let it die. And now Lupita's hijacked it."

"What else can you tell me about her?"

I look down at the busted old town where the Main Street parade happened long ago, if it ever happened at all.

"Nothin'," I say.

Lee props my wrist on her knee. "If I were to walk past her, who would I see, Arlo?"

"No offense," I say. "I'm just no good at this."

"It's all right," Lee says.

As she loops the braid around my wrist, a strand of her hair brushes against my forearm. I'm extremely aware of it. Just when she's about to cinch the knot, it breaks.

"Shoot!" She flings it away and gazes down at all the slag and rust that once was Sally Nickel. Broken. We're all broken. Knots, towns, people. It's just the normal state of things.

"I'll tell you a story," I say.

"Please do," Lee says, reaching for more stalks of grass. This time, instead of snapping them off, she slides them out by the roots, for added length.

"One time — when I was five or six — we were up at my Grandpa Spencer's place. It was blowing pretty hard. I had a new toy, an action figure named GI Joe or Sergeant Savage, something like that."

I'm watching Lee's fingers as I speak. The way they move, like pistons, is almost hypnotizing.

"He came with a parachute. I took him down to the barn, climbed the ladder to the loft, opened the hay door, and tossed him out into the wind. That little guy sailed quite a ways before hitting the ground. Man, I was hooked."

"I'm sure you were," Lee says.

"I kept tossing him out that hay door to see how far he could fly. Each time, he went a little farther — fifty feet, then eighty. Well, the last time, a gust scooped him up and carried him away. I went down and searched the ground all around. Must've walked a hundred yards in every direction. He was just gone.

"After a while, my mom started calling from the house — 'Time to go.' But I wasn't about to leave without GI Joe.

"Finally, she came down to the barn. 'What's wrong, Little Texas Slim? Why are you crying?'

"I told her.

"'C'mon!' she said. 'We'll find him.'

"We climbed to the loft. She knew exactly where to reach for a swallow's nest, up on the high rafter out of sight. Right away, she found a feather. Cut off the end with a tack knife.

"'You go back down,' she told me. 'I'll toss this out — like you tossed your paratrooper. Be sure you follow. Don't lose sight of it.'

"So I went outside and watched her launch that feather from the hay door. It caught the wind and just flew. I ran all the way down the ravine, with her cheering me on: 'Go, Texas Slim! Go!' I scrambled over some rocks and followed that feather around a bend. Just a few feet from where it landed, I found my GI Joe.

"So you wanna know what she was like? That's the best I can do."

Lee fits the braid around my wrist. This time, she's able to tighten the knot. She pats my arm. "All done."

I hold up my wrist to inspect. "Thanks," I say. "A lot better than those stud bands the Hells Angels boys wear."

I roll to my feet, dust my ass, and take a goodbye look at Sally Nickel.

"She left us quick as lightning," I say. "It changed everything. We're all different people now. Maybe I should miss her more. Maybe I should feel like I've been kicked in the gut. Or had scalding oil poured over me. But it doesn't feel like that at all. I'll tell you why — because she's all around, more now than when she was alive. Guess I'm crazy."

I go over to my bike. Strap on my helmet, saddle up, and slam down.

"You comin'?" I shout.

Lee gets up and walks over. Reaches for her helmet. Before she puts it on, she looks straight at me.

"I like honesty, Arlo. I'm all over it."

« « « » » »

WE GO ALL DAY. Now the sun is down. Purple-yellow sky. Moon cradling Venus.

We bomb the last miles up the canyon road and bump across the cattle guard. Dad's pickup is parked in front of the house. Good. Means I can hitch a ride back. Give my old Yam a rest.

We pull up behind the barn, hose the dust off the bikes, and head for the house. I can see Dad through the living room window. He's sitting on the couch dressed in a white shirt and bolo tie. Lupita drops beside him. Dad stretches an arm along the back of the couch. It stops just short of Lupita.

"Hold up!" I say to Lee. "Where's this going?"

We stop and watch. It's not exactly going anywhere. But it looks like it might. I want it to go somewhere. It's been a long, dark season for Dad.

"Um, this is none of our business," Lee says.

"Maybe not but still . . . "

I grab her hand and drag her tiptoe up the steps onto the porch. I drop into an armchair — an old Adirondack — and pull her into my lap. Her eyes practically land in mine.

Through the window, we hear:

"How many times you been married, Lupita?"

"Twice, Hec. You know that."

"Somehow I thought it was more like three or four times."

Lee gives me a little swat — punishment for eavesdropping. Normally, I'd agree. But this is Dad. And he's got on a white shirt and bolo tie — *damn!*

"Had a couple live-in sets of spurs," we hear Lupita say. "Kicked the last one out two years ago."

"How come you're all alone now?" Dad asks.

"I'm not alone, Hec. Got my niece. And Siouxsie. The girls are wonderful company."

"You know what I mean," Dad says. "You could snap your fingers and any one of ten honchos would drop his saddle and come running."

"I've had it with honchos dropping their saddles," Lupita says.

I clasp the lapels of Lee's jacket, pull her to me. Kiss her — peach soft, plum shiny. Her hair cascades around me, all that red-gold holding the scent of dusk, wheatgrass, and the beautiful brokenness of life. We sink into the Adirondack.

They go on talking, but who the hell cares.

After a while, I hear Dad say:

"Don't you miss it?"

"Miss what?"

Lee lifts her head, listening too.

"Being with someone," Dad says.

"My weakness is for stallions," Lupita says. "The frisky kind. But stallions have a way of going lame on me. Nowadays one trots up, I shoo him away."

"Get yourself a gelding," Dad says.

"Ha!" Lupita says. "Not interested in geldings."

Lee laces her fingers behind my neck. Man, am I starved.

"*Whoa,* Arlo!" She pushes me away and catches her breath. Buttons her shirt. Gives me another little swat, bad boy that I am. Fact is, nothing much has happened. And yet everything has happened.

We hear Lupita say:

"Tell you what I do miss."

"What's that?"

"Picnics," Lupita says.

"Picnics! You speaking metaphorically?"

"Oh, go stuff your metaphors," Lupita says. "I mean real picnics. Driving up the canyon to the spring. Spreading a blanket under the sky. We forget, this is the Land of Enchantment. The most beautiful place on earth. We bog down in our lives and forget that."

"We sure the hell do," Dad says.

"How 'bout you, Hec? What do you miss?"

"Gettin' naked."

Lee lands me another little swat, like I said it.

Lupita chuckles. "Listen to you."

"I used to be a stallion," Dad says.

"Used to! What happened?"

"Death. Life. The whole shebang."

"True love is damn painful," Lupita says. "Still, life is nothing without it."

"I disagree," Dad says. "Life is just fine without it."

"You're the dumbest man I know," Lupita says. "Get your ass over here before the kids come back."

"Why? What are you gonna do to me?"

"Spell something out."

Whatever Lupita spells out must be in Braille, because we don't hear a single letter. Then Dad gasps.

"My God!" he says. "Now I can die."

"There'll be no more dyin'," Lupita says.

Dad tries to laugh, but for a mere second he chokes on a sob. Lee hears it too.

"Too bad Siouxsie's just down the hall," he says. "Otherwise . . ."

You can hear the wink in his voice.

"Hec," Lupita says, "I could thrive on your bullshit."

Lee snorts into my shoulder.

Me, I'm feeling good.

I'm feeling great.

Lee grabs my hand and pulls me to my feet.

I add a stomp to my step, and we go inside.

CHAPTER 48

MOST MARES LIKE TO BE ALONE before they foal. Not Blue Dancer. She likes having me there. She's in the big stall now, pacing, stamping, switching her tail.

She's lathered. I move the heat lamp farther back. Talk to her, low and easy. Her udder looks waxen where the drops have leaked and dried.

At ten p.m., I fill a thermos and climb into my bed of hay and kittens, flashlight and book. Give her all the privacy she could ask for — and the soothing of my voice when she wants it.

Just after midnight, her water breaks. I call Lupita.

"Hunker beside her," she tells me. "Stroke her neck. Love her. I'll be there soon."

Half an hour later, Lupita arrives with Lee and Siouxsie. Dad swings open the gate so they can watch. But not too close.

Only Lupita and I get close.

"Be a lot easier if she just popped it out like a kitten," Siouxsie says.

"Kittens are pretty low tech," Dad says.

"Push, baby," Lupita urges.

Blue Dancer strains. Her sac starts to bulge. What I think

is a nose turns out to be front hooves and nose clapped together.

"Oh my God!" Siouxsie says. "It's watching us."

And, yes, it is. Being born, Blue Dancer's baby looks right at us through the skin of the birth sac. The eyes seem to follow us.

Lupita grasps the legs and tugs. "C'mon, push!"

All that pushing, and then the foal slips out in a gush. Lupita peels away the sac, and we see a wet, shaggy, ears-back baby horse.

"*Ha*—a stallion!" Lupita says.

She clears the nostrils and mouth. Feeds it oxygen from a little tank she's brought along. Blue Dancer lifts her head and begins to lick her newborn.

"Come over here, Siouxsie. Don't make any sudden moves."

Dad lets go of Siouxsie's hand, and she steps into the stall, gets down on her knees, and squeezes a hoof.

"Weird," she says. "It feels mushy."

"That's right," Lupita says. "It's nature's way of protecting him from cutting his mom's uterus. Those hooves'll be hard soon enough. Slim, hand me that knife."

Lupita cuts and ties the umbilical. For an hour or more, we watch this licked-shiny, milk-stuffed, spindly-legged baby stumble around the stall.

Eleven days later, Cornflakes foals—a chestnut filly with four white socks.

And in the last week of January, Queen Zenobia gives us a colt.

"Look at that great big chest," Lupita says. "Here's our champion. Watch out, Kentucky!"

All these births are about waiting, breathing, and pushing. About peeling away a sac to reveal a tiny horse itching for life.

From the start, I get along just fine with these babies.

All they want to do is run.

All they want to do is fly.

CHAPTER 49

"THERE'S NO SUCH THING as a point of no return," Uncle Sal tells me. "You can bail now or right up to the last second. I'll support you one hundred percent."

We're up on Burro Mesa with the crew of the hit reality TV show *CrazyDirty&Extreme.*

The guy from Price Waterhouse is here too. He's the "neutral third-party representative," or official observer, whose job is to make sure that nobody cheats or fakes. He checks out the Ducati and Flying Squirrel and then gets a little too close to my parachute pack.

"Hands off!" Uncle Sal snaps.

Uncle Sal's in no mood to like these people. And he's barely talking to me. "Why am I here?" he mumbles to himself. Then he answers: "I'm here because I'm here."

Bill-William Cooper has been pacing. Now he walks up to Uncle Sal and me. "Whatever happened to all the glorious sunshine in New Mexico?"

He's right. Nothing glorious about this tin-plate sky. The wind, too, is kicking around. It's definitely not a great day to fly off a mesa—or to film somebody flying off a mesa. Mr. Cooper consults with an assistant, then tells me to "be prepared mentally" both to jump and to cancel. Thanks a lot.

The herd — a few dozen browns and their calves — has retreated to the south end of the mesa. I don't blame them — there's no peace here at the north end. Especially with a helicopter chopping all over the place.

« « « » » »

IN FACT, IT'S MY SECOND time on Burro Mesa with the *CD&E* folks. We came up here two weeks ago to scout and plan. Uncle Sal was with me then too. "Can't let you enter the lion's den alone," he told me.

That day, it was me, Uncle Sal, Bill-William Cooper, and a stunt coordinator named Thumper.

"How'd you get the name Thumper?" I asked.

"The hard way," he said.

Mr. Cooper photographed the north rim from various angles, uploaded the photos, then created a graphic map. He and Thumper gazed up, around, and out. But they didn't seem to notice the fresh-cut square of earth near their feet, about twenty paces back from the rim. When they weren't looking, I rubbed some of that grit and sand into my hands and pocketed some more.

"We only get one shot at this," Mr. Cooper said. "So we gotta get it right, and we gotta get it all."

We huddled around his laptop, and he pointed from the screen to the place where I would start — about eighty yards from the rim. Then he showed us where the cameras would stand. "There, there, and there," he said.

"We'll also film you from a zip line as you accelerate," Mr. Cooper said. "We want to catch your kinetic energy—that rush as you twist the throttle. I'll be in the helicopter, just off the rim, with the aerial crew."

"I'd like to ride in the helicopter too," Uncle Sal said.

"Fine, fine."

Thumper explained how the two minicams would work. "We'll mount a sportcam on your helmet—for the bird's-eye view. And we'll U-bolt a sportcam to your handlebars, pointed at your face, so we can catch your expressions—and believe me, you *will* express. This camera will fall with the bike, which, of course, will get annihilated on impact. But the camera will survive, because we'll encase it in polycarbonate."

Mr. Cooper then launched into an explanation about reality TV. "What we're trying to do here," he told Uncle Sal and me, "is make the experience feel *real-real-real.* The guy sipping a beer in his armchair in Wheeling, West Virginia, should experience the same rush as you, Jett, as you fly off the mesa. His stomach should be dropping right along with yours. The bigger challenge, however, isn't up here, it's down there. God knows how far you'll go in that wingsuit of yours." He swept an arm across the horizon. "Where do you think you'll land, Jett?"

I pointed to the river glinting in the distance. "Probably about there."

Thumper laughed. "The Rio Loco! I highly doubt you'll get that far."

Uncle Sal flashed a glare. "Only a fool would doubt Arlo Santiago," he said.

"Arlo San—?" Thumper looked puzzled. "I thought your name was—"

"His name is Arlo Santiago!"

« « « » » »

MAKING A HIT REALITY TV SHOW is basically all about waiting. Everybody tinkers with this camera, that light, that microphone, then retinkers; then the wind changes, so they retinker again. The helicopter needs more fuel. The assistant director needs more coffee.

Hurry! Wait.

Take two: Hurry! Wait.

On and on.

Only problem is, waiting breeds doubt.

Doubt breeds fear.

My own philosophy is: Don't wait—go!

I wait.

« « « » » »

IN THE LATE AFTERNOON, the sun splits the clouds and the wind tapers off. Mr. Cooper gets everything he could hope for—the ancient turquoise sky of New Mexico, the distant spiked peaks of Colorado, the bled-dry mesas, and the shadows getting longer.

"Let's get the shot before we lose it!" he shouts.

The crew rushes about with new energy. Thumper barks orders into his radio.

I peel out of my jeans and flannel shirt, zip into the Flying

Squirrel, strap on my parachute. Uncle Sal posts himself in front of me like a sentinel. When the man from Price Waterhouse comes sniffing around again, Uncle Sal blocks the way.

"What the hell!" he tells the man. "How do you fake something like this?"

"Time to board the chopper," Mr. Cooper tells Uncle Sal.

"Hold on a minute," Uncle Sal says.

He puts an arm on my shoulder, and we step away.

"Let me see those hands, Arlo."

All of me is shaking, but my hands are seismic.

Uncle Sal looks ready to cry.

"Arlo-Arlo-Arlo, say the word and we walk away. Who gives a damn about these reality TV people? Who gives a damn about their money or market share? None of it matters — none of it. Say the word."

I don't say the word.

Maybe if I were doing it just for me.

But I'm not.

"C'mon," I say. "Let's go."

« « « » » »

THE CHOPPER LIFTS OFF and flies out over the north rim. It swings around and hovers there. A *CD&E* cameraman sits in his safety harness in the open door, aiming his camera at me like an assassin.

I unzip my leg pocket, scoop out the sand and grit that I've stored there, and rub it into my hands like chalk dust.

Slide on my helmet, throw a leg over the Ducati, and fire her up. Grind pepper like Burro Mesa has never heard. The Monster is wide awake.

Thumper guides me to my mark.

He radios the crew one last time. Reaches over and activates the sportcams on my helmet and handlebars. Pats my shoulder. His mouth moves, but I can't hear him. I throttle down.

"What did you say?"

He cups his hands to his mouth. "Anytime, Arlo."

Anytime! Easy for you.

Because all the bells and alarms—all the evolved, life-saving no's and don'ts—are screaming inside me.

Not to mention the guilt.

My biggest fear isn't what might happen to me; it's what might happen to Dad.

I could power off and walk away. It's definitely the logical-rational thing to do. It's one thousand percent what Dad would want me to do.

Instead, I shove the thought out of my mind.

Nature sure knows how to draw a line, because the north rim of Burro Mesa is as straight as a ruler. Beyond stands the Front Range of the Rockies. Below stands nothing at all—just gaping space, three thousand feet straight to the floor of Colorado.

It's the same line Mom galloped toward long ago, knowing her horse would balk. Or did she?

Anchor of earth, spiral of sky.

It's all so beautiful. Wish I'd noticed before—truly noticed. Why does it take maybe dying to see the world like this?

I clasp my fingers around the grips.

Grind!

GRIND!

So loud my mind goes silent.

Empty.

I focus on that line — that perfect horizontal.

Drop into the Zone.

Full drone.

Yea, though I fly through the valley of the shadow . . .

I jerk my wrist.

Buck into a wheelie.

The earth churns under me.

Shudders.

When I hit speed, everything smoothes out, like a gallop.

I open the throttle all the way.

Ride into the sky.

CHAPTER 50

Oh, I have slipped the surly bonds of earth,
And danced the skies on laughter-silvered wings. . . .
Topped the windswept heights . . .
Chased the shouting wind . . .
And done a hundred things . . .
You have not dreamed of . . .
Put out my hand and touched the face of God.

That's how Pilot Officer John G. Magee felt when he flew his Spitfire over England in 1941.

And it's how I feel the instant rubber meets sky.

Only it's an understatement.

The wind rushes up. "Where ya been?" it seems to say. Like it's been waiting all this time. The brother they never told me about.

The Monster slips weightless out of my hands, its tractionless roar twisting into a high-pitched scream, a whiff of gasoline my last contact.

I punch my arms forward and spread my legs.

Colors pour into me. The dusty-green of the far hills. The

powder-blue of the forest — black where fire singed it. The broken gray of the talus shelf. All swirling into veined rust, which is the color of the tumbling mesa — the color of life.

My webbed skin puffs out like a sail.

I fall, lifted,
my mind shouting
awesome-awesome-awesome-awesome.
I soar beyond the face of Burro Mesa,
glimpse the Monster windmilling below,
my fear oxidizing into joy,
into dazzling awareness.

« « « » » »

FROM HIGH UP, THE BANKS of the Rio Loco look sandy and smooth. But when I drift in, I see that all that "smooth sand" is actually spiny yucca and brittlebrush, crowded with saber shoots. I can't spot a decent place to land, so I spill air and splash down in the river.

Big mistake.

The Rio Loco billows into my chute. Before I can unhook my harness and peel out of it, I plow into a rock. I brace my arms and legs and push off, tasting nylon as the canopy plays out behind me like a noose. The current grabs hold and sucks me toward boulders. Water sucks up all around me.

What saved me in the air will kill me here.

Pit of the gut, I'm scared.

The lines snap taut, and I'm jerked under. Held and hammered by the overflow.

I think of Dad, aware that my last thought is of him. Not by conscious choice, it just is. Aware of how much I've hurt him. How sorry I am.

Then the lines slip, and I burst to the surface.

Gasp giant air.

The river thunders in my ears. The chopper *whop-whop*s around me.

I fumble with my leg pocket, grab my knife, and slash the lines. Swim for the bank and drag myself out.

The chopper takes a last look, then peels off.

I'm ice cold. Shaking all over.

I stumble up the bank, slicing my hand as I push through the yucca. But it's nothing. Just blood. I can't even feel it.

The chopper finds what I couldn't — a clear patch to land. Mr. Cooper and the cameraman rush toward me.

"Big numbers, Arlo."

These are the first words I hear. The next are: "We're definitely scheduling this for Sweeps Week."

"T-t-t-totally frozen," I stutter.

Mr. Cooper wants to do an interview now. Catch me dripping and shaking. He stands me with Burro Mesa off my shoulder and the river behind me. I can see Uncle Sal coming across the field.

I'm sucking the blood off my hand when the camera light goes on. The interview goes like this:

Mr. Cooper: "Arlo, can you describe how it felt?"

Me: "Aw-aw-awesome. No words."

Mr. Cooper: "Talk about fear. How afraid were you?"

Me, pointing to Burro Mesa with my bloody hand: "Up there, h-h-huge." Pointing toward the river. "D-d-down there, even more. I almost died. But in the air, n-n-not at all."

Mr. Cooper: "How do you explain that?"

Me: "C-c-c-can't."

Mr. Cooper: "Anything special you can share?"

Me, shaking like a leaf: "No words. No words."

"Enough!" Uncle Sal shouts, coming up.

Mr. Cooper nods, and the cameraman powers off.

Uncle Sal helps me out of the Flying Squirrel and throws his jacket over me. It's full of his big warmth.

"We'll promote the hell out of this," Mr. Cooper says. "Sweeps Week is coming up. I can promise big numbers."

Here's what I would've said if I hadn't been frozen, and if the cameraman hadn't been pointing his camera in my face. But most of all, here's what I would've said if they'd tried to help me out of the river. Because you don't give your best stuff to people who shoot video of you while you're drowning.

Say, for example, Cam had asked me the same questions. I would have told him:

"The instant I crossed that line, I wasn't alone anymore.

Wind, sun air were alive around me.

I felt this in every atom and molecule.

Connected.

I'm part of all this!

Mesas, mountains, stars.

Me, part of all this!

I slipped out of my skin.

Broke through."

« « « » » »

MR. COOPER WAVES TO US from the chopper. "Time to get on board," he shouts.

The pilot and cameraman are already buckled in.

"Let those bastards wait," Uncle Sal says. "Follow me."

We pick our way through the spines and sabers and go down to the river. From the bank, it looks more innocent than it really is.

Uncle Sal reaches into his shirt pocket and pulls out a cigar.

"Pre-Castro, Arlo. Hundred bucks a stick. Reserved for only the finest occasions. Too bad you don't smoke."

He holds the cigar at arm's length and surveys the valley. Sights on Burro Mesa, now monolithic in the creeping dusk.

"Why the long face?" he asks.

I shake my head. "It was too close," I say. "Even for me."

What I don't say is, a dead son is not what a father needs. A dead brother is not what a sister needs.

"That's the last one," I say. "Never again."

Uncle Sal runs the cigar under his nose. "Music to my ears, Arlo."

"Dad's gonna be mad as hell," I say. "He'll tell me I'm crazy."

Uncle Sal lights the cigar, puffs a few times, loosens his jaw, and blows a smoke donut.

"Funny thing," he says, touching the donut with the tip of his cigar and sculpting it into a pretzel. "One man's crazy is another man's courage. I suspect your dad will come around when he hears the outcome. After all, you're rich."

"Not rich enough," I say.

Uncle Sal takes a puff. "Nobody's rich enough, Arlo. But what you did — you earned." He winks. "Hey, whaddya say we call him now, in the spirit of the moment, and tell him the news?"

"Bad idea," I say.

But Uncle Sal's already punching the number. As he waits for Dad to pick up, he blows another donut. Me, I look across at the mesa — at the dusk and shadow, the cut and fall — and feel a weight lift.

"Hello, Hector!" Uncle Sal says, his mouth quirking into a grin. "This is Sal Focazio, your favorite uncle. Now, listen — listen up. I'm here in Colorado — standing on the banks of the Rio Loco . . . Why? Never mind. Just listen. I have some good news and some bad news. It's about Arlo . . . Hold on — hold on! — I'm about to tell you."

Uncle Sal takes a long pull on his cigar and blows a cloud. "The good news is, Arlo will be depositing a large sum of money in the bank on Monday morning. The bad news is . . ."

He steps to the river's edge, squats, and holds the phone an inch or two above the gurgling water. I can't see his expression, but his shoulders are shaking. Then he stands and puts the phone to his mouth again.

"The bad news, Hector, is that the funds won't be available for twenty-four hours."

Click!

"Nice one," I say.

Uncle Sal flicks an ash. "Let him stew on that for a few hours. You can tell him the rest when you get home."

CHAPTER 51

CAM, LOBO, AND I are lounging on our bikes in the school parking lot. The bell rang five minutes ago, and everybody's scattering to go home. Normally, we'd blast out of there, but today the sun hypnotizes. We soak it in.

Nobody knows about my big jump off Burro Mesa yet, except Dad and Uncle Sal. I keep it to myself—partly because of what the ancient Greek Herodotus said: "All arrogance will reap a harvest rich in tears." And partly because what happened—on the mesa, in the air, and in the river—is still working its way into my pores and molecules. How can I talk about that?

Anyway, the whole damn town will know soon enough. Sweeps Week is coming up.

Lobo's phone pings. He peers at the screen: "*Slam!* Got him!"

Cam yawns. "Got who?"

Instead of answering, Lobo gets off his Bandit 350, plants his legs apart, and shouts. "USA!"

Some kid across the parking lot echoes, "USA!"

"What the hell!" Cam says. "What's got into everybody?"

I have a pretty good idea. And now Lobo confirms it.

"They just nuked the king of all terrorists," he says.

Cam shudders. "You mean—?"

"Exactly," Lobo says. "Obliterated the living shiz out of him."

Cam spikes a fist in the air.

The news is landing on other phones. The reaction is like super-accelerated Darwinism. In a blink, kids evolve from bored knuckle-draggers into swaggering *Homo erectuses.*

Horns get honked. A tree gets climbed and shaken. A shirt gets peeled off and waved.

"USA! . . . USA! . . . USA!"

Me, I don't evolve.

I sit on my bike, frozen.

Lee rushes up. "C'mon, Arlo. Let's get out of here."

She fires up the 125.

We blast out of the parking lot.

Gone.

« « « » » »

"If you're just joining us . . ."

Ethan Shackleton stands with the broken hills of the Swat Valley behind him.

> *"Approximately two hours ago we learned from our intelligence sources that Caracal, the insurgency's top commander and mastermind of some of the most horrific atrocities of the past decade, is dead. A missile fired by an aerial drone reportedly killed him as he fled up a mountain road on the back of a motorcycle."*

The camera zooms in. All I can make out of the blurry images are a pit in the road, bloody clothes, and twisted metal.

"The strike was carried out by a special ops team working in consultation with the U.S. National Security Agency and CIA."

Ethan gives a summary of Caracal's life, during which they flash photos of him as a kid standing beneath Big Ben in London; as a student standing outside the U.S. Capitol; and as a rifle-toting warrior standing in some dusty hills.

Then the photo of him and his family pops up — wife, son, and tiny twin daughters.

"His death brings the United States and its allies one big step closer to completion of its military mission on the North-West Frontier."

Tears are tracking down Lee's face. I know she's thinking about her dad and that he might be closer to coming home.

Me, I'm thinking about a phone call I got from Major Anderson.

He woke me in the middle of the night, and I told him what he didn't want to hear — that no matter how much extreme and lasting good it might do for me and my family, I couldn't take anybody out.

Not even Caracal.

It's not who I am.

And besides, you never take out just one person.

A perfect hit goes beyond a single target. It goes wide. And it goes deep.

So my answer was no.

"Second best can do it," I told him.

And I was right.

Seeing these images on TV, I feel no joy — zero.

Maybe I didn't push the button, but I primed it.

Lee sweeps back her hair and shows me her tears. I slip my hand into hers, and our fingers twine together.

"Caracal achieved near-mythical status in the borderlands, where he orchestrated a fierce, decade-long campaign against U.S. and NATO forces.

"He was the last of a triumvirate of leaders accused of plotting and executing terrorist strikes on three continents."

Ethan lowers his eyes, takes a moment. Then he looks straight at Lee and me.

"On a personal note, in the cadre of correspondents in which I serve, no question has been asked with greater frequency or urgency than this:

"'Where is Caracal?'

"Today we know the answer:

"He is dead.

"This is Ethan Shackleton, BBC World Update, *reporting from the North-West Frontier."*

CHAPTER 52

LIKE MR. COOPER PREDICTED, the numbers for *Crazy-Dirty&Extreme* are big.

"Thirty-eight percent market share, Arlo," he tells me by phone after the segment airs during Sweeps Week. "That's nearly three million more viewers than we usually get. Do you know what that means?"

"No idea," I say.

"It means, Arlo, that you're famous."

"Interesting," I say.

And that's exactly as excited as I feel.

I've never gone looking for attention. But attention seems to find me. Maybe Uncle Sal's right — destiny is a huntress, and she's hunted me down.

CHAPTER 53

LEE WANTS TO SEE WHAT Drone Pilot is all about. We agree to meet me at TunzaFunza — the caffeine and cyber heartbeat of Orphan County.

When I get there, it's packed with day-off wranglers wearing their go-to-town cowboy hats and sipping Americanos. Uncle Sal has opened the terrace. It's sunny and warm outside, but the wranglers huddle inside in the shade.

I get catcalls:

"Hey, everybody, it's Arlo!"

"Nah, it's Jett Spence."

"Arlo! Can I borrow ten thousand bucks?"

"Jett, autograph my ass!"

On and on.

I bump a few knuckles. But I don't autograph any asses.

Uncle Sal has hung a poster-size picture of me on the wall above the espresso machine. It shows me flying off Burro Mesa on the Ducati. I'm still gripping the handles, but my wings have puffed out. I've crossed that line.

Uncle Sal took the picture from the chopper using a fisheye

lens. He caught the burnt colors of the high mesa, the golden-red sun, and the thousand shadowed shades. New Mexico paints this for you better than any artist who ever lived.

People tell me it's a great picture, and I admit, it's pretty good. But when you've been there and opened yourself up like that — your pores, atoms, and molecules — all you can think is, it doesn't catch a tenth of it.

Lee waves to me from the game station. I go over and squeeze beside her — two asses, one chair. Mine, the bony ass. Hers, the perfect one. It's a good fit.

"Listen up," I say, logging on. "Anybody can score the points. But you gotta score 'em every time. That's what separates the cowboy from the cows."

Lee bumps me. "It's called consistency, Arlo."

"Nah, it's called customizing," I say.

As I go through the setup, Lee studies the international rankings. SergeiTashkent has fallen many notches. IpanemaGirl has climbed to second place. She's seriously breathing down my neck.

"Hey, isn't that you?" Lee says, pointing to my username: ClayMadSwooper.

"Just so happens."

"Wait! Does that mean you're . . . the best?"

"Doesn't mean anything," I say. "Ranks change all the time."

Today, we're playing the newest version of Drone Pilot, just released. Now you can tap into a full global menu of geolocation options.

You can build your own battlefield, or strike zone, anywhere in the world, from Timbuktu to Kalamazoo. You're not limited to the same old war holes. My guess — these topo maps have been ripped off from the Pentagon. Drone Pilot simply layers animation and lots of cool features on top.

Couple clicks and we're over Orphan County.

Lee traces a finger along the Cimarron to where it flows into the Rio Loco. Another click and we're over Clay Allison. From the satellite, the town looks like a round waffle iron.

"Kids!"

Uncle Sal walks up carrying two large glass mugs brimming with his latest invention, the Arlo Santiago Mesa Blaster. The Arlo consists of two shots of espresso, one shot of mocha, steamed milk, a dash of cayenne pepper, a splat of whipped cream, and a final shot of espresso poured macchiato-style on top, for extra power.

I could do without the cayenne pepper, but it's Uncle Sal's signature ingredient, so I say nothing. Plus, it's on the house. And always will be.

"Thanks!" we say.

His eyes shine bright.

Today, I'm flying an MQ-1 Mamba — a pure hunter-killer. Alpha-aggressive to the core.

"Three rules," I tell Lee. "Just follow these."

"What are they?" Lee asks.

"Rule number one," I say. "Customize."

Why customize? Because the more you distance yourself from the average default idea of you, the higher-farther-faster you will go. Just a few people truly get this. If more did, the competition would be ridiculous.

The default arms me with four missiles. I delete three and shave the remaining missile from one hundred pounds to seventy-five. On second thought, I trim it to fifty. All I need is one pinpoint sting. Anything extra is a waste.

Drone Pilot teaches the law of opposites — the smaller the cloud, the bigger the bang, at least in points.

"Gonna do this fast and furious," I say. "We'll launch just down the road, at White Sands."

Lee stifles a yawn.

The soundtrack comes on — the Hawaiian steel guitar that is both sweet and haunting at the same time. The guy with the kick-ass bass voice intones:

"Yea, though I fly through the valley of the shadow of death . . .
I will fear no evil."

I fire up my engines and blast into the blue.

Right off, a pod of enemy fighters pops up. One by one, each fighter peels away and dives on me.

"Rule number two," I say. "Switch it up — shatter expectations."

Why? Because when you switch it up you confuse the enemy, and his confusion is your opportunity. For example, when an enemy expects defense, hit him hard.

The best defense can be offense.

Pretty soon, we see the rim rocks of Chicorica Canyon. I skim low and follow the dry creek, blasting over Lupita's pastures and sliding into an air trough, just feet above the ground.

The dam rushes up.

Picking the moment to fire is pure adrenalized instinct. On gut, I push the button, fire my fifty-pounder, and pull into the blue.

Even before my missile strikes I shudder, knowing that I've hit my mark.

But when I circle back, the dam is still intact, standing as obnoxiously as ever. This means I've overestimated my firepower. It will cost me. Hugely. It's IpanemaGirl's lucky day.

But when I look down again, a thin stream of water is pissing out of the face of the dam. As I watch, a concrete block spits out, like a tooth, and water geysers through the gap.

Now it happens — the dam begins to blow out, piece by piece. In a burst, all that pent-up water — water that the city of Clay Allison would happily siphon away from Lupita and the other ranchers of Chicorica Canyon — vaporizes the concrete. A wall of thrashing foam races down the dry bed onto Lupita's thirsty land.

Game over. My points roll up. Good score — in fact, a great one.

"Rule number three," I tell Lee. "Be humble in victory."

Why? Because I've seen too many good players get full of themselves and self-destruct. Arrogance is an enemy.

"So what do you think?" I say, bumping Lee.

She folds her arms. Ponders the dead screen.

"One thing's not working for me, Arlo."

"Yeah, what's that?"

"The symbolism."

"Symbolism?" I say. "What symbolism?"

"Think about it," Lee says. "You took that dam out in five minutes. But Lupita's got to live with it for the rest of her life. You can blow it up a thousand times, but it's still up there. A symbol of . . ."

She searches for the words.

"You mean, a symbol of town greed and all that crap?" I say.

"More than that," Lee says. "A symbol of the way things ought *not* to be."

"So what's your point?" I ask.

She weighs whether to say it.

"My point — and I'm just being honest — no offense — but this is a pretty stupid way to spend your time, if you ask me."

EPILOGUE

TOWARD THE END OF APRIL Mr. Wasserman's fancy rig arrives from Colorado. Two wranglers load the mares into the trailer, stalling each next to her offspring.

"Well, that does it," Dad says, peeling off his gloves. "I'll get dinner started."

I watch the rig roll up the drive, turn on the access road, and lurch toward the interstate, bound for pastures north.

Easy as that, they're gone. Who knows, maybe I'll see them again someday. Will they remember me? The years. They pass. And after all, they're just horses.

In my life, I've been loved by six individuals. No matter how much I mess up. No matter how much I don't deserve it. No questions. No hitches. It's just there. Inside the marrow. Deeper than DNA.

Mom with grace.

Dad with distraction.

Siouxsie with distance.

And the mares.

Six. It's no record. But it's not bad.

« « « » » »

THIS TIME OF YEAR, THE road up Burro Mesa can be slick with melt and drainage. Dad's pickup has been known to bog down. But it's easy on a dirt bike.

Just before you reach the top, some benevolent dirt-bike god has placed a bump. Hit it right, and you sail over into the grass.

That's what I do now — hit it right.

Sail.

Land sweet.

Brake and wait.

Pretty soon, Lee pops over. Rolls up. Takes off her shades and looks about.

It's her first time on Burro Mesa.

Sea of grass — sea of sky.

To the north, the Front Range — by some trick of light crystal close today. You can practically touch those glaciers.

A small herd of browns dots the mesa, a couple dozen cows and their calves. El Guapo will have a field day today.

We're at least a half hour ahead of the others, so we cruise over to the rim. Stand our bikes and walk to the monument.

Dad tried for months to write the epitaph — or whatever you call it. Phrases like "Etched by golden sunlight" and "Gone for now, here forever" got favored and rejected.

"Pained by life and beauty, yet deeply strengthened by it" — that was another.

"Arlo," he told me, "I've come around to your way of thinking. Words fall short. They simply do not do justice. Maybe if I were Shakespeare, but — forsooth! — I ain't."

So it's just plain, unchiseled rock. Rib-cage high. Shoulders wide. Cut from the yellow earth of Bandelier, New Mexico. Dad, Cam, Lobo, and I hauled it up here two weeks ago. Dad ground every last ounce out of the pickup.

We stood the rock just back from the north rim, twenty paces or so. Used a winch, a pulley, and old-fashioned sweat. Then Cam and Lobo pocketed their hands and drifted away. With all the respect that friendship knows.

In the end, family buries family.

Dad and I packed and smoothed the base. Combed every last grain of sand.

Then I drifted away.

« « « » » »

LOOKING NORTH, I FEEL AGAIN the whole soaring-falling flight.

Impossible — *impossible!*

Easy.

Far below on the piney forest floor lies a twisted mess of dead metal. No more roaring down the interstate, a monster.

Just getting swallowed by rust and time.

"Arlo, don't get any closer," Lee says, pulling me back from the edge.

We stake out a picnic site. Sprawl in the grass. Lee snaps off some stalks, and her fingers go to work.

Cows are curious — natural investigators. We must look to them like pillars of salt, because those grazers start to lumber toward us.

Lee glances up. "What the—! What're they up to?"

"Nothin'," I say. "They just want to run us off the edge."

She picks a shooting star to add to her grass braid. Soon we are surrounded by gawking thousand-pounders. Blue-eyed Elsies.

"I feel like I'm on public display," Lee says.

"Hey, I can do something about that."

I place a hand over her eyes.

Kiss her peach soft.

Plum shiny.

We fall back into the perfect alfalfa.

Later, through bovine legs, we see the pickup rolling across the mesa. The cows twitch, the circle opens, and there is El Guapo standing in back, forepaws perched on the tailgate, snout poked into the breeze.

So eager and primed that he plunges out and lands in a tumble. Then he's up and off, full tilt, ducking toward this cow and that, beelining joyously, skittering and scattering them, filling the air with moos.

Dad pulls up and gets out. "That's one fine workin' dog," he says. "Hold up, Siouxsie. I'll just be a minute."

Dad and Lupita offload the picnic stuff. Then he gets back in and drives Siouxsie over to the monument. Lifts her out. Carries her to the yellow hunk of standing rock. It's getting harder and harder for her to stand alone, so they hold on to each other.

Lee snaps open the blanket. Lupita starts to set things out.

I drift over to the monument.

Step up beside Dad and Siouxsie.

Into all that silence.

All that remembering.

Siouxsie pulls off her headband — the tie-dyed one with the rippling shades of blue — and places it on top of the monument.

"Now you guys," she says.

"Hmm," Dad says. "Didn't know this was on the agenda. Wish I'd come prepared."

He digs around in his pockets.

All I have in mine are my bike keys. I take off a spare to the old Yam 125 and place it beside Siouxsie's headband.

Dad contemplates his wedding ring. Slips it off and puts it there.

"Nice," Siouxsie says.

He helps her back to the truck, and they ride over to the others.

Me, I linger a while.

The wind rolls across the grass, carrying the memory of distant glaciers and the promise of summer.

I can see all the way to Pike's Peak.

Turning, I can see halfway to Mexico.

Up here, it's just space, space, space.

Green, blue, and forever.

That's epitaph enough for me.

THE END

ALSO BY CONRAD WESSELHOEFT

Since his brother's death, Jonathan's been losing his grip on reality. Last year's Best Young Poet and gifted guitarist is now Taft High School's resident tortured artist, when he bothers to show up at all. He's on track to repeat the eleventh grade, but Jonathan has friends who refuse to be seniors without him, and the music that never lets him go. All that's left of Telemachus are memories and Eddie Vedder's guitar. Maybe that's enough.

Use this QR code to download chapter one of Conrad Wesselhoeft's *Adios, Nirvana.*